Sensitive Skin

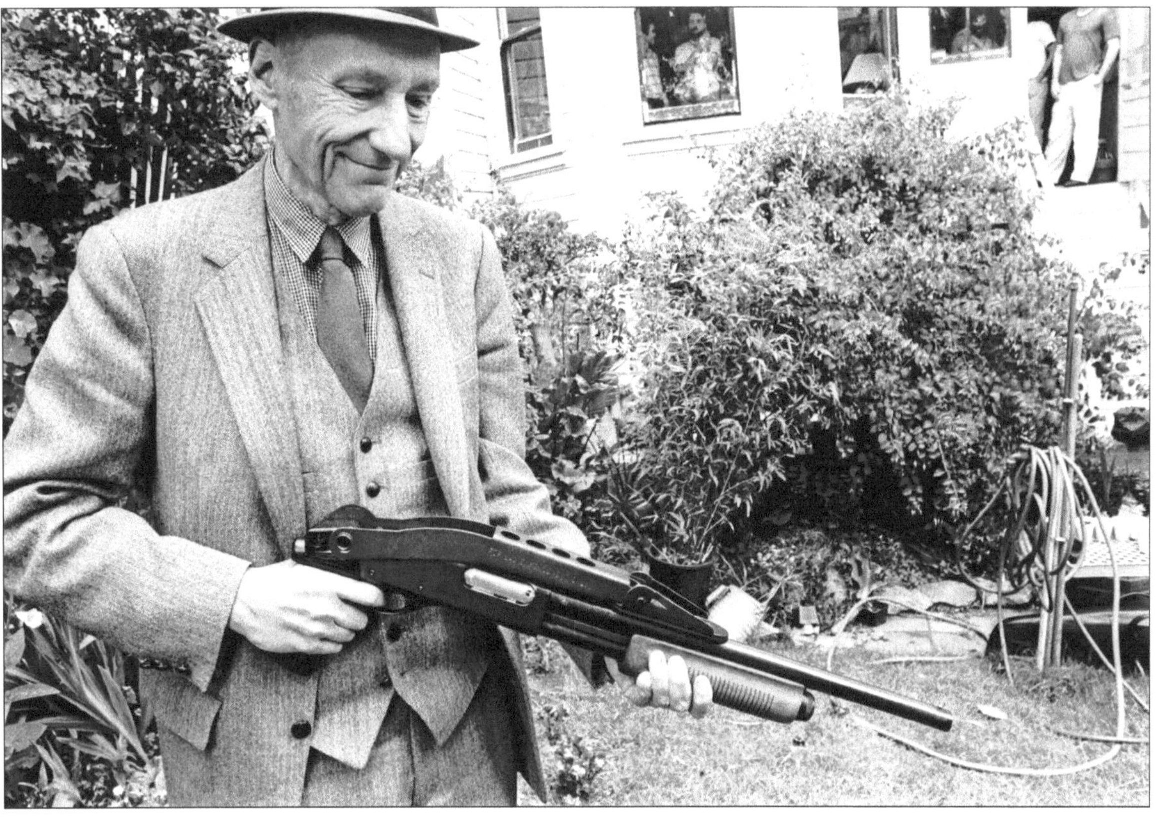

Sensitive Skin Magazine is published twice a year and is available online at **www.sensitiveskinmagazine.com.**

Publisher/Managing Editor: Bernard Meisler
Associate Editors: Rob Hardin, Mike DeCapite & B. Kold
Music Editor: Steve Horowitz
Contributing Editors: Ron Kolm & Tim Beckett

Cover photograph: *Burroughs and the Wild Boys,* 1981, by Ruby Ray
Back cover painting: *Another Green World,* by Justine Frischmann

You can find us at:
Facebook—**www.facebook.com/sensitiveskin**
Twitter—**www.twitter.com/sensitivemag**
YouTube—**www.youtube.com/sensitiveskintv**

We also publish in various electronic formats (mobi, epub, etc.), and have our own line of books. For more info about **Sensitive Skin** in other formats, **Sensitive Skin Books**, and books, films and music by our contributors, please go to **www.sensitiveskinmagazine.com/store**. To purchase back issues in print format, go to **www.sensitiveskinmagazine.com/back-issues**.

You can contact us at **info@sensitiveskinmagazine.com**.

Submissions: **www.sensitiveskinmagazine.com/submissions**.

ISBN-10: 0983927154
ISBN-13: 978-0-9839271-5-0

Contents

The Opportunity of a Lifetime

Mike Hudson

The canyon was broken and hilly, with shallow arroyos cutting north to south and green agave plants and small stands of Joshua trees providing the only color there was against the relentless grey of the desert and the dirty white snow that clung at the peaks of the mountains on either side. The Funeral Mountains, they were called on the map.

But I wasn't looking at the scenery. Instead my focus was fixed on a beat Ford pickup parked about 15 yards in front of me. Through the filthy windshield, I could see the old man, skin and bones, naked from the waist up and gesturing wildly with his hands, sitting in the back under a windowed truck cap. Ten minutes ago, he'd been eating his dinner. Now I waited for him to make a sudden move for the gun he had stashed back there. No one would live alone in the back of a pickup out in the middle of the Mojave Desert like that without a gun.

Not that I would have minded seeing Kenny get shot. He was a major league asshole who'd fled Buffalo for Vegas one step ahead of the creditors and bill collectors and leg breakers he owed money to. In Nevada, he parlayed a few hundred dollars he'd stolen from his mother into a tiny patch of desert with an ancient mine shaft sunk into it, and was currently attempting to extract a hundred grand from Frankie Donatelle, promising untold riches in return once the mine was reopened.

Now he was screaming and threatening, calling the guy every name in the book. He thought he was a tough guy and the fact that he was 100 pounds heavier and 25 years younger than the old man only encouraged him.

No, I wouldn't have minded seeing Kenny get shot at all. In fact, if he'd have started beating on that old man, and it looked like he was getting ready to, I might have shot him myself.

But Frankie had gone to the back of the truck as well, trying to settle Kenny down and defuse the situation. And since I was there specifically to look out for Frankie, it wouldn't have looked right if he went home in a box.

I motioned to his girlfriend Anna to get back to a little ruined shack that was behind us and picked my spot, a shallow depression in the earth fronted by a small growth of sagebrush in case I needed to drop down. I had the old Army Special .41 on my hip and I unsnapped the safety strap and tucked it back between the holster and my belt and I waited.

On the ground around me, there was a shovel and a geologist's rock pick and a couple five-gallon Army surplus fuel cans filled with water. Nearby

---

A person could get away with killing a guy out here, I thought. Some of those mine shafts were hundreds of feet deep. Nobody would have missed either of them. It would have been easy.

---

there was a pile of empty cans the old guy had eaten out of already and a burned area, about five feet across, where he made his fires.

He'd been prospecting and, from the looks of it, he'd been there a week or more. From what I could hear, the angry debate centered on whether that particular patch of desert belonged to Kenny or to the federal government, which controls most of the land out there and allows prospecting.

The sun was beginning to set, and the two of them were perfectly silhouetted against the windshield right there in front of me. A person could get away with killing a guy out here, I thought. Some of those mine shafts were hundreds of feet

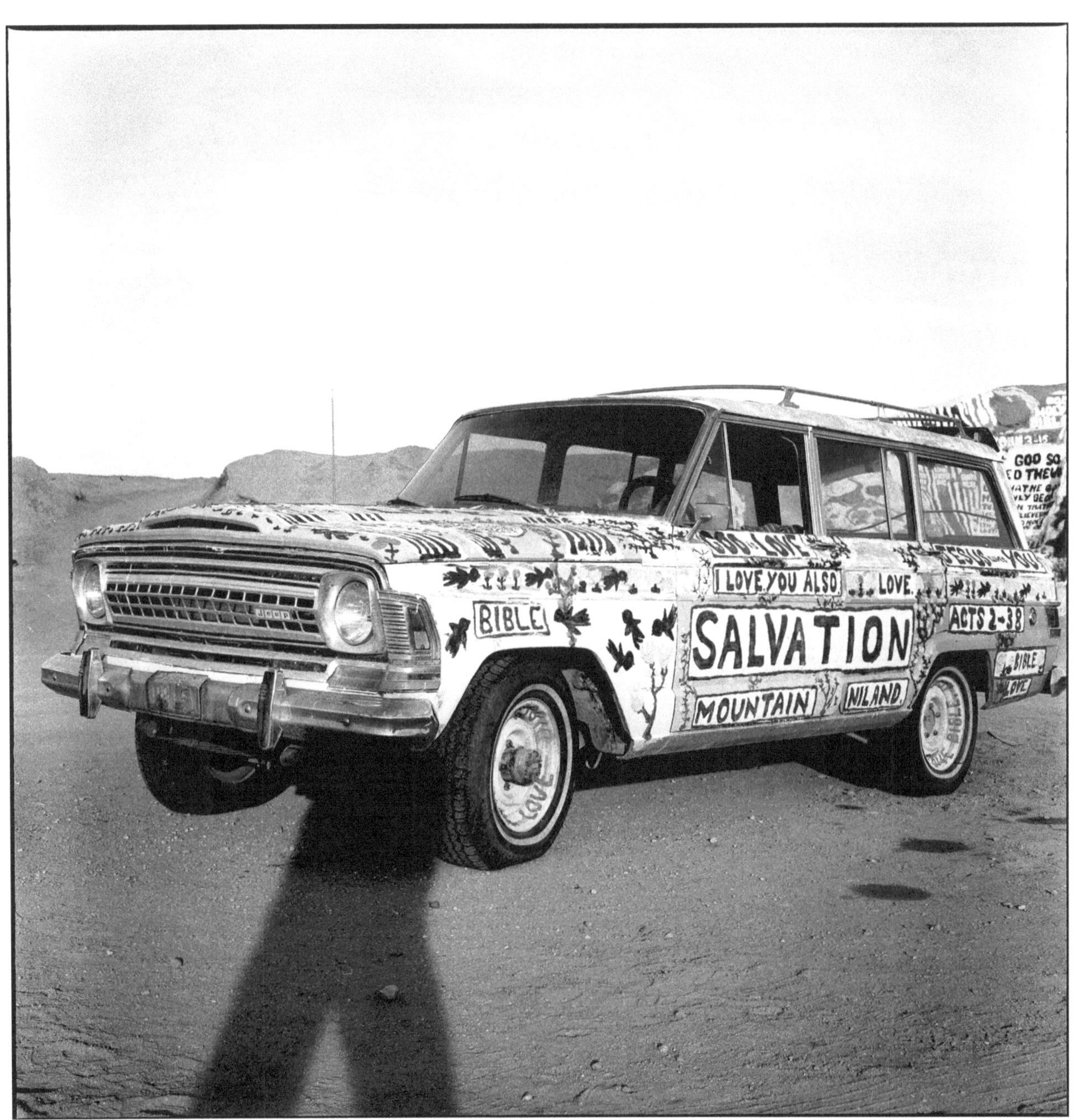

Salvation, photograph by Ted Barron

deep. Nobody would have missed either of them. It would have been easy.

Finally Frankie broke away from the argument and walked back toward me.

"What do you think, Tom?" he said.

"Get Kenny the hell away from there before it gets out of hand," I said. "I'll kill the guy, but I don't want to kill the guy, you know?"

"Yeah."

I snapped the safety strap back over the big Colt and let my jacket fall back over it. The old man nodded, then looked away.

When I got back to the vehicle, I took the holster off the belt and slid it underneath the front seat before climbing in the back. It was almost dark as Frank pulled out onto the road, and Kenny launched into a long soliloquy about what he would have done to that old man, how terrified the guy

I thought briefly about shooting him again, but when I reached under the front seat my hand found the bottle of bourbon Frankie had bought earlier in the day.

Frank walked back to where he'd been and after awhile Kenny came away from the truck.

"Let me have the gun," he said as he walked up.

"No," I said, not even looking at him, and he kept walking.

Before he returned, Frank had calmed the old guy down and convinced him that he should gather up his gear and move on. Maybe he even gave him a couple bucks, I didn't ask. The guy got out of his truck and began picking up his stuff and I relaxed a little. Anna came out from behind the ruined cabin and walked over. We were standing downwind, and the stench of the old man's body and clothes wafted over us.

"Dude needs a fucking shower," I said. Anna laughed a little.

"Yeah," Frank said.

"I'd have shot Kenny, you know."

"Yeah," he said again.

They began walking toward the Land Rover, parked back up by the road. When the old guy approached, he looked at me.

"The guy's an asshole," I told him quietly. "Just do me a favor and get the fuck out of here, OK?"

was and how he'd have been well within his rights no matter what he did. I should have put a couple rounds through the radiator on the guy's truck just to fuck him up, he told me.

Finally, Kenny remembered what we were all doing out there in the desert in the first place and he forgot about the guy and switched back to his stupid con so quickly it was difficult to follow.

"I'm just doing the brotherly thing here," he told us. "I figured I could give my bro Frank a cut because there's more than enough millions to go around. This is the opportunity of a lifetime here, for sure."

The night air brought a chill and the stars began to shine above.

I thought briefly about shooting him again, but when I reached under the front seat, my hand found the bottle of bourbon Frankie had bought earlier in the day. The Land Rover was a rental and it was in Frank's name and doing it in the car would have caused a lot of trouble, so I took a long pull from the bottle and sat back in the seat and closed my eyes.

If You're So Special, Why Aren't You Dead?

James Greer

ALPHONSE SAMSON STOOD BEFORE THE mirror in his bathroom for a long time before deciding to. The mirror had no frame but its edges were beveled and the soft light from the neighbor's bright room shining through a small square heavy-glass window above his head on the right wall produced a doubling of. The scissors, he concluded after staring at them longer than was necessary to arrive at such a conclusion, were too small. He would need. He put the scissors on the back left edge of the ceramic sink and opened the medicine cabinet by pulling on the right edge of the mirror, which was hinged. Inside were four bottles of prescription drugs, all of which remained sealed. To deal with the problem later. To ignore, as long as possible, the ill effects.

There were three outcomes, and none of them. Anything else was a reflection only, the shadow of action. According to his disintegrating paperback of *At-Swim-Two-Birds*, [TK quote at very end of book which you stole and repurposed for the end of *Artificial Light*]. Or to put it differently, as TK had done in TK *Voyages en Afrique*, and obviously Roussell's [sp?] *Voyages en Afrique* [check both these references, obviously the books weren't called the same thing or even either of those things, but there was *Afrique* in the title of both, or at least in my memory there was, which is the point], the which both of which to say precisely the same thing but in different ways and. In the pile of books on his office desk. The photo of James Joyce walking along the strand in Dublin he had framed and propped on the desk against the yellowing wall. The photo of Nabokov reading by lamplight which he had framed and propped against the pale green wall next to the photo of Joyce. Most people assumed these were relatives. Is that your grandfather. Yes I said yes it is. [May have used this joke more than one too many times.]

In France they call scotch tape *le scotch*. For a long time Alphonse used to go to bed early, but then he finished the final volume of *In Search of Lost Time* and there seemed no point. He started going to bed a little later, maybe ten o'clock instead of eight-thirty or nine, but he still woke up without fail at five in the morning. This was the best time of day for getting things done. The most productive. This was the most productive part of the day. For Alphonse, the early morning hours were. There was a wasp buzzing a wasp buzzed outside of his office window buzzed a wasp or possibly a bee [can one tell by timbre of buzz? check] whose low hum sounded like an old man talking on the phone, or to himself, about something private. As if there were words just under the threshold. A kind of meaning. Like the amnion of unbirthed sun the pregnant dark from which the filigree of colors from which soon would burst the slow heat from it would soon be dawn. The desk lamp produced a semicircle a circle a half circle a crescent of silvery light shone silvery light on silvered light on the small stack of books and the worn wood of his desk. There was also a paperweight a round paperweight with a bird a black bird looking at red at red holly berries on a branch against a yellow background and a silver heart-shaped box containing in which could be found a pewter heart-shaped container an ornate, beaded box in the shape of a heart with a heart embossed on its lid which when opened contained revealed a polished pink quartz heart in a blue velvet lining lined with blue velvet the box was lined with blue velvet and contained a smoothly polished pink rose-pink quartz heart. Index cards and sticky notes and nearly twenty pens of various kinds and multicolored pens of various types: ball point and felt-tipped and. A pencil-sharpener, electric, and a three hole punch, manual. The pewter box containing the rose-pink stone heart was a gift from Caeli Fax from whom Alphonse had received many gifts and.

The walls of the office were lined with books arranged haphazardly arranged in no particular order disorder desultory disarray that followed a system only he could understand because he had invented the system of his own design which he had himself invented in fact was a system there was in fact a system behind the disorder a method. [Not a method.] C. M. Bowra's book on heroic poetry was next to nestled against Richardson's *Clarissa* which itself in order you could find C. M. Bowra's volume on heroic poetry, Richardson's *Clarissa*, Burton's *Anatomy of Melancholy* [not that again you are always using it or misusing it in fact] *The Poetical Works of Shelley*, *Stephen Hero* by James Joyce [no you have a picture of him on the desk that would be too obvious something better like *The Journal of Albion Moonlight*], Mao's *Little Red Book*, and Newton's *The Principia* [doesn't that have a longer title in other words didn't he write more than one *Principia* but on different subjects for Christ's sake you have a PhD in physics you ought to know these things this is one of the worst aspects of aging is when your memory goes. I used to be able to picture everything as in a photograph, I used to refer to my memory as eidetic "but only when I drink" hilarious you stupid fuck now it would be better described as idiotic . . . eidetic, idiotic. Not the worst *jeu de mots*. Why does Barth always use such bad French in his books? He uses a lot of French, too, in every book there's some little snippet of French either appropriated or appropriate to the scene. *The Sot-Weed Factor* that chapter where they go confront the Jesuit or the secret Jesuit and Burlingame in disguise speaks to him in French to prove his bona fides but the French is completely wrong. Almost Google Translate–level wrong. As if he didn't care. Or didn't know any better. At least he didn't have the excuse of relying on Google Translate as it didn't exist back then but whatever high-school -or college- (should these be capitalized?) level courses he may have taken did not stick. UNLESS the awkward or just incorrect French is deliberate, in which case it is always deliberate, down to his last book latest most recent book novel *Every Third Thought* where he makes elemental *masculin-feminin* errors. That would be a device were it the case, but even as device towards what end?]

Godard's *Histoire(s) du cinéma* apparently has been or is going to be released on Region 1 DVD this year. Finally. The Artificial Eye UK version is very

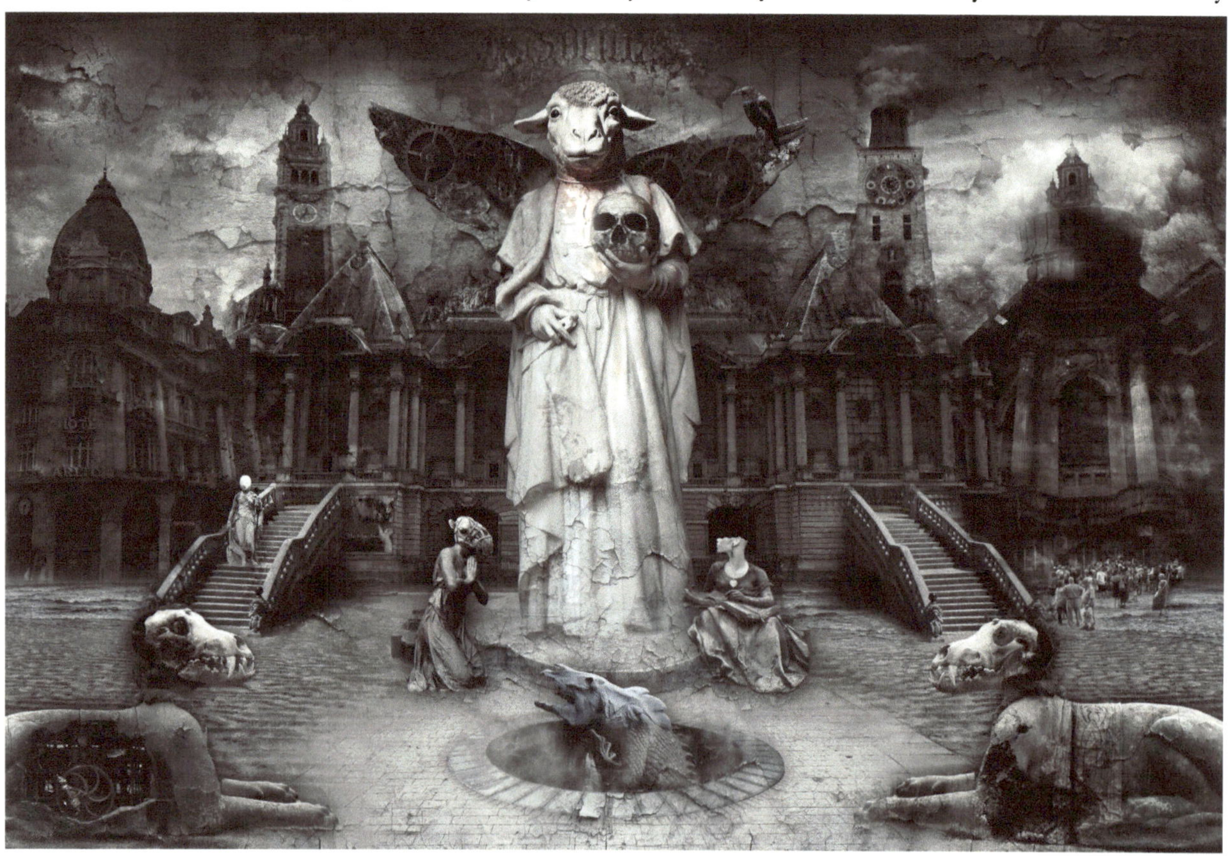

The Great Architect of Dystopy, by Marcin Owczarek

good of course but you can't turn off the English subtitles which is frustrating. The greatest achievement [maybe] in film ever and you can't watch it the way it was intended and the subtitles don't add anything on top of which they're distracting. Also it plays in the wrong aspect ratio on every all-region player I own. Presumably a Region 1 version would play in the correct aspect ratio. And the transfer could use some work, too, though its having been produced for television I doubt the image quality can be improved drastically. The constant bombardment [word choice] of image and text and sound, the layering, the incredible montages, these. What the fuck is kombucha anyway? What exactly is it supposed to do for you? *Bacillus coagulans* GBI-30 6086: 1 billion. S. Boulardi: 1 billion. 1 billion what? Units? Strands? Molecules? Bacteria? And why would I want to put 2 billion anythings into my gut and since I have apparently done just that what is going to happen to me? Will I get any of my memory back? Will it rewrap the frayed synapses in my gray matter? It will not no it won't it will at best one can expect it will produce noisy eructations. The which I may well have produced independent of the 2 billion somethings or other that I recently introduced to my body.

And a stapler, also manual. The stapler was Alphonse's most prized possession partly mostly due to its longevity: he had stolen it from an office where he had worked as a clerk when he was sixteen and the staples as well which he still had, in boxes, in the bottom drawer of a credenza from probably Ikea [try to stay away from brand names, in twenty years Ikea is not going to mean anything, it's like saying "Xxxxxxxx Xxxxxxxx" already nobody remembers that band, and rightly so, awful band, if only he had hired a singer instead of trying to sing himself. No one else in the band could play except the drummer, so why not be satisfied with over-dubbing forty thousand guitar parts and writing simplistic not-great melodies to go with your reductive me-versus-the-world lyrics and have someone who can sing do the singing?]. The staples were in their original boxes of blue-and-white cardboard, 5000 staples each in long rows stacks of rows of 500 each and had not rusted or lost their appeal over the years [see that? it's your nose. And this is sitting on top of it] nor had the stapler ever required maintenance. Alphonse would not argue with anyone who said that things in general used to be better made constructed more sturdily built to last because in his experience or at least in his experience as regards as concerns regarding the stapler that was true the case more often than not. He was in the habit of drawing general conclusions from specific knowledge which is why the world has become is becoming will become a dark and savage place.

He squinted at his reflection in the mirror. All things in this best of all possible. In his left hand a weight, a thing with weight, an object that weighed. His fingers curled around the. People say now or never but that's not. Never is an awfully long time. From the monochrome streetlights of Alphaville to the tangerine night sky of Alphabet City to the dusty unripe brown pear lid over Los Angeles and back and forth we go up. We go down. To be or not to be is false equivalence. Not every answer is binary. Between being and nothingness stretches a fantail of options, each with the same consequence with a different consequence the same completely different similar result and the end is the end after all is never the end. A golden spiral trapped in a glass paperweight with a black bird looking at red berries against a yellow background and you bring the object to your throat and squeeze but suppose but I suppose thought Alphonse that having made it this far there are as many compelling arguments *pro* as *contra*, in the absence of absolutes which we may take as granted or at least for purposes of argument granted by deficit by the God.

To be able, for all and ever, to stop explaining oneself. To stop justifying, excusing, apologizing, lying above all lying. To stop. To stop talking. There is in every human heart an impulse towards irony that is both the making and unmaking of us. No other animal can act irrationally on purpose. Can self-harm knowing the damage that will be done. Can drive at high speed into the ass-end of an alley full-stopped by a brick wall, on a motorcycle, without a helmet, in Paris, because just because.

Alphonse Sampson cut his jugular with a razor three times and scrawled with a dying hand on the mirror good-bye, good-bye, good-bye.

New Work, 2008–2012

Tom McGlynn

The term "social sculpture" is most readily identified with the German conceptual artist Josef Beuys, who has said: "an enlarged understanding of art could work and could break through the borders of isolation which the present culture stands in . . . ." —Nova Scotia, 1974

Much has changed since then, in the overall cultural reception for art, and sculpture is no longer solely represented by isolated modernist gestures. How art "represents" and is received, nevertheless, still tends to get a rarified treatment and is generally cordoned-off—if not literally, then figuratively—behind dense thickets of aesthetic and social theory.

In my approach to the conception and execution of these works, I considered the specific social context of their situation as part of their formal genesis—not in a didactic way, but with an intent that might focus spontaneous interaction with the pieces and with other viewers.

—*Tom McGlynn*

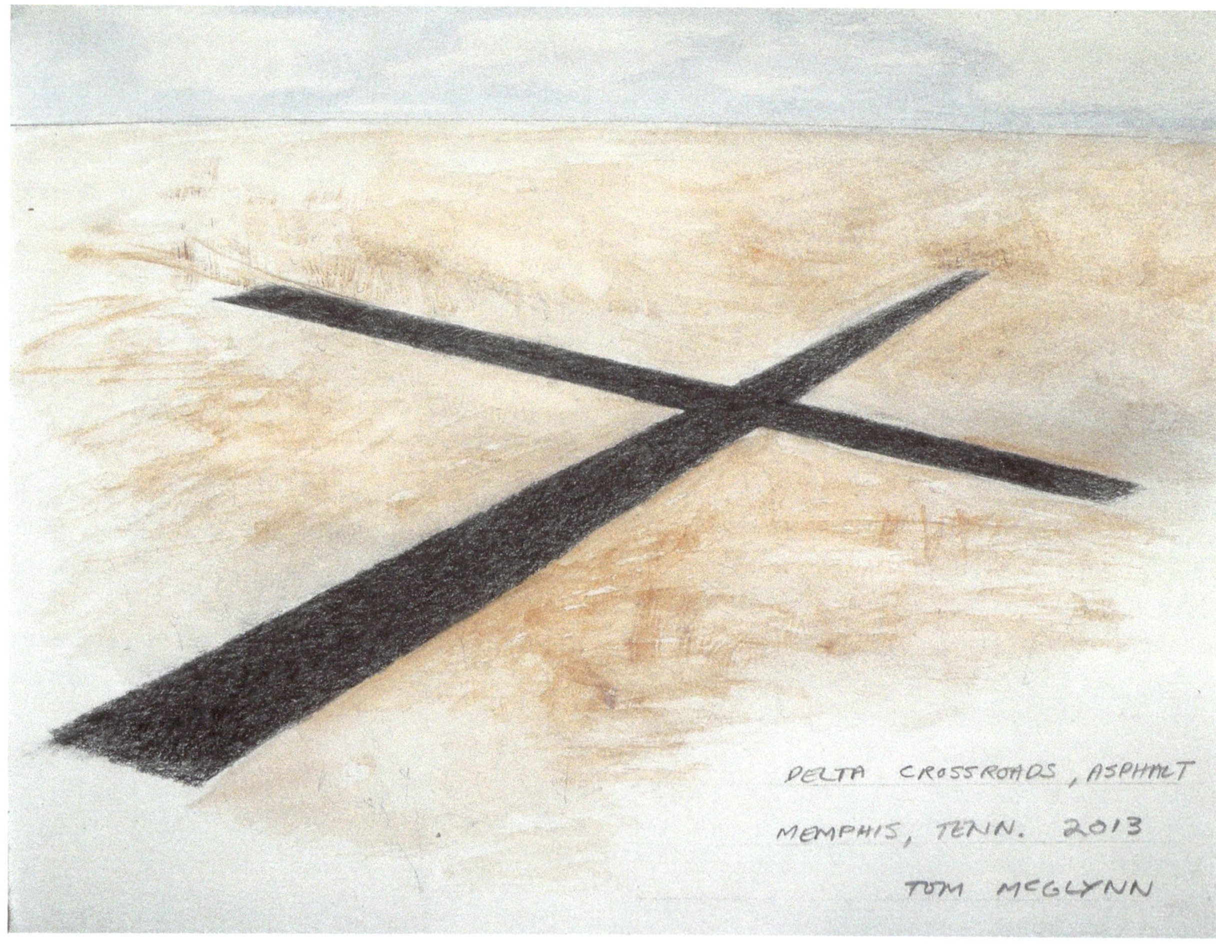

Delta Crossroads, 2013, drawing of proposed sculpture, Memphis, Tennessee. This work will be paved in place, in asphalt, on an abandoned site in as part of *Memphis Social* exhibition, slated to open in the spring of 2013.

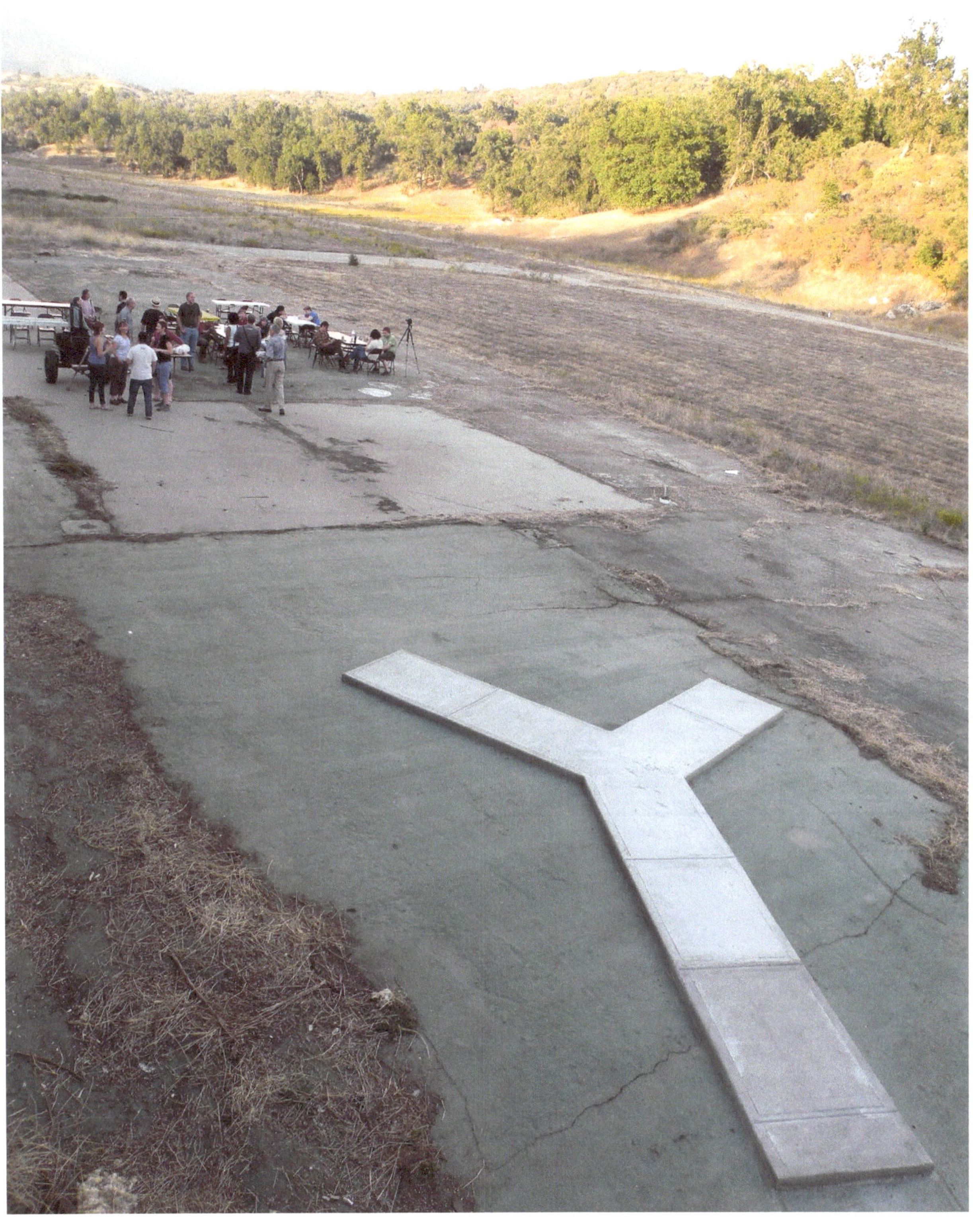

Forked Path, 2011–present, concrete, cast in place, in the Sierra foothills, California. Permanent installation, adjacent the runway in an abandoned cult compound, and part of the *East of Fresno* exhibition, September 2011.

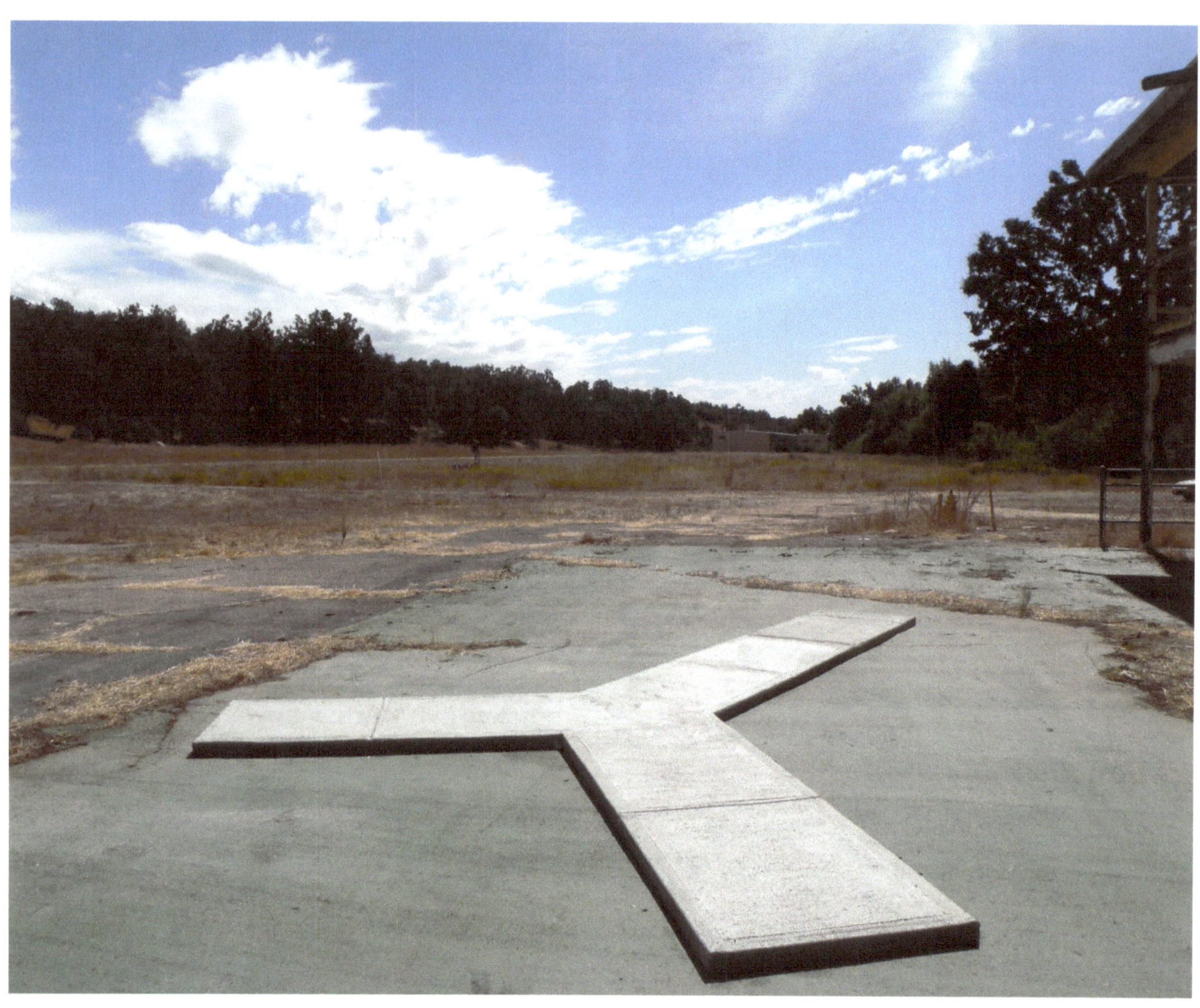

Another view of *Forked Path*, 2011–2012.

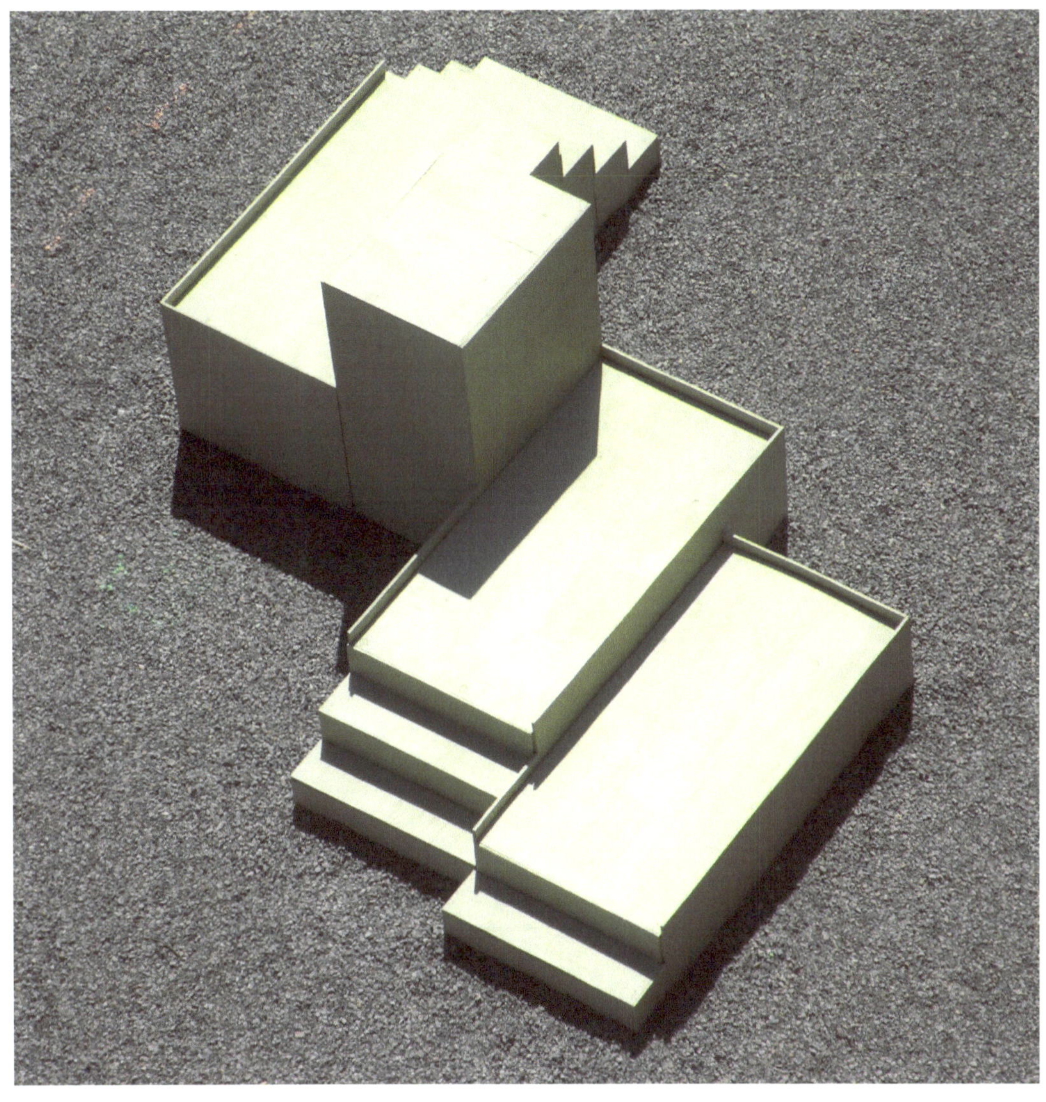

Pilgrim's Progress, 2010. Plywood. An interactive social sculpture as part of the Golden Door sculpture park in Jersey City.

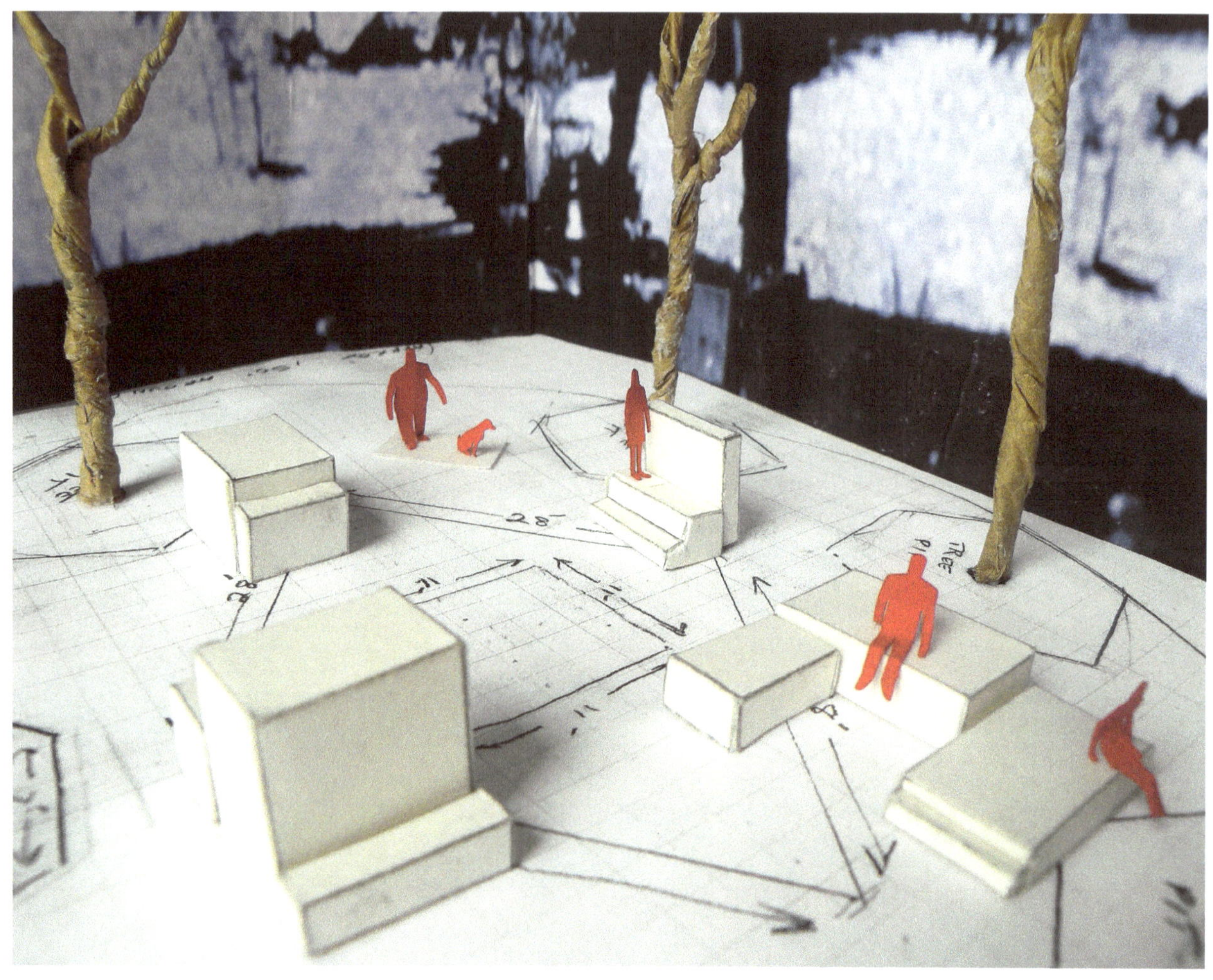

Whitman's Steps, 2010. Proposal model for a modular sculpture at the northeast entrance to Fort Greene Park, Brooklyn, NY.

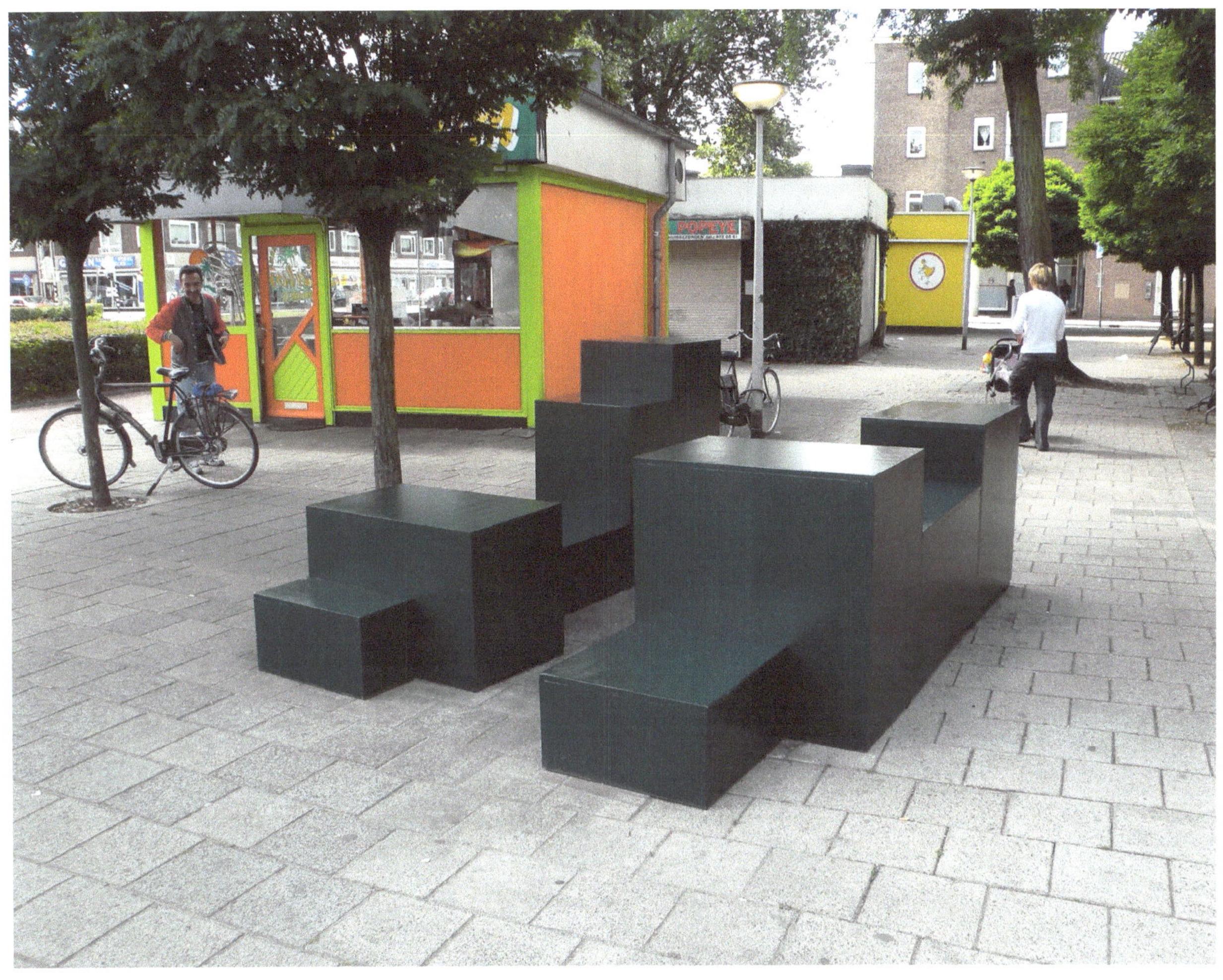

Rotterdam Stages, 2009–present. Plywood. An interactive sculpture in the urban setting of a street corner in Rotterdam, Netherlands, as part of the *Kuf/Mold Rotterdam* invitational exhibition.

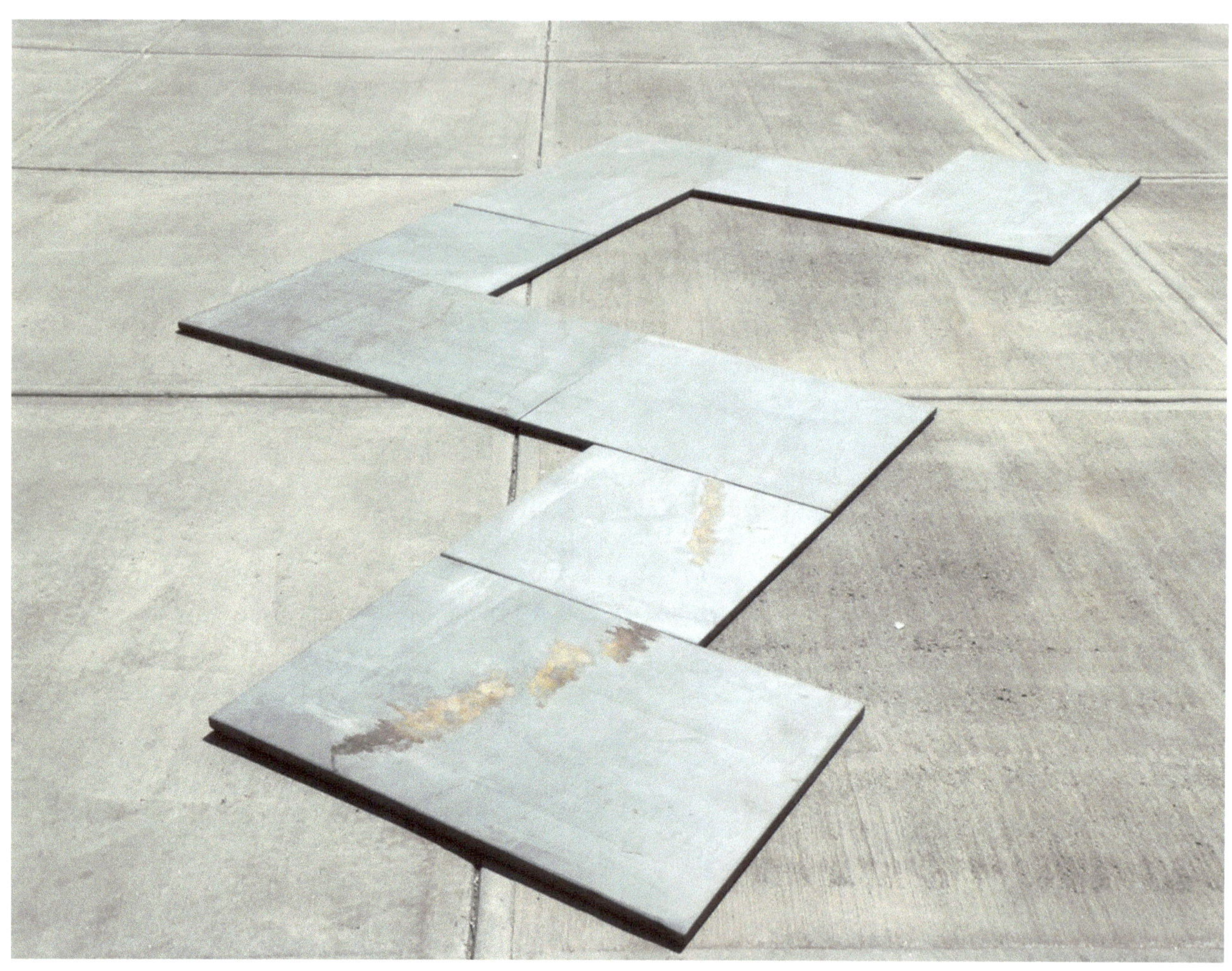

Slate Path, 2009. Installed at Castleton State College, Castleton, VT.

Pardon My French

Thaddeus Rutkowski

When I arrived in Paris by train, I tried to place a call to a friend, someone I knew from my home city. Surprisingly, there was a phone service with a human attendant in the train station. I gave the phone woman the number I wanted to reach, and she dialed it.

Suddenly, she started yelling *"Occupé!"* at me. I thought she was telling me to get lost, so I started to walk away. She yelled more loudly and pointed at the phone. Slowly, I came to understand that *occupé* meant "the line is busy." Presently, she put the call through.

* * *

My friend came in a car to pick me up. He had the car for his job; he ran errands for a commercial production company. As he drove, I watched green rectangles and monumental buildings swing through my field of vision.

Soon, we arrived at the commercial director's home: a converted storefront near the Bastille. The apartment was large, with a spiral staircase connecting floors. I lugged my backpack up the steel steps and laid it in my friend's bedroom.

When I looked for food in the kitchen, I found a baguette and some pâté. The baguette was the thinnest bread stick I'd ever seen; its diameter was that of a U.S. quarter. Moreover, the pâté came in the smallest tin I'd ever seen. Undeterred, I popped the top and dug at the pâté with a spoon, then spread it on a disk of bread.

* * *

A young woman was staying in the same place. I didn't know what she was doing there. When I first saw her, she was watching a television show. The characters were college students who kept losing their pants and falling down.

One time, my friend played a game with the young woman. He lay on his back, held her hands and pushed against her stomach with his feet, so her body was balanced over him. Then he laid her on her back and knelt between her legs. He put his hands behind her knees and lifted her pelvis toward him. They stayed that way for a while, rocking. I wondered if this was the French version of Twister.

* * *

I thought Paris was small, but actually only the amount of ground I covered was small. I would walk from one point to another and think that I'd gone from one side of the city to the other. The reality was, I'd passed only from one district to another.

The place I visited most often was the adult strip of the rue Saint-Denis. The shops there showed films that played continuously. If you stayed past the end, the clip would loop back to the beginning. The effect was one of perpetual sexual activity.

I found an aggressive vignette featuring a black-haired woman wearing leather boots and a headband. I was convinced she was a Native American. I imagined that she'd been separated from her tribe. Off the reservation, she was confined to a small room, with only a sawhorse as furniture. This was not her lucky day.

The problem was, the film was only about ten minutes long, so the repetition soon grew tiring. After the third loop, I couldn't watch another round of brutal activity.

* * *

I went back to where I was staying. The baguette and pâté had been eaten, so my friend and I went to a restaurant. The problem was, we couldn't read the menu. We guessed at a selection and ended up with a plate of snails, which were not bad, not at all. They had obviously just been harvested from a damp lawn. I could taste the dew.

Later, we found a better place to eat: a cafeteria. The food there was plentiful, varied and cheap. In addition, the place was located near the rue Saint-Denis—a big plus, in my opinion. At one point, as we sat there, my friend asked me for some coins. “I need them to open the stall in the men’s room,” he explained. “There’s some action back there.”

“What do you mean by ‘action’?” I asked.

“A guy met my eyes with his eyes. You know what that means. Do you have any change?”

“How much?”

“Two francs.”

That, I knew, was about 50 cents. I gave him the coins. I didn’t mind. I was off to the rue Saint-Denis.

* * *

Another time, my friend and I were sitting in the apartment with the main tenant, the commercial director. The two of them were smoking a hashish-and-tobacco cigar and talking about someone they knew, Annie, but her name was pronounced Ah-NEE.

“I stayed the night with her,” my friend said, “but she scraped me with her nails, and I got an infection.”

“She’s a bitch,” the director said, grinning.

I helped them finish the hash cigar, and all of us meditated on Annie.

* * *

Later, my friend and I went to visit Annie in her apartment across the river. Her place was luxurious, with a polished wood floor and a grand piano. Through the large windows, we could see a park with trees and the Eiffel Tower.

Annie wasn’t unfriendly or friendly. She just sat there with us. “There are two kinds of people,” she told me, “intellectuals, and those who follow their instincts.

“I’m the second,” she continued. “I can meet someone on a train, get off at the next station, have sex with him, and get back on the train.”

“I followed her here,” my friend explained to me. “She’s the reason I’m in Paris.”

Shortly, I left the apartment, but my friend stayed. I hoped Annie would not scrape him again with her nails.

* * *

When I finally took the subway, I noticed that the trains ran quietly. They didn’t shriek with the sound of metal against metal. My friend told me that was because the trains had rubber wheels, and I believed him. I imagined that the tracks were flat, and wide enough for tires to pass over. I didn’t look closely as a train went by to see if it had steel wheels—which, of course, it did.

The trains didn’t shriek with the sound of metal against metal. My friend told me that was because the trains had rubber wheels, and I believed him.

I took one of the trains to meet a French couple I knew from New York. But when I got to the address they had given me, they were not home. Someone I didn’t know was there, but he was hospitable. He served me a greenish-yellow liqueur. I disliked the taste but drank it anyway. Unable to converse, I sat in the small, unfamiliar apartment for a long while, sipping at my glass of chartreuse, nodding occasionally at my host, but the couple I knew never showed up.

* * *

Back at the storefront apartment, I got the young woman to sit while I drew her portrait. Her face filled a page of my sketchbook. I thought it was a perfect face, but on second look, I could see its flaws. The mouth was too wide, the eyes, too big. Those distortions, however, might have been due not to my model but to my own lack of skill.

At night, my friend brought out an envelope of drugs. “It’s Paris-brand junk,” he said. “It’s stronger than what you get in New York.”

I sniffed some of the powder and immediately felt sick. I ran to the WC, but by the time I got there, the wave of nausea had passed. Feeling all right, I returned to my friend’s room and lay down. Again, I felt the sickness, so I got up and returned to the WC. I repeated this pattern, of getting up and lying down, for most of the night.

* * *

IN THE DAYTIME, I went out walking. I still believed I could get anywhere I wanted on foot. I walked to the cathedral in the middle of the river. The structure had flying buttresses and craning gargoyles. The animals' heads stuck out on long necks, ready to spew boiling oil on anyone who approached.

I wanted to go into the cathedral, but a private event was being held. It was my last day in the city. I walked around the outside of the structure, looking at the buttresses and gargoyles, enjoying the flow of the river and my freedom from Paris-brand junk, then went back to where I was staying.

* * *

THE NEXT DAY, I had to take a train to another city. The train ran all night, and there were no seats, so I slept standing up. I leaned against a wall and dozed until my knees buckled. Before I fell over, I woke up. Then I leaned back and dozed again.

In a waking dream, I saw two women behind the glass door of a nearby compartment. They were sitting on opposite sides of a small shelf-table. One of them was holding a carrot with a Band-Aid wrapped around its middle. She pointed at the bandaged root, and her companion looked at it closely. The carrot was large and well wrapped. The companion gestured in turn at the erect carrot, and both women started to laugh uncontrollably. The first woman held the carrot over her head and waved it while both women pointed and giggled.

As the train covered ground, the names of towns changed. Mulhouse became Mulhausen, Bale became Basel, and la Suisse became Schweiz. At first, I really thought I was getting somewhere. I thought I was entering a different country. But soon enough, I realized I was still in France.

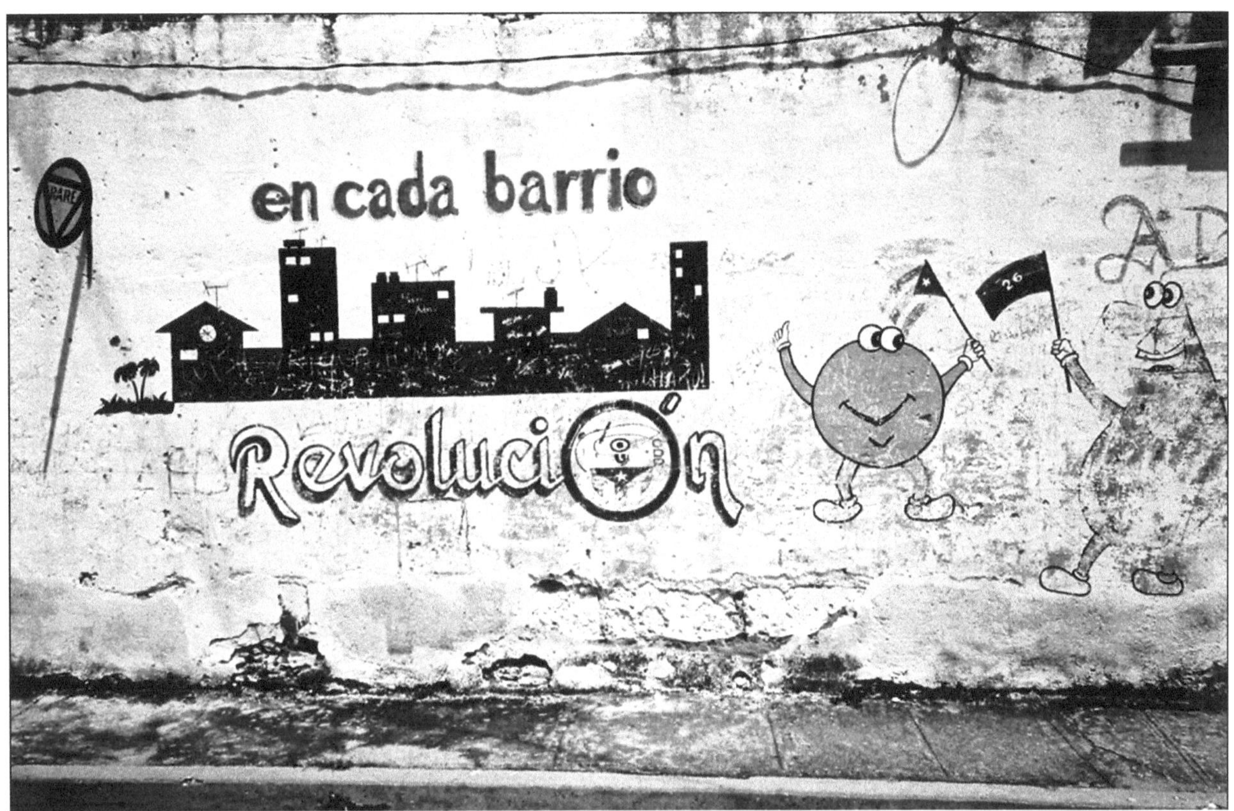

photograph by Cédric Monot

Eight Poems

Todd Colby

Peace & Good Order

Okay dear, whatever you can manage
will be propped up in a boat next to you
full of apologies and texts from some cabin
pumped with nitrous oxide next to the ocean.
You can't regret stuff when your mouth
is lick-jacking the petunias. In this instance
the poltergeist is actually the heat in this room.
That shit's got a real ghostly presence here
on Baltic Street. I'd like nothing more
than to see the future spread out on your bed
in chambray and muscles but I'm stuck.
This is like some other things,
but I like this one better.
You know what I am saying.

Orange Tan

What a ridiculously hot day can do
is make you sweat all over me.
All of this realism is what makes things
sort of interesting for the people
who can't be here right now.
By referring to real things
throughout the day,
you can start behaving
like you have a real body
that can do fun things.
I would like to sit down
on the roof and watch
you fly away to some realistic
land just down the block. Brooklyn in the heat
is so meager in the Department of Hope.
I am leaping into position, ready for the
delight that people with orange tans provide.
I will think of the circumstances that led me here
and, when I'm done, I will craft an excuse
not to be here at all.

How to Initiate Human Contact

You could arm wrestle with a perfect stranger
on a beautiful day like today. Okay, try this:
Walk into a deli and put a gallon of milk on the counter and ask
the cashier to arm wrestle. Simply put your elbow up
on the counter next to the milk and challenge the cashier
with your inside voice. Maybe there's a truck idling outside
and some kids are walking to school,
maybe a man is standing behind you
with a package of cookies. It's all coming together now.
You need to initiate contact with some fellow humans,
but you're going about it all wrong.
You're too aggressive and there's not enough sweetness or fun
in your leisure activities. Here, let me show you how.
I hope this is a magical year for you.
I miss you a lot.

Hello

Imagine a city
underwater where you
swim around in fancy pants
lock arms with total strangers
surface gasping as your lungs blaze
surrounded by bright orange air
you are nearly magical and sincere
children drive silver jets
that they pedal with their tiny legs
and then more summer
and simple movements
almost like dancing
around the sun on a goofy planet
here we are whispering our day
over the phone hexing new developments
holding on for one more day.

King of Time

I'm going to use the words you love
write something that smells like beer
light a bonfire on the roof
toss pine cones at the neighbor
kids I'm going to shout into a dirt clod
like it was a microphone
in a laundromat I will go back to my school
and jump around the auditorium like I never
did once I should have stuck my finger
in a socket in the Principal's office I will leap
into the air from the water tower spray
some paint over a "Rimbaud" stencil
on the back of my V.W. light the action
in the aftermath of glory comes platinum
oh you inspectors of cruelty I'll have none of your
sparkled hairdos and misshapen identities
you can keep your hot pounds and your celebrities with glass eyes
go throw yourself into a wall I prefer to chat with my mouth
or chew into an apple of deeper beats in this backwater of life
uninterrupted by death I have a hand waving
get me out of here.

Radiant & Dazzling

I want something really vast and soft
and radiant and dazzling to lift you into
the day so that you feel a real sense of panic
start to recede. There will be gorgeous spiders
and bits of blue skin and something really
sweet like peach pie and honey and pomegranate
jam and stuff like that. Huge flakes of snow
won't piss you off like they do me when you
walk in the field in Prospect Park someone
is there won't you watch them watch you
walk to me? I can't control what you do
in your free time but I can make a helpful
suggestion or three. Won't all the days you thought
would never end finally end and become
planted in your memory as calm shivers? A shark never
stops moving, not even for you, so why should
you stop getting jacked up before bed, if not for me?
The city is all moist and expectant
like my hand on your cheek as you sleep,
I certainly hope so.

Red Onion in the Snow

An elegant blitz of slush
is something I can wake up to.
My sheets have jelly on them.
All my books are marked with severed
pinkies. Out in the living room someone
spilled corn on the pillows
and stinky green multivitamins
are strewn on the floor.
What's going on here?
I'm alone with the
crisp metallic clang of the radiator and the sounds
of snow removal machines humming
together creating a wobbly harmony.
The day is blank. Someone put
a red onion on the snow outside
my door, like that would help
change things, like I would ever
make out on the F Train again.

Who Let You Go?

All the people are getting even with my
new panic button because they are revved up on
capitalism. A battering ram at my door like on a cop show,
with theatrical urgency, because they know they're being filmed.
I don't want to wake up to that, ever. It's good to mention
what you feel too but what about my door? It's fucked.
An eagle on a nature show eats some fungi
and mistakes himself for a fist with wings
(he flies pretty good for sick eagle though).
Oh for the days of simply whistling while I floated
down a river with my ass planted in an inner tube.
Oh to never again frisk a litigant, or sell something
to someone I don't even know. I'm trying to be fabulous
all the time. I've ordered some super special diamond dice
from the internets that are just for licking, you. Of
wetness and the bridge of your nose, of workers
knocking things over, of dreams that show
no signs of beginning. Oh, who let you go?

If You Play and If You Die

Jim Feast

Artemis Brewster owned a large retail store in New Jersey, the Bargain Toy Mart (Toys for Less!) And he loved science fiction as much as what he sold. But his was not the doting, immature love of the geeky fanboy, it was the mature, robust love of the connoisseur. In fact, he loved a little too much, often playing the role of mentor to his favorite authors: writing letters (judicious ones, he thought) to sometimes chide them "for letting themselves and their genre down." Occasionally his missives went on a bit too long—and sometimes they were more than just a little bit negative.

For example, take his letter to Thomas Disch, whose early story, "Descending," printed in *Fantasy and Science Fiction* in 1964, he particularly treasured. On rereading it years later, he felt compelled to contact the author, pointing out a glaring defect in the otherwise powerful piece. In the story a penurious writer, who has been living on instant noodles, finally makes a big sale. After cashing the check, he goes to a large department store to buy a paperback novel as well as some snack food. He is so ravenous, both physically and intellectually, that he tears open a bag of pretzels and begins reading the newly purchased tome simultaneously as he rides down an escalator. Immersed in these two activities, he stays on the moving stairs even after everyone else has gotten off, eventually traveling deep into the store's nether regions. And this is what Brewster took issue with.

"It's implausible," Brewster wrote Disch. "People have omni-active peripheral senses. No matter how engrossed you are in a particular pursuit, you'll be immediately snapped back to reality if there is a radical shift in your surroundings, say, going from a peopled to unpeopled terrain. Given this internal alarm system, it is simply out of the question that a character would descend multiple stories into a basement without noting that fact. Don't get me wrong," Brewster ended. "I only make these complaints because your story has affected me so deeply—haunting me, even—that I want you to redo it to make it perfect."

Disch didn't reply to his letter—perhaps he never got it—and, as time went by, Brewster forgot he ever sent it.

That Fall, Artemis went to the annual Guangzhou Toy Fair in south China—he made this pilgrimage every year to order toys to restock his store. Anything he bought in the U.S. was usually overpriced, so the money he spent on air fare was always more than made up for by the profit he would make on the toys he was buying. Besides, he truly enjoyed being in China with his translator and partner, Mr. Chu.

After placing several large orders, Brewster decided to take a stroll through the streets surrounding the toy fair to relax. Unfortunately, Mr. Chu was sick, so he wasn't by his side. Artemis walked down Beijing Lu absorbing the abrasive rhythms of the marketplace. A shopping area like this one, with its streets closed to traffic, had a lot more commotion than one found in the streets of, say, Philadelphia. The numerous small clothing shops had no proper storefronts, only pull-down shutters that left their entrances open to the air; they were clogged with customers fingering the fabrics and teenage girls standing on the bottoms of overturned buckets in front of each one clapping along with the music that issued from chest-high speakers as they chanted, "*Hoy my. Hoy my.*" ("Come, buy. Come, buy.")

As Brewster elbowed his way through this cacaphony, he stayed in the arcade, avoiding the even more raucous closed street where shoppers converged on such cynosures as a giant Coke can that lay on its side serving as a soft drink stand. By doing this, he avoided the touts who approached foreigners with laminated sheets showing a variety of high-end watches they were trying to unload. After a few minutes, tired of the sensory overkill and the mid-afternoon heat, Brewster sought refuge in the imposing GrandBuy department store.

He checked out the toy floor and, feeling proud of himself for having navigated that labyrinth so well, got on the elevator to descend to a lower level. There were two buttons at the bottom of the panel:

1 門口
1 土庫

Just by chance, the whole car emptied on the upper 1. The crowded displays on that floor didn't appeal to him, as there weren't any toys in sight, so he proceeded alone down to the lower 1. The door opened to reveal a dark aisle filled with packing crates. He seemed to be in the basement.

Immediately on the elevator's settling, its lights blinked out, including those on the control panel. He felt around, pressing all the buttons in the dark, but nothing worked. The door remained open. He felt all over the walls, getting more and more frustrated. It was then that he recalled the Disch story and his resultant letter.

Figuring he'd better find the stairs, Brewster hesitantly made his way down the aisle, bumping into the large cartons that were on all sides in the dim grayness. They were the kind that could hold hundreds of Barbie dolls apiece and they sat unevenly stacked on pallets, each box stamped with what looked to be identical Chinese characters—the world's worst case of overstocking.

He continued straight ahead, hearing no other sound than his own footsteps in the vast space. Turning a corner, he glimpsed a lighted door in the distance. He picked up the pace and finally reached it, a door that opened onto a stairwell. But now there was a decision to be made. Next to this exit was another elevator, which had its door open, was lit up and seemingly awaited his pleasure.

He didn't have to think long. Why walk? He got aboard his "escape vehicle" and faced another indecipherable array on the control panel. There were no English numbers at all. Again he moved impulsively, hitting the second button from the bottom, assuming this panel mirrored the one in the conveyance he had gotten off. The door closed smoothly and the elevator

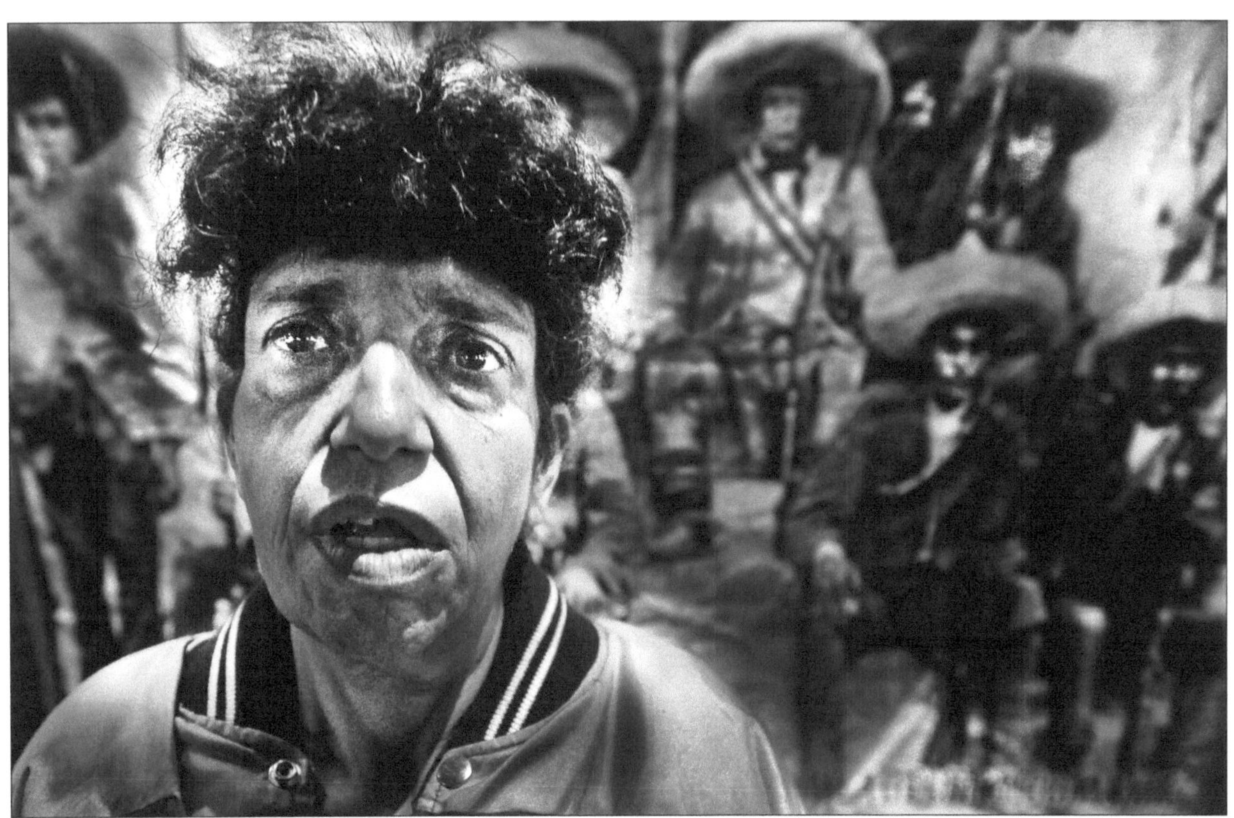

photograph by Chris Bava

dropped down one level, opening on another vista of packing crates.

He was shaken, to say the least. It appeared this elevator only went down. As he was staring at the control panel bewildered, without having time to react, the door closed again and the car descended further.

When the door opened this time, there was not the same array of packing crates but a vast plain of automobiles: row upon row of compact cars, new ones from the look of it, though their bodies were dull in the bleak light. He blocked the door with his own body to keep it from closing and looked around to see if anyone had perhaps summoned the elevator. He yelled out in vain, getting only an echo in reply. He stared at the rows of cars receding into the dark distance; ominous in silence.

He stepped back in, jabbing the very top button that logically should have taken him back to the floor he'd left, where he could try the stairs this time. But he had a new problem. The door started to close, ran most of the way across, then retracted. Had his holding it open jammed something? Nothing he did would make it work; it stayed open, not budging at all.

In a panic, Brewster decided to take any stairway he could find, so he ran out into the sub-basement looking for one. Fear was starting to overwhelm him. This was not the way reality should be. Normally, there was nothing he loved more on his factory visits than walking through serried rows of Baby Boo dolls or Maximus Man action figures, feeling the vastness and power of manufacturing, but the endless rows of cars buried many stories underground were only threatening. He sped past the brooding headlights.

As he was crossing the vast cavern, he realized he was making a mistake. It would make more sense to hug the walls, making a circuit of the room till he found access to a stairwell. He backtracked, and then turned to his left, finally coming upon a locked door with ideogrammatic labeling, which, for all he knew, might have been a storage closet. He couldn't open it. He passed a closed elevator, then stumbled onto a door labeled with the universal symbol of stairs.

But it was locked and he didn't have anything with which to pry it open. A sudden inspiration hit him. He could hop in one of the parked cars and, if he could start it, drive over and crash into the door. Screw the damages. He tried opening several car doors, but they were sealed tight. Even their trunks and hoods were locked. Moreover, he could see through their windows that none of them had keys in the ignition.

This was getting him nowhere. He decided to walk the complete circuit before he got too fixated on this one exit door. There might be other options, but the chill in this dank basement was getting to him. What did he know of the car trade? Perhaps cars were stashed in such out-of-the-way facilities for months without being disturbed. And no one knew he had come down here. No one even knew he was in this store.

"Be systematic," he told himself. That had always been his way, whether coping with a downturn in the business or family problems. He would make a complete tour of the premises and, if that didn't yield an open exit point, slowly and untiringly check every one of the few hundred cars to see if any had been left open. Very likely someone had gotten careless and not locked one of them.

And if that didn't work, he would get back into the elevator that brought him here and pound on the walls until someone above him heard it. One of these actions would have to yield fruit.

Even as he spun these options in his head, he quickened his pace, almost trotting to get his initial survey done. He was trying to stay focused, but his frantic haste was not rational, not guided. He forced himself to slow to a jog. Then a paralyzing, crazy thought shot through his head. "This is the revenge of Disch's story." And even though it was the kind of lunatic idea one only gets in a panic, it sent a chill sparking down his spine. That frightening idea didn't last long. In the next minute, he saw a new elevator, a big one this time. The inside was brightly lit and it was open. In it sat an automobile.

He hurried over and scouted the situation. The sedan's right front door was open and the keys were in the ignition. Okay. He breathed deeply, his mind working systematically, flipping through possibilities as if he were rifling through a Rolodex. No sense trying to ride this elevator. He'd just get in the sedan and, assuming it started, drive around the basement till he came to the stairway door, which he would crash into gently, freeing up his exit.

But he had another thought. What if he got in the car and the elevator door suddenly snapped closed? He removed his shoes and suit jacket and braced them at bottom edge of the elevator door so it couldn't shut completely.

Then he had another thought. Usually there were panels in the ceiling that could be popped open. He climbed up on the car and examined the roof of the service elevator. It was unyielding.

He sat down on the hood to rest. Why did they leave the car in the elevator with keys in the ignition? Chinese workers, like the Americans he'd known, were loafers. When it was quitting time, whoever was handling this car had decided to find a place to park it tomorrow.

To escape, he simply had to hop in, start the engine, motor out and drive over to the door he needed to break down. But nothing was simple down here.

Brewster slid feet first down the hood of the car and firmed up a plan of action. To escape, he simply had to hop in, start the engine, motor out and drive over to the door he needed to break down. But nothing was simple down here. He got in the car and, offering up a little prayer, was about to turn the key when he paused again. What if the car door he'd just closed had jammed? He quickly tried the door—it opened. He twisted the key and the motor sprang to life. Then another problem arose. There were no markings on the gearshift. He'd seen this on some American models. The shift indications were displayed on the dashboard. However, look as he might, he couldn't find any.

Trial and error, he thought, gingerly moving the shift one notch and tapping the accelerator lightly. The car lurched backward, banging the back wall of the elevator sharply. All at once, before he could pump down on the brake pedal, the wall buckled without breaking, the lights went off, the whole enclosure tilted back, and the elevator door started to close.

Trying desperately to remain calm, he switched off the ignition or, rather, tried to switch it off and snapped the key instead. He watched in horror as the elevator door went past where his shoes should have stopped it—shoes which had now slid from their place when the floor tilted—though it didn't close completely, leaving a hairline crack. The door was barely held open by his jacket, which was slowly being forced into the cavity.

He was shaking but still thinking clearly, almost clinically. He just had to get out and force the door open.

In the crash, the car had shifted to the right wall, so he had to switch sides and exit on the left, but the door on that side wouldn't open at all. He could still break the window, squeeze through and crawl over the roof—which he did. He was woozy from the exhaust fumes, but remained focused—his consciousness crystal clear, his actions sure and quick—as if he'd been transformed into one of the Maximus Man figures he liked to sell.

He staggered to the crack and drew a few pure breaths through the chink, while trying to shove back the door. It was immoveable.

New plan. He could reenter the car, shift a second notch down and drive into the door, ripping it right out. He mounted the hood, but after a minute's exertions, he staggered back to suck more clean air from the door space. He realized he would surely pass out if he tried to get back in the driver's seat.

Then he was hit by an inspiration. He went to the front of the car, found a latch and wrenched up the hood. He would yank off the fan belt and kill the engine. But before he could do that, he slumped to the floor, almost overcome. Had to get back up. He tried to stand but stumbled sideways, careening off the elevator buttons, then sat down again. The whole structure began shivering and groaning. With a tremendous screech, the back wall rubbed against the shaft. He was going upwards jerkily, as if drawn by a demiurge or, as flashed through his mind, a Maximus Disch lifting him to toy heaven.

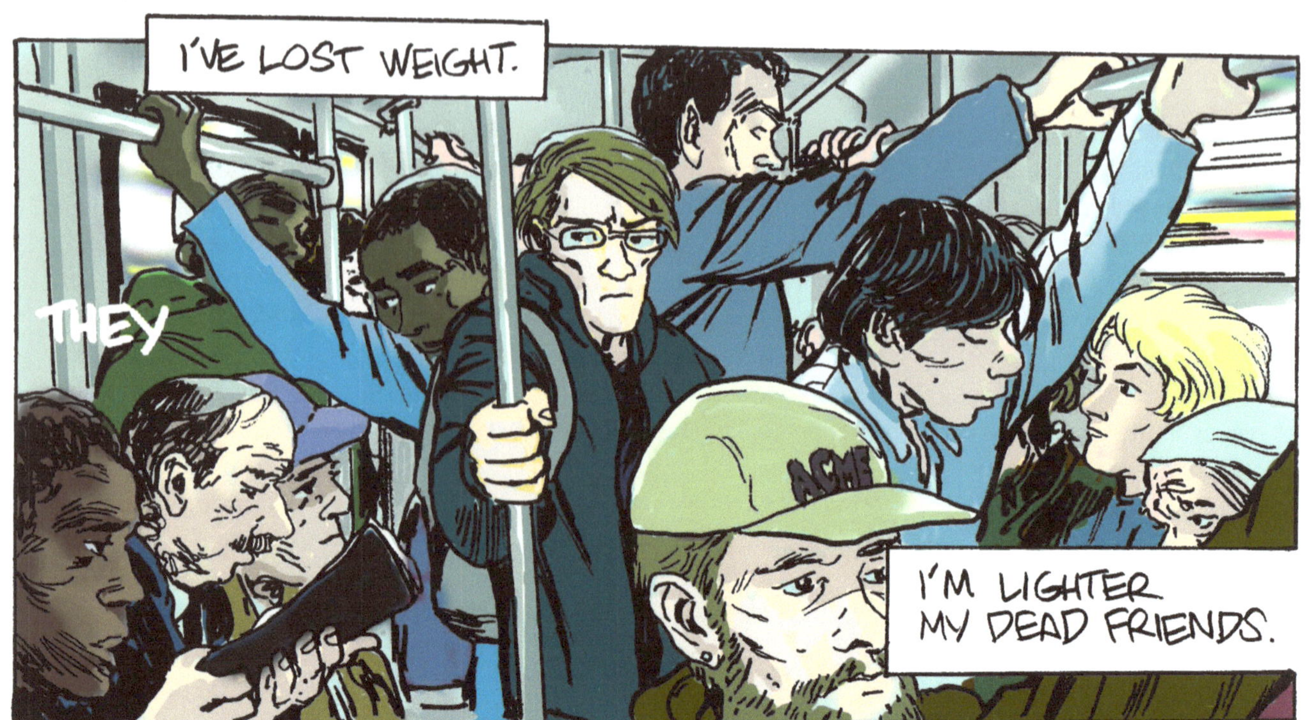
I'VE LOST WEIGHT.
THEY
I'M LIGHTER
MY DEAD FRIENDS.
ACME

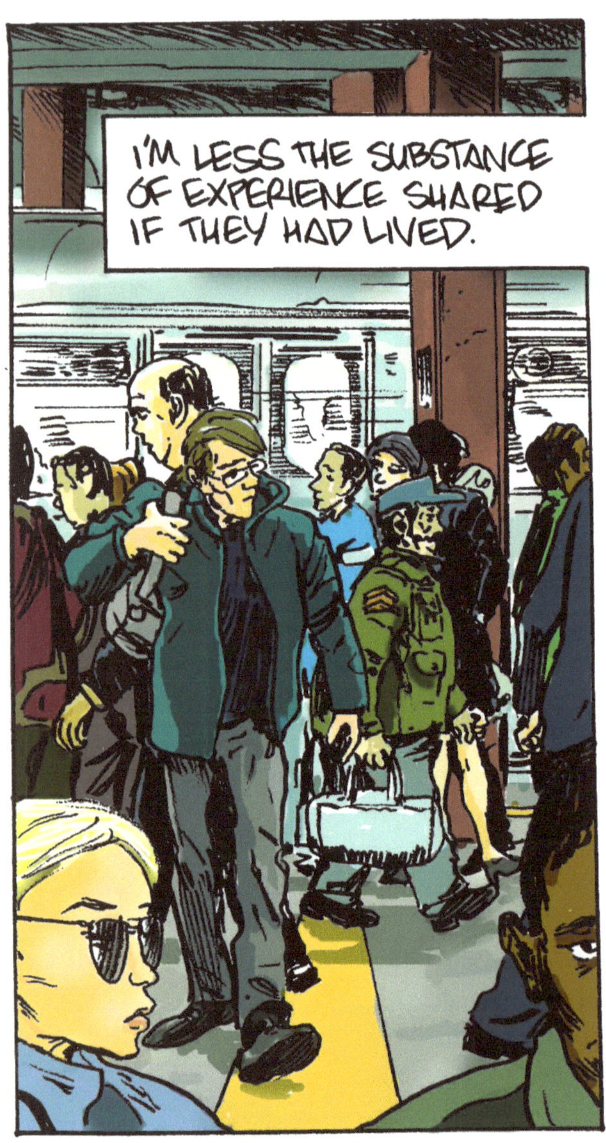
I'M LESS THE SUBSTANCE
OF EXPERIENCE SHARED
IF THEY HAD LIVED.

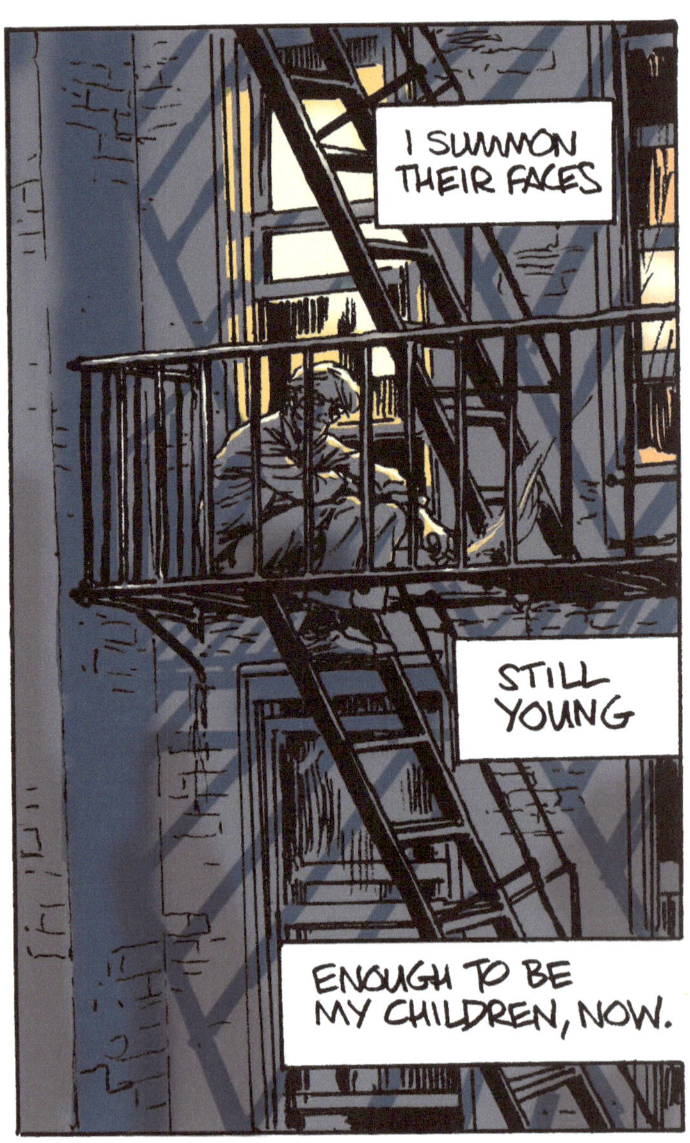
I SUMMON
THEIR FACES
STILL
YOUNG
ENOUGH TO BE
MY CHILDREN, NOW.

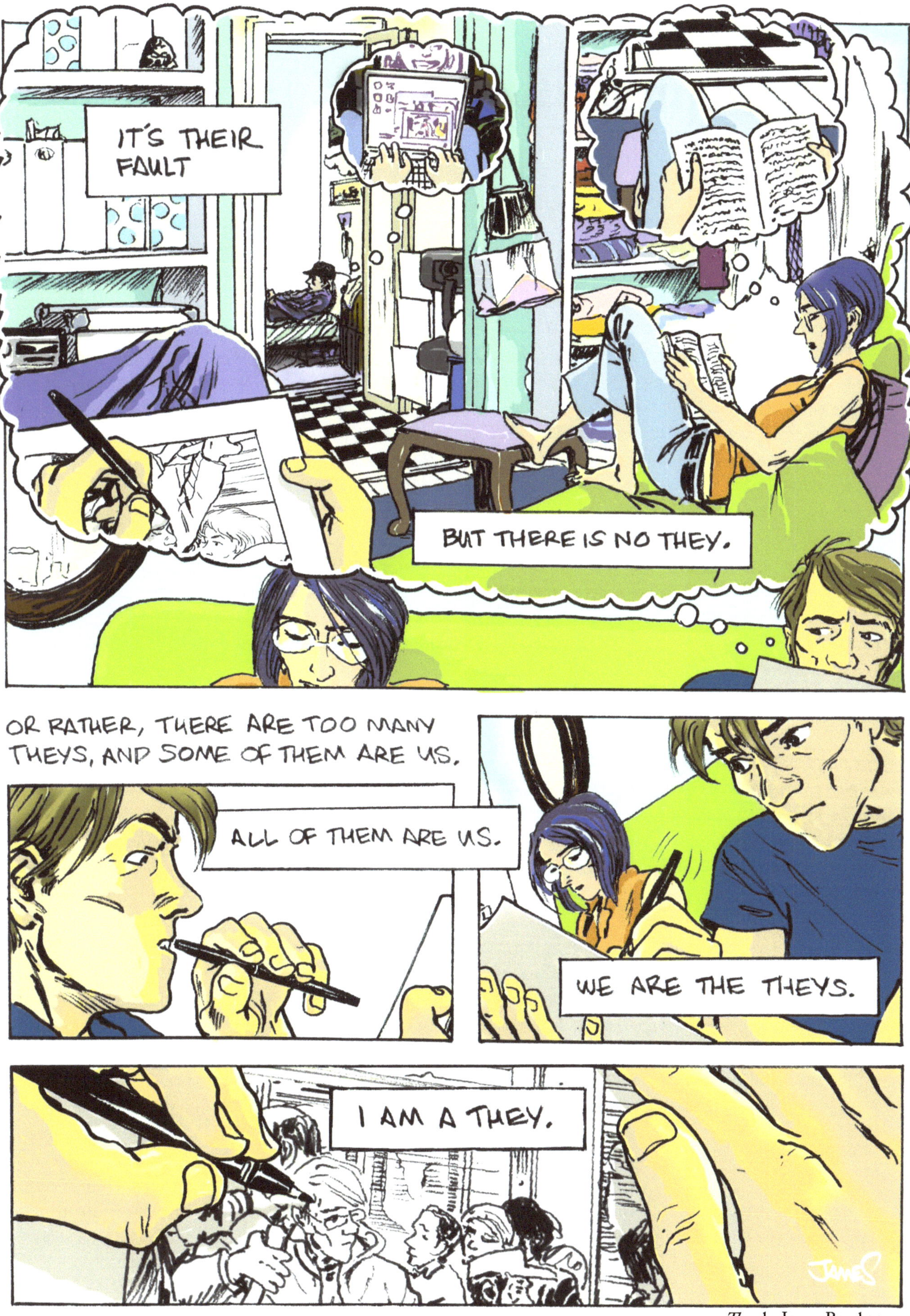

IT'S THEIR FAULT

BUT THERE IS NO THEY.

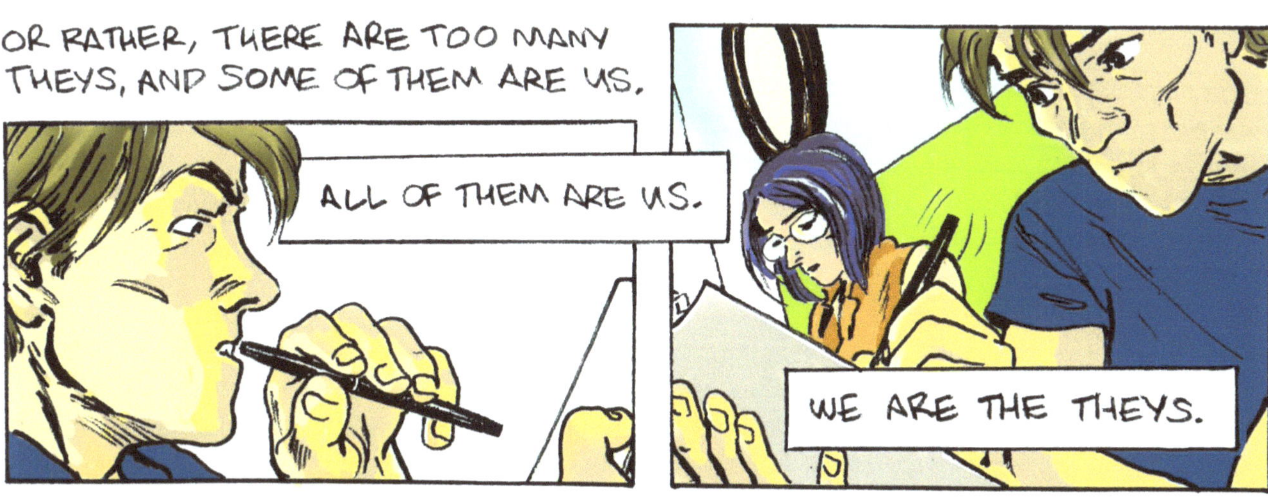

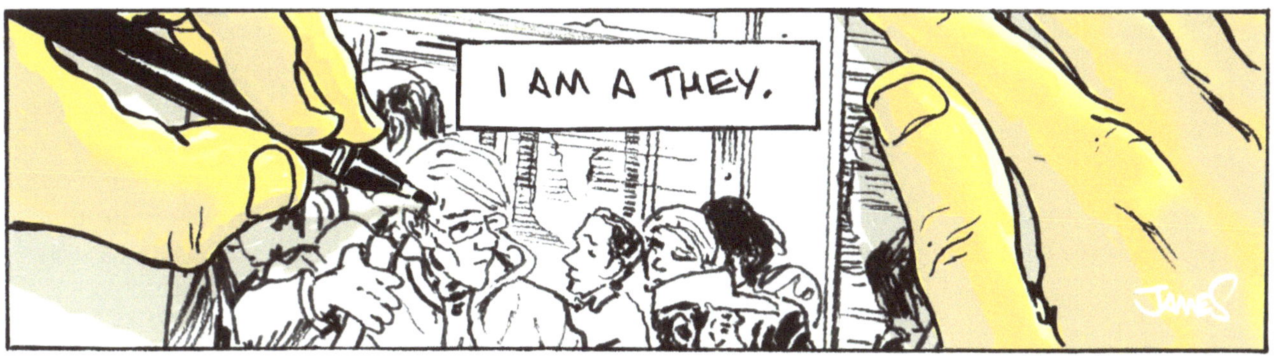

They, by James Romberger

William S. Burroughs: Interview

Allen Ginsberg

Editor's Note: *Circa 1995, one of the editors of the original* Sensitive Skin, *Mr. E. Oso, handed me the following manuscript, in turn given to him by an assistant to Allen Ginsberg, Ginsberg having blessed it for inclusion in the magazine. Unfortunately, at that time, to paraphrase W. B. Yeats, shit was all fucked-up and bullshit, so we never got around to publishing the piece. So it sat in a drawer. When* Sensitive Skin *came back on line in 2010, I remembered the Burroughs interview—but I couldn't find it. I looked for it everywhere, but after a cross-country move, it—along with all of the OG files from issues past and projected—had gone missing. As the French say,* "Emmenez-moi votre mère, pour que je puisse vous refaire!"

Then, six months ago, in the fall of 2011, while poring over ancient CD-Rs, searching for an old scan, I stumbled across all the missing files, including the Burroughs piece! Huzzah!

Shortly thereafter, the painter David West approached me about publishing his book, Music: Drawing Down the Muse. *He told me to go see the book's designer, Ruby Ray, in San Francisco, to check out the galleys. So I met Ruby and, looking around her apartment, quickly sussed out that she was a photographer. As a matter of fact, she's* the *photographer, the one who took those iconic Burroughs shots for* RE/Search *magazine back in the '80s. Turns out she had some unpublished photographs from that session, which she generously gave me permission to use. When I told David about it, he sent me the original illustrations he'd created back in '95 to accompany the article, so they're included as well. Sometimes the universe tells you what to do. . . .*

I recently learned this interview had *been published, in a collection called* Burroughs Live: The Collected Interview of William S. Burroughs, 1960-1997, *from Semiotext(e). The book was published in 2000, I don't think it's widely known (6 reviews on Amazon), and hey, we had it first. So here it is. . . .*

—B. Kold

The preface is from Allen Ginsberg's Journals. Steven Taylor transcribed the many hours of taped conversation which took place in Lawrence, Kansas, from March 17–22, 1992. Steven Taylor and Allen Ginsberg made the initial edits, from which a very small selection follows.

[*I WENT OUT*] LAST NIGHT WITH BILL BURROUGHS and friends to a stone house in which Bill used to live on a hilltop outside Lawrence, Kansas. William Lyon [*a professor of anthropology who apprenticed 14 years with Wallace Black Elk, a Sioux medicine man*] now rents the same house and has dug beside it a sweat lodge to work with a Navajo Indian shaman named Melvin Betsellie.

We sat with towels in the black dark smoky plastic igloo bower, laced with twig skeleton covered with black plastic, a fire pit in center. Bill sat by the entrance as the big-bellied shaman went 'round the tent thanking each one there, Bill first, for inviting him to share the grandfathers' medicine and again giving him the opportunity to drive the bad spirit out of Bill's life and body. Then he prayed to the grandfathers, water, earth, rocks and green coal. So Melvin prayed to the creator, the grandfathers, the elements, to help Bill on his way, make his way easy when it's time for him to go back to the creator, make him strong to live a long long time, and to us all to think of Bill and send him our healing thoughts, get rid of the bad element that was in the coal, send the bad spirit back to the one who'd put it in Bill, maybe an animal, maybe someone angry. The spirit was caught, jiggled in the shrill flute & blown into the fire. Put the spirit into the rocky fire pit still glowing, steaming with cedar-fragrant smoke in our eyes.

Last round of pipe and tobacco were passed 'round, sweet mild tobacco. We puffed three or four times each from the long-stemmed stone-headed heavy

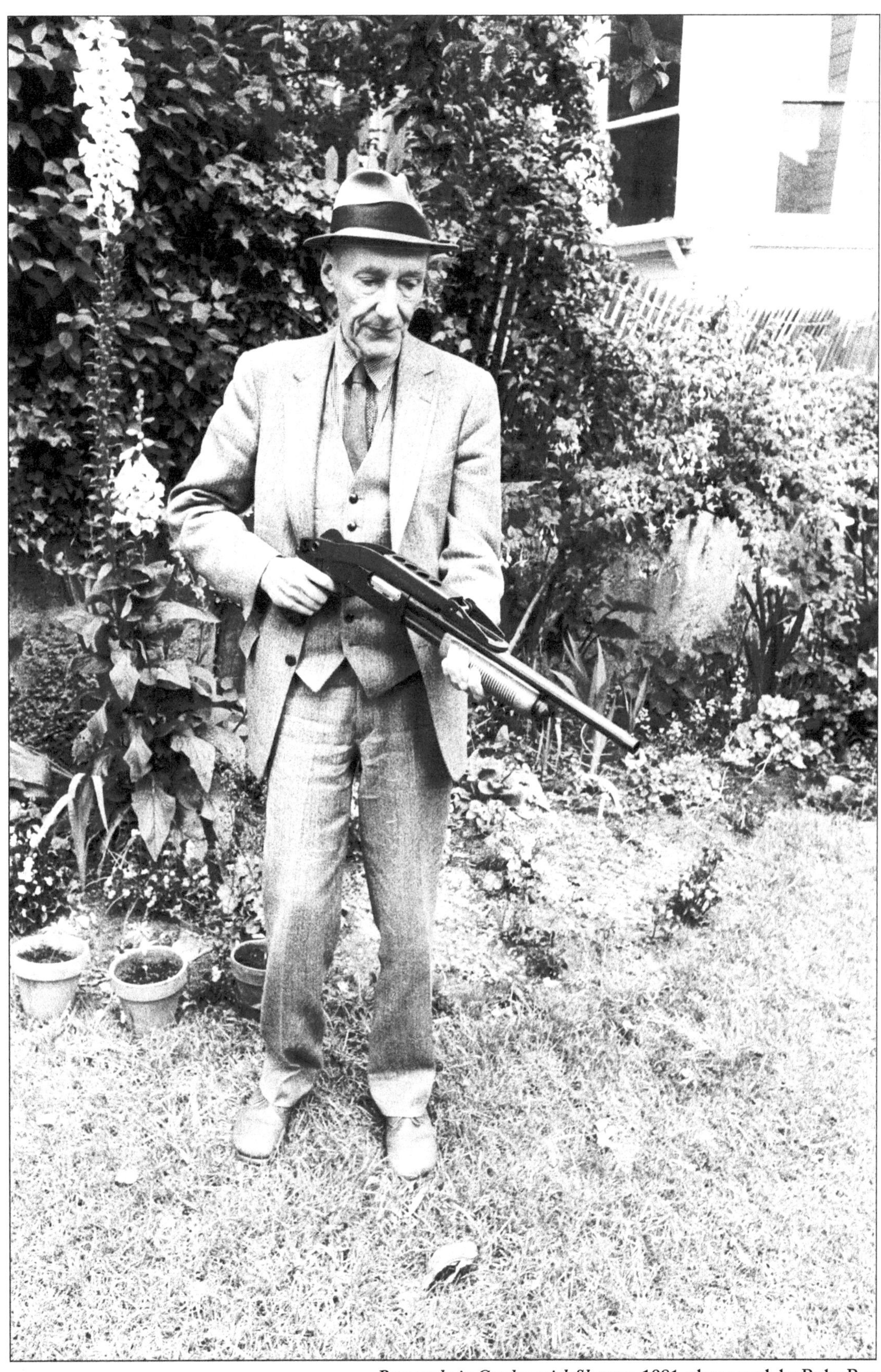

Burroughs in Garden with Shotgun, 1981, photograph by Ruby Ray pipe. Thank ancestors, thank water, stone, sky, wood, varied elements, spirits, crawling spirits, insect spirits, all asked to help us and help this old man on his way have a strong heart and clear head and a long happy life, peaceful life from now on, the bad spirit gone back to where it came from, who it came from.

I was naked in the darkness as was Bill, except for his shorts. He kept saying: "Yes . . . yes . . . of course, thank you, I'm grateful," with good, subdued, conscious manners, quietly responsive 'till, at the end with the heat and suffocating smoke and occasional heart pity, "Please, please, open the door, some air." And a couple of times: "Please, let me out, I need to go out," till he lay down with his head close to cooler floor where there was more clear air. His chest wrinkled, the scar of coronary bypass skin colored brown, tan like on his arms and breast which sat wrinkled on his frame. Thin body, the back of him was stooped, soft-muscled but vigorous at 78 years. He said, "I always thought poets were lazy prose writers, writing paragraphs and sentences and breaking it up into lines.'"

The Shaman prayed to help Bill on his way, make his way easy when it's time for him to go back to the creator, and to get rid of the bad element that was in the coal, send the bad spirit back to the one who'd put it in Bill, maybe an animal, maybe someone angry.

Climax of long ceremony, on his knees, Mel chanted several long long prayers. Then he repeated anaphoric words in his native Navajo tongue . . . and waved the smoke at all of us separately and prayed repeatedly to the bear spirit, the four-legged people, the two-legged people, the crawling people, the insects, the families, the brothers and sisters here and everywhere, the relatives and their own brothers and sisters or relatives. Family, all one family, no matter what race we come from. All relatives together in a room.

Finally, ceremony over, we all ate, big servings of pot-roast meat, baked cheese potato slices, salad, coffee, a homemade sweet icing cake.

Now next morning, Bill's up talking to his cats, feeding them. I'll get up and see him on his way to Kansas City 7:30 AM, later read him this account.

* * *

Breakfast table talk, AG and WSB at table.

AG: How did you feel emotionally or psychologically during the exorcism ceremony? That was quite moving, I thought, all those people really wishing you well.

WSB: Oh, that's what I felt too. They were really great and I just felt, you know, sort of . . . laying myself open, just completely, undirected thought, undirected thought. I did nothing, no sort of intellectualizing.

AG: What occurred to me is that we were focusing on your well-being, but also, I was realizing at the time. . . . I don't know if you realize how many people really love your work and feel a great deal of affection, but it must be hundreds of thousands or millions of people.

WSB: Yes. Well, yeah I feel it. I feel it very deeply. I like the shaman very much, the way he was crying.

AG: Later, in conversation with the shaman, you were agreeing that, in order to get a spirit, you have to see it.

WSB: Oh yes. If you see it, you gain control of it. It's just a matter of, well, if you see it outside, it's no longer inside.

AG: In other words, unless error were allowed enough play so that it manifested itself visibly—

WSB: You would never see it. In exorcism, a verbal argument can never do anything. You can't ever beat the entity in a verbal argument because that's what he wants. It's only through a confront, a non-verbal confront, that anything happens. It has to be non-verbal. Otherwise, they'd argue and argue going around and around and around for a hundred thousand years. But the arguing has nothing whatever to do with what they're really doing.

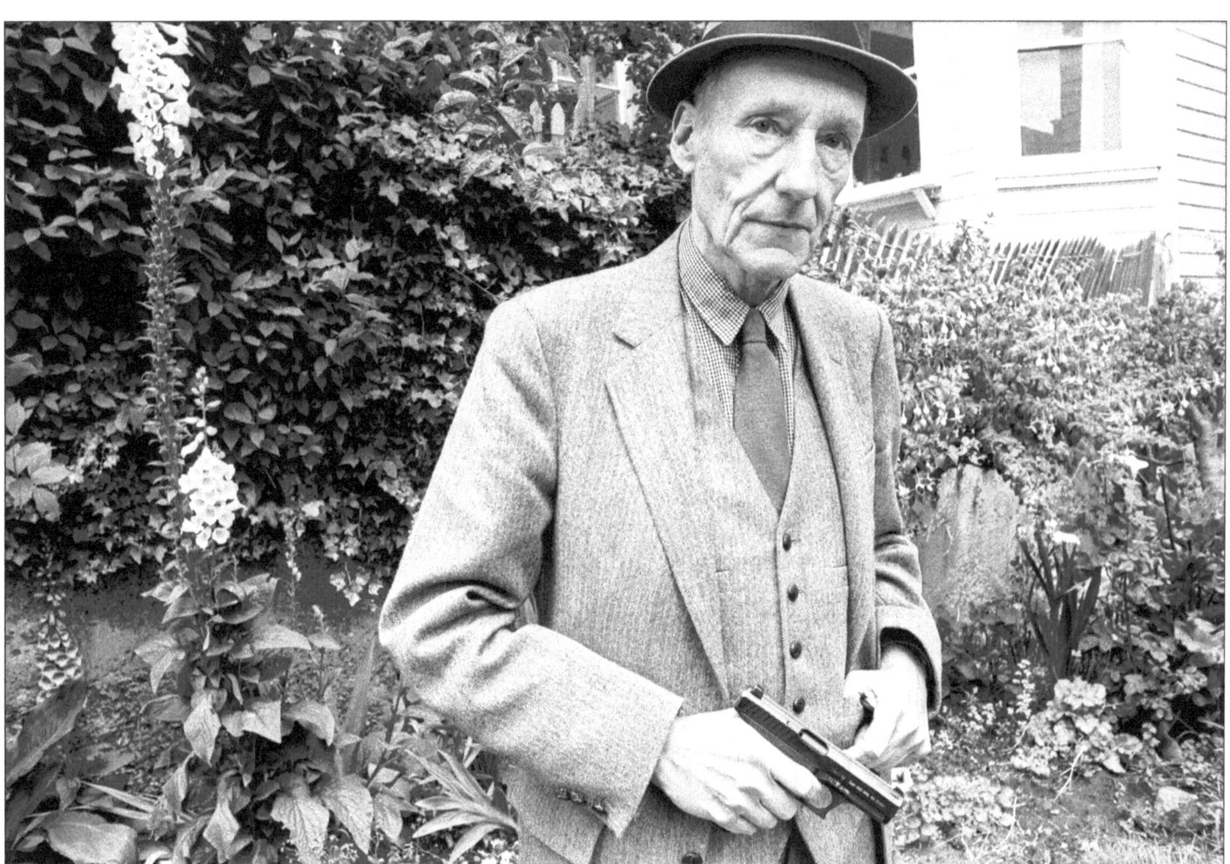

Burroughs with Colt Commander, **1981, photograph by Ruby Ray**

AG: So now how would you have confronted the Satan in the Ayatollah and his followers, about this price on Salman Rushdie's head and the killing of his Japanese translator?

WSB: That is not a question. You think in political terms or justifications, never get anywhere.

AG: Well, the method of confrontation is now that many of the publishers got together to put out *The Satanic Verses* in paperback. That's not an argument, that's a deed.

WSB: Yes, it might be something. But never, never a verbal argument, it will never never go anywhere except in circles. Because you're not talking about the issue at all, you're talking about words.

AG: Uh-huh. I like the idea of the idea as a virus. In marketing research, that's exactly what they do. Like for political purposes, make a little three-word virus slogan.

WSB: Why, sure. Now I know you've heard about the computer viruses.

AG: Yeah, now what do they do, spread through telephone modems?

WSB: It can get in the program. And then it's hard to get rid of. They have to kind of call in the priest to exorcize the computer.

AG: What do you think the shaman, Melvin, was seeing in you? What do you think he was getting?

WSB: He described it as a spirit with a white skull face, but no eyes, and sort of . . . wings, like that.

AG: A-ha! And did you get any glimpse of such a thing?

WSB: Well I have many times.

AG: Yeah, and you've painted it in a way.

WSB: Yes, I brought it out in some paintings and he would say, "Well, there it is, there it is, and there it is," in the painting. Come in here and I'll show you some of the paintings that I showed him.

* * *

They move into the painting studio.

AG: Here are some journalistic questions: Why did it take so long for your books to be published?

WSB: Well, there were lots of reasons.

AG: In those days, there was very direct censorship.

WSB: See, I had published *Naked Lunch* in 1959, it was published in Paris. Then, when it came to the question of publishing *Queer* (mss. 1952), I didn't have the manuscript. Alan Ansen the poet had the manuscript in Venice. And I wasn't in a hurry to publish it because I felt it was amateuristic, you know. I'd gone much further by then.

AG: You already had material for *Soft Machine*, and—

WSB: *The Ticket that Exploded*. You see, *Naked Lunch* was from about a thousand pages of material. A lot of it overflowed, then, into the cut-up trilogy including *Nova Express*.

AG: And then a big huge manuscript, *Interzone,* that Kerouac had helped type, which was the first draft of *Naked Lunch*. But there was another reason, as I remember, which was that *Howl* was not published till 1957. In the *Howl* case in San Francisco, the judge said that literary merit was a critical consideration. Up to that point, *Queer* would have been too . . . colorful to pass censorship. And then since '58, in a sequence of cases beginning with D.H. Lawrence and Henry Miller and culminating in '62 with the *Naked Lunch* victory, the courts affirmed over and over again that literary merit was a defense against censorship for obscenity.

WSB: Yep.

AG: And that had never been established. Like in Britain, Vizetelly was persecuted in the 19th century for publishing Emile Zola, and was ruined because the statement of literary merit was not allowed in court. And then in the '20s in England, Radclyffe Hall's lesbian *The Well of Loneliness* was condemned, though the entire Bloomsbury circle went to court, including Virginia Woolf, Leonard Woolf and E.M. Forster. They weren't allowed to speak for the literary merit of the book—which they didn't think had that much literary merit—but they went to bat for it because, though it was controversial, it was legitimate.

WSB: Yes, and the Sitwells, too.

AG: Yes, but British court at that time said that literary merit would not be admissible as any sort of evidence. The question in British law was whether or not the book was obscene, not whether it had merit.

WSB: Yes.

AG: In the American James Joyce decision of the '20s, the judge said that, if the definition of pornography or obscenity is that it tends to excite or arouse lust, then *Ulysses* is more of an emetic, so does not arouse lust.

WSB: I think it was Judge Learned Hand. Well, he was a cultured, intelligent man.

AG: So the sequence of trials that Grove Press funded in the '50s, culminating with yours, actually broke the back of literary censorship, because at that point, it was not a question of whether or not it aroused erotic interest, or gave you a hard-on, or got you sexually aroused. It was a question of whether this arousal was on the basis of something that had artistic or literary merit. OK. [*Reading*]: "How come *Naked Lunch* was started in Tangier?" Actually, *Naked Lunch* was started before. Originally, Interzone and the Market had their origins in notes you wrote when we were editing *The Yage Letters* together in New York in late 1953. I always thought the Interzone Meet Café was the seed of *Naked Lunch.*

WSB: Absolutely. Yes.

AG: I thought *Star Wars* stole that seed when they had that Meet Café, the interplanetary bar.

WSB: Oh, yes, well I wouldn't say that they stole it.

AG: Well, the vision certainly was keyed-off or "appropriated." [*Reading*]: In '57, Orlovsky, Kerouac and Ginsberg visited Burroughs in Tangier. Did Burroughs receive any influences from that event to write *Naked Lunch*?"

WSB: No.

AG: No, what you received . . . we came bringing manuscripts and Kerouac bringing his typing and editing skills. Did he type *Interzone*, or what?

WSB: He typed quite a lot of it. Fast typer.

AG: Yeah, a hundred twenty words a minute.

AG: [*Reading*]: Please tell us about Brion Gysin [*painter and Burroughs collaborator*]. How was the cutup technique created? What was Mr. Burroughs intention in creating this technique? How did they collab—

WSB: I did not create it. It was created by Brion Gysin. It's really a painter's technique, an extension of the collage technique, which was pretty old hat in painting at that time. It is closer really to the process of human perception. You see, should I stand in front of a landscape and paint it, I'm completely ignoring the factor of time. While I am painting it, it's changing, clouds are changing, all sorts of things. So there's the myth there of someone creating in a timeless vacuum. Now, so I say, take a walk around the block, come back, and put what you have seen on canvas. What have you seen? You have seen fragments. You've seen a man cut in half by a car, you've seen reflections in the shop windows.

AG: Uh-huh, and you've seen your own thoughts, if you daydreamed also.

WSB: Yes, of course, and how they intersect with reality. And I found that if you notice what you were thinking when you saw something, you'll see that what you're thinking is reflected in what you see. I was thinking about New Mexico, and I rounded the corner in New York, and there was a New Mexico license plate: "New Mexico, land of enchantment."

AG: Now, Gysin's suggestion was that "writing was fifty years behind painting," from the point of view of the Dadaist and early collage artists.

WSB: Yes. Also, this is closer to the facts of perception. Every time you look out the window or walk down the street, your consciousness is cut by random, seemingly random . . . Life is a cutup. And to pretend that you write or paint in a timeless vacuum is just simply . . . not . . . true, not in accord with the facts of human perception.

Life is a cutup. And to pretend that you write or paint in a timeless vacuum is just simply . . . not . . . true, not in accord with the facts of human perception.

AG: Portions of *Naked Lunch* were sent to Maurice Girodias [*original Paris publisher of* Naked Lunch *at Olympia Press*] in the order of their typing.

WSB: That's right.

AG: And so the arrangement of those chapters was in a sense random or cutup.

WSB: The idea was that we would decide the order when we looked at the proofs. I remember Brion saying "Well, why change it? It's perfect the way it is, the way it came from the printer." Made one major change, that is, the first chapter that came from the printers, which would be the beginning, we moved to the end. The first chapter became the last chapter. There's no actual cutups in *Naked Lunch*.

AG: What did you think, in the movie, of the use of that autobiographical section?

WSB: I thought it was quite . . . quite all right.

AG: To shoot the actress twice, I thought, was treading on territory . . . though by doing it twice, it sort of made it more imaginative and less close to home.

WSB: Well, that's what I meant. The use of all the biographical material became part of a bizarre surrealist structure. That was the reason that Cronenberg didn't want me to take any part in the film as an actor. That would destroy the whole illusory structure—to put somebody in there that the audience would know, know just who it was—it would be a bad note.

AG: So the film is basically an hallucination on the basis of some autobiographical material already fictionally hallucinated in the book.

WSB: Yes.

AG: I like the idea of generalizing the narcotic thing by making it black meat addiction.

WSB: Yes, so you can't say it's a film about drugs, all the drugs are made up. Nor can you say it's a film about sex because, well, there are all sorts of sexual references, as there are in these other films. It was not explicit human sex. It's kept totally inhuman, people turning into centipedes. It is not—

AG: So it's not specifically homoerotic, either.

WSB: No, no.

AG: The big giant insect, that was the most realized thing. The typewriters were amazing, cause that combined the Talking Asshole and the typewriters.

WSB: Yes, but I never would have thought of that. That is, the importance, the symbolic importance, of the actual instrument with which you write, the typewriter. Never occurred to me.

AG: Well, it's already implicit. It's an extension of your idea that the writer writes the future or writes reality or writes what is going to happen. And in that sense, the typewriter "tells the fortune" so to speak. The typewriter imagination tells the writer what to write.

WSB: Exactly. Yes.

AG: So the typewriter is both the machine and the imagination itself. But it also combines it with what looks to be an anus, which talks out of turn, which is in the classic Talking Asshole routine, and it also combines it with an anus addicted to bug powder pleasures [*laughs*]. So he actually made a composite image. That was an invention worthy of your prose, I thought. But I had one strong objection to the acting, which is that the figure of Martin, which is based presumably on me, is a wimp, and I don't mind that, because I did feel somewhat wimpy, [*laughs*], still do, but reading the Market section at the beginning, when [*the Kerouac character*] is screwing your supposed wife . . . and I'm sitting there making believe I'm ignoring it and reading or encouraging it by reading the Market section, or this character Martin is doing it. And it's read in such a flat, toneless, uninteresting voice! It doesn't bring out the vigor and humor and color of the soliloquy.

WSB: Yes, but always remember, there's no point trying to be faithful to the book because film and writing are just two completely different things. Any film stands on its own, apart from whether it's based on a novel.

AG: Does this film stand on its own as logically as the book? In other words, the book has that logical frame. The film, I couldn't tell. It was sort of like . . . Yeats has the phrase *Hodos Chameliontos,* chameleon-like, in that you don't know where the beginning or the middle or the end is, so it's an unrelieved hallucination, because you don't know where you're coming in and you don't know where you're going out. It ends, you're going into the hallucination, or maybe coming out of it, I don't know. Annexia might be waking up from having committed killing or waking from a dream of having committed killing or maybe a continuation of the hallucination. It's kind of an indecisive moral, or an indecisive resolution of the condition of hallucination. In the book, you touch on the reality. Here reality is touched on when Martin . . . the two writers come in occasionally.

WSB: Now remember that there isn't any Kerouac in the book.

AG: Yeah. So that's just added in from biography. And what other elements? So they took from *Queer*. And they took from *Exterminator*. The opening chapter of *Exterminator* with the addiction to bug powder.

WSB: Bug powder, yes. There's a book called *Mummy* and the people actually seem to have become addicted to mummy dust. And mummy dust was somehow made from people who've died of the most loathsome diseases. It's too bad that Cronenberg didn't see this book, see I only saw it after the film was made. It might have been of interest to him.

AG: Who do you read now, among American writers? You read Mailer's *Ancient Evenings*.

WSB: I read Mailer's *Ancient Evenings* with great interest because I was interested in . . . the seven souls structure, which was very helpful to me in *Western Lands*. And also in *Place of Dead Roads*. So that's Mailer. But I read a lot of books for information, like doctor books, spy books. . . .

AG: Like this book actually. Exorcism.

WSB: Exorcism is a subject that interests me, and books on shamanism, I've read through.

AG: You read a lot of spy novels. Did you see Mailer's new huge spy novel, *Harlot's Ghost*?

WSB: I have seen it yes.

AG: Have you read it at all?

WSB: Not all.

AG: Looked a little like Dos Passos. You know, that composite of realistic news and news headline and journalism and fiction. But apparently, he's come to funny ambivalent feeling about the C.I.A., both admiration and loathing or something. Sort of like life itself, complicated and . . . a big complicated organism that you shouldn't kill, necessarily.

WSB: [*laughs*].

AG: Did you read *The Naked and the Dead*?

WSB: Yes.

AG: It's a good read, a solid novel. I liked *From Here to Eternity* better. It got more of the army . . .it's about what it means to be a peacetime soldier, a 20-year man. Whereas Mailer's was about a wartime army with all sorts of miscellaneous people who were not professional army men at all. Did you read *The Catcher in the Rye*?

WSB: Caulfield, he was a wretched specimen. Talk about a wimp. He really turned my stomach.

AG: And *The Old Man and the Sea*? I thought that was very good when I read it.

WSB: It's good from a mythological point of view. All this talk about the noble fish and all that crap.

AG: Well the guy strives so hard and he gets his fish home but it's been eaten to a skeleton by then. So you get what you want, but . . . now I have enough money to travel wherever I want, but I haven't got the health.

WSB: Well, exactly.

AG: I've got enough money to live where I want, but I don't want to move. It's too hard. [*laughs*]

WSB: Exactly exactly exactly. I've gotten enough money, so I could travel if I wanted to, but I can't.

AG: Why can't you?

WSB: Well what am I going to do?

AG: Go out and have sexual adventures in Burma.

WSB: Yes, I . . . lost interest in that, and there's the question of . . . various questions. My health and so on.

AG: Hobbling into the bathroom to take another pill? What pill is that? Actually I like the image of *The Old Man and the Sea*, of striving and succeeding but finding that the success was ghost success. In other words, in the long run, after a certain age, the motives for success, pride or oppressing people or getting power—

WSB: They're gone.

AG: The desire to have power dissolves. The desire to dominate people for love dissolves. On the other hand, it's a relief to realize you can let go.

WSB: That's true, too.

[*After watching* Naked Lunch *together at the cinema in Lawrence.*]

The first person who really showed me the ugly spirit was Brion Gysin. "The ugly spirit shot Joan because. . . ." and I never found out why. This Brion wrote out on a piece of paper in a sort of trance state.

AG: Well, congratulations, Bill. In some ways the movie was quite good, a far-out piece of imaginative fantasy.

WSB: That's it, yes.

AG: To get on screen with the Talking Asshole, quite a feat. And it's certainly going to be a cult film that people will be seeing. The combination of drugs, homosexuality, some good prose recited on screen. . . . In the sweat lodge ceremony we went through, did you get any glimpse of the Ugly Spirit, what that was historically or biographically?

WSB: Well, I know what it is.

AG: The nurse, your governess, or . . . ?

WSB: No, no, she was just a very minor . . . the first person who really showed me the ugly spirit was Brion Gysin. "The ugly spirit shot Joan because . . ." and I never found out why. This Brion wrote out on a piece of paper in a sort of trance state.

AG: So the phrase "ugly spirit" was from him, but did you ever locate the specific quality or character or historical personage or spirit?

WSB: Well, no. It's very much related to the American tycoon. To William Randolph Hearst, Vanderbilt, Rockefeller, that whole stratum of American acquisitive evil. Monopolistic, acquisitive evil. Ugly evil. The ugly American. The ugly American at his ugly worst. That's exactly what it is.

AG: But then that's the character that has possessed you?

WSB: Yes. That's right.

AG: So would that be a family thing from Burroughs?

WSB: No, not necessarily.

AG: That would apply to moving your hand with Joan? That's how Brion was locating it, that way.

WSB: No, he said "ugly spirit shot Joan *because.*" To be cause, shot Joan to be cause. . . .

AG: Well, in the preface to *Queer,* you spoke of it as the ugly spirit that entered you and depressed you beforehand and after.

WSB: Yes, certainly.

AG: And his phrase was, "for ugly spirit shot Joan because," and that it's a case of your possession. So I was wondering, with the shaman, did you get any glimpse of the action or operation or persona of the ugly spirit in you when he was exorcizing it?

WSB: Well, he said it was the toughest case he'd ever handled. And for a moment he thought he was going to just lose.

AG: Then I remember yesterday you were saying, "He had to face the whole of American capitalism, Rockefeller, the C.I.A."

WSB: Yes, yes.

AG: J.P. Morgan, ITT. . . .

WSB: All of those. Particularly Hearst.

AG: Hearst the word man, the original image manipulator.

WSB: Yes, precisely. They say something is true, it is. "We don't report the news, we make it!"

AG: Yes.

WSB: Well, that's what the shaman said. He didn't know what he was up against. He didn't expect the strength and weight and evil intensity of this spirit, this "entity," as he called it. The same way the priest in an exorcism has to take on the spirit.

AG: I remember, during your hypnoanalysis experience with Dr. Louis Wolberg in 1947, you uncovered various levels of personae in yourself. But didn't he get to the ugly spirit?

WSB: No, he couldn't have handled it.

AG: What if there never was such an invasion? Do you still think there was some specific event?

WSB: Of course there was.

AG: That was not reachable.

WSB: Not with such means.

AG: And would the memory of the event be necessary for exorcism?

WSB: No, not necessarily.

AG: Or memory of the feeling. In other words, did you get anything from the shaman's sweat-lodge ceremony?

WSB: That was much better than anything psychoanalysts have come up with. Something definite there was being touched upon. He did more than. . . .

AG: So what could it possibly be? You got any idea if it's a definite event?

WSB: It's the means, the moment at which the spirit gained access.

AG: So the "ultimate secret" would be that moment when the spirit gained access.

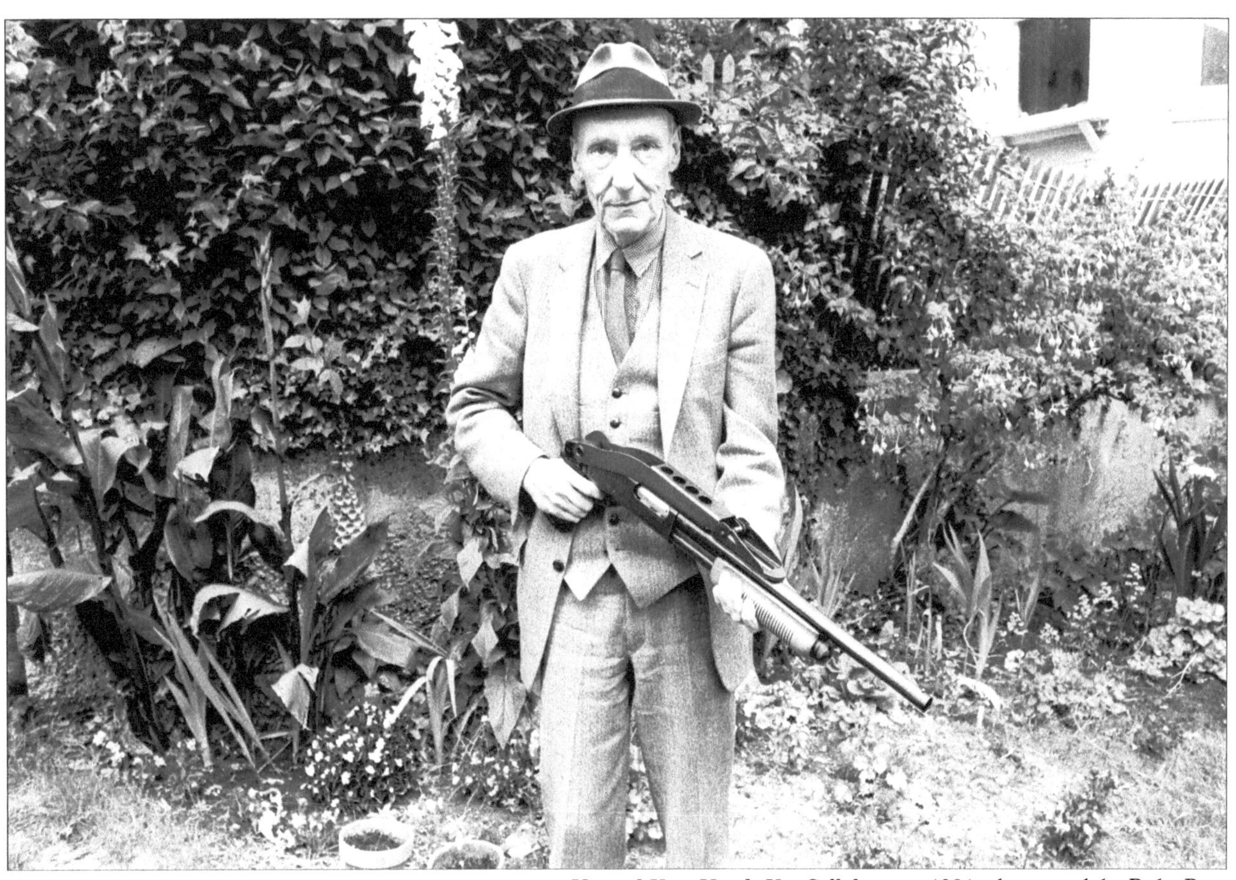

Up with Your Hands, You Collaborators, 1981, photograph by Ruby Ray

WSB: Well, presumably, if you see it at the moment it gained access, then it'll be dropped.

AG: Dissolves.

WSB: This, you see, is the same notion—Catholic exorcism, psychotherapy, shamanistic practices—getting to the moment when whatever it was gained access. And also to the name of the spirit. Just to know that it's the Ugly Spirit. That's a great step. Because the spirit doesn't want its name to be known.

AG: So Brion Gysin was the one that actually named it.

WSB: Yes, yes.

AG: What year was that?

WSB: Well, it'd be 1959.

AG: In Paris. How did that question arise, then?

WSB: Well, he saw it.

AG: So Brion was a kind of shaman.

WSB: He was a shaman. A very potent shaman.

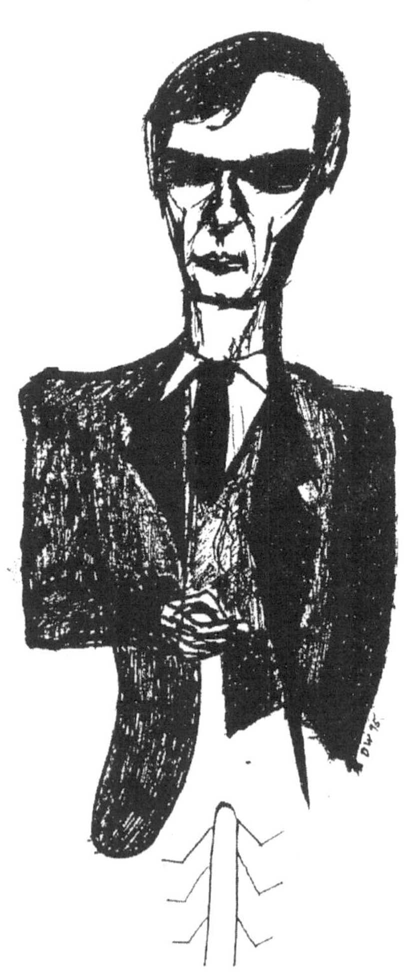

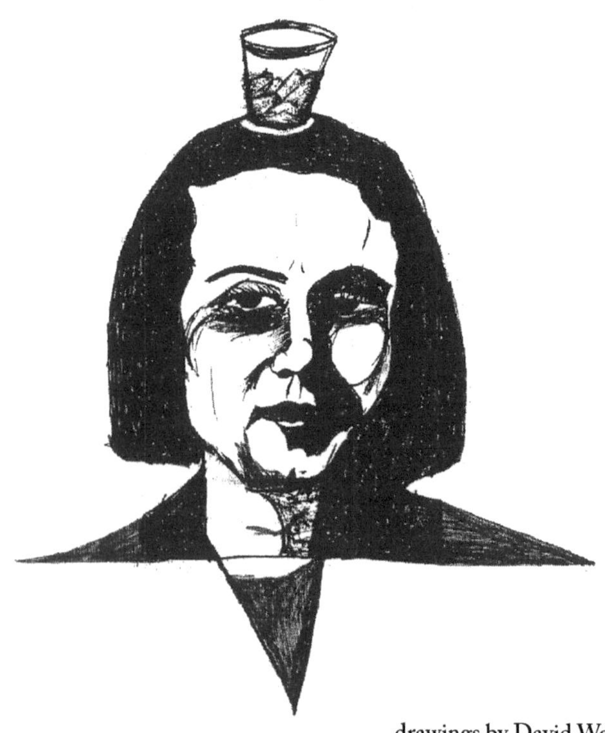

drawings by David West

The Soul of the Doll

Rob Hardin

Being the Recollections of a Late Inmate (1931–1946) of the Dalmarnock Asylum for Children in Glasgow, Scotland

THE EYES WERE WHAT CHANGED AND flayed me above all else—the eyes or, rather, the doll's eyes' dead caress. Black glass in a placid head opened similar holes before me, offering streams of amnesia through crawlways gone smooth and useless. Down cephaloid miles uninflected by edge of iris or glare of sclerae, I dove and drank. I was the infant mole who plummeted inward. It was as if I were looking into the dollhole of my past and could go nowhere but backward, into the lobotomized lull its gaze evoked. I drank and yet I feared my impulsive thirst. I feared the therapist's doll not because of its physical presence but rather the psychic excavation the eyes invited. They were tunnels of history and I was loath to gain entrance.

I feared the therapist's doll not because of its physical presence but because of the psychic excavation the eyes invited. They were tunnels of history and I was loath to gain entrance.

A day, a year ago, I didn't know which: A nail-file with amber fluid drying along the edge, a snarl of flaxen hair, a crying matron, a fist to the back of my head, the blood-tint of hemorrhage sifting intricately behind closed lids. Vertical metal bars ringing against searchlights, chill fingers clamoring across my knees, silverfish or frozen rodents come to life in sickness' thrall. No parent's care, no window, in that prison—just parched light drying on a concrete facade. When I brushed against its coldness, I saw caverns; I flowed with the facefall of my shame into a moonbleached gallery where, past that poultice, I plundered hungers. Clumsy and numbed, I tripped on ripcords, strangled on coral, grasped at strands. I peered over undersea bridges and caught glimpses of my sickness, ink fanning outward over an ocean bed. I wasn't afraid of becoming a chimera, since monsters are still ordinary men. Rather, I was afraid I'd be proven too weak to become anything else—that past ignominies had stained my self-perception until I couldn't recognize any truths at all, which always hid among monotonies of gray.

And then I found Isabel. She stood dilated and distressed in Dalmarnock, awaiting me in the playroom after I withdrew from the cliffs of sickness.

The bisque head tilted back to glare at me from the cupboard. Isabel's putty fingers found my neck and traced the perforations, the forkholes, at the base. I didn't cry out, as her touch was almost familiar. I squinted and crinkled my eyes. I do not trust myself, I said. I do not trust my hands.

Light through a sticker of red cellophane spread across my limbs, rinsing my face with the chamber music of sunset, crimson dye and shadow, a complex erasure that drew my hand closer to Isabel's nascent breasts, slight and evocative, things I'd imagined, old castaway that I was at fifteen (a confusion of premature nostalgia disillusioning me still). Performing some cliché ritual and yet still trembling. "Here's where you stabbed yourself." Fearing discovery and capture in the therapist's office, knowing how insensitive the nurses were to their own nuclear presence, omniscient nurses as severe and stylized as Templars, with their scorching discoveries and scalding collargrip, with disapproval that detoured and dead-ended our explorations even when the nurses themselves proved absent, leaving unalterable marks in ambiguous places, numb spots to ponder later, when exploring our skins in bathroom light, tracing cattlebrands of trauma at some future decaying age. Who did that? Wasn't me. It isn't me now.

We sang some putrid song that seemed like an anthem then, and lowered gowns, the ritual making me queasy. Nausea's music. I tried to concentrate but couldn't, I couldn't stop thinking in words. That's when Isabel spoke to me, spoke because she knew I needed her enveloping voice, a sheet drawn over my features.

She was distant, too, I knew. She didn't actually hear me. But neither did I, for that matter. I wasn't in my skin and hadn't slept for weeks, worried by some cruelty I'd inflicted or imagined or couldn't remember. I'd set fire to a slug, thinking it was dead. But it wasn't. The slug was alive.

"The slug is alive," I told her. And then I watched my fingers leave slime-trails across her pelvis and over her thighs, their wakes' tingle a salve to her nerve-ends. It was something she could feel instead of my fascination with her numbness, instead of/in place of trajectories of guilt.

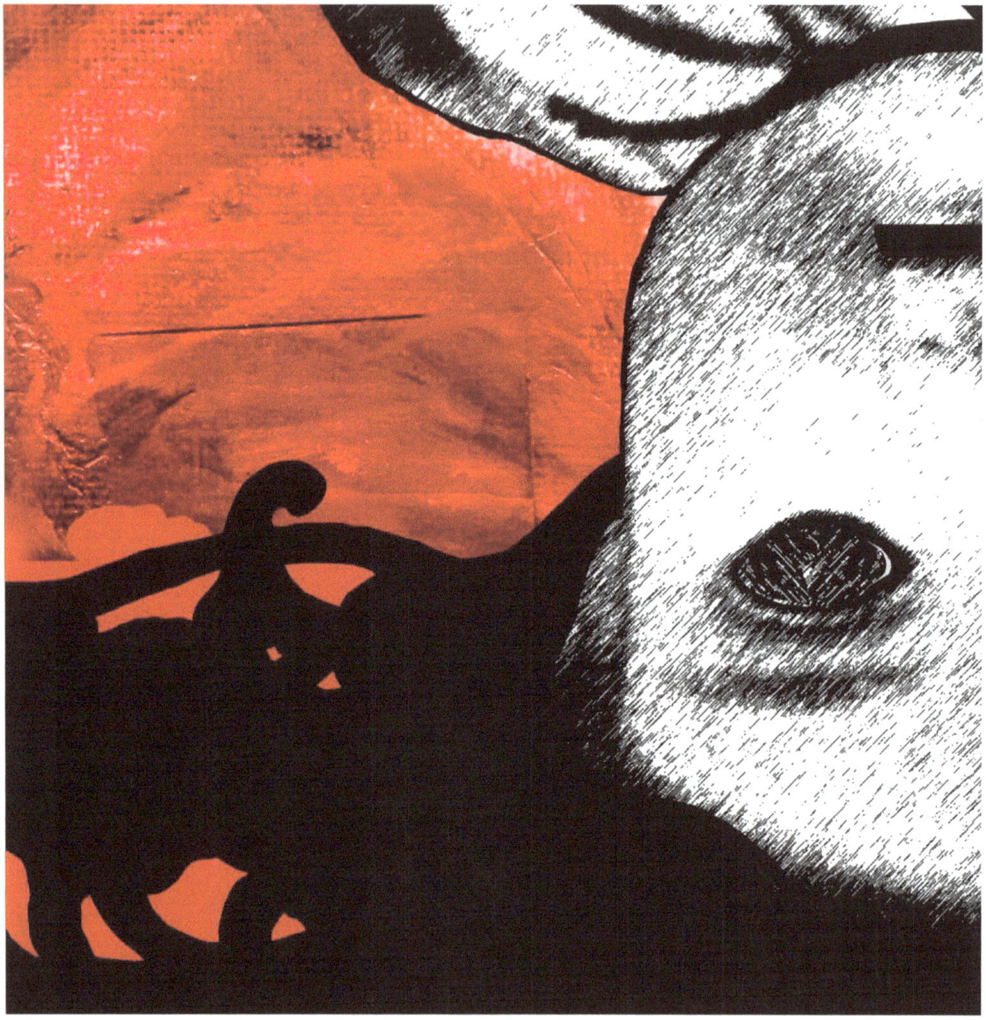

She Sees Us, mixed media, by Leslie Hardie

The doll gazed at the slug trails like a camera photographing us, just as I was being photographed by my own mind or, rather, as my mind recorded her body's reaction to thought. Thumb wrinkles touched the edge of the reading desk, and then she stared up at me, delighted and gone, and I almost forgot the shunt cell where Father sagged against my sickle, or so they swore at the inquest, or so they lied, and I told myself to be quiet, I'd wished for this.

Then clay spread across her arms and everything felt viscous, easier and more exciting and somehow worse. The mental color of disgust slid into view: Purple, an overripe surface dyeing the light three shades past crimson. And I told her no, I exclaimed she should wait and not sweat, and she stiffened, then stopped, but it was too late, I was inside her, sheath of warm liquid distracting me somewhere. I didn't feel I was doing it the right way, as a normal, less disgusting boy might have done it to her.

The sky turned more violet than my dream of zygotes wriggling. Motes of light flickered in darkness around me, scotomas caused by peering at the lightcrack under the door. Who was there? What would I do if the Templars burst in? Could I bring myself to withdraw, could I control my rigid stump, or would I keep grinding, would Isabel be shamed when they shined the flashlight on us and banished each to a quiet room and told us never to touch? Would she feel sufficiently shamed to kill herself, or would she suicide over another groping boy? My mind blurred with the distraction of her hand touching my testicles. I shoved her hand back—don't do that!—fearing I might shriek. Then I placed my fingers around her neck and squeezed just a little, just enough for her to know. And as she gasped for air, and removed my hand and kissed my fingertips, I pretended we lived on a secret island where trees sprouted cakes and sleep did not exist. And anyone who needed to dream floated physically toward wishes that rose in clitoral peninsulas, and no one on our insomniac island knew what I'd done to my father and mother, nor what I was doing to Isabel this moment. She'll be damaged for life, damaged or dead, I whispered. And if she heard, she pretended not to understand, and studied her own palm as I pumped her and finally let go, hitting my own face as I tingled, my own cheek to avoid hitting hers, punching my eyes and letting rhapsodies of discharge fade to the flicker of throbbing lids, some correlation of bone and skin making pain feel mechanical, an alert resonating through the calcium stick-man inside. And I reached over our heads and up to the cupboard and tried to bat the doll's scrutiny away, but the figure tumbled down on us and Isabel shrieked softly and leapt off me, disengaging and disengaged. My orphaned cock floated below her, chilled by vertigo, and I picked up the doll and rose to a standing position. I knew I could never put it back in exactly the right place—after all, we had fucked in this room, so everything in it would now look different to the Templars, we had made everything stink with our sex stink and we couldn't wipe it away, and the Templars would sense it just as they sensed now in their slumber that we were here and I was touching the doll. The nurses knew and my days would now play out dully, would consist of panicky sleep as promised by the doll's disapproving eye, by the sucking tunnel, by the leeches inside head's hollow.

What would I do if the Templars burst in? Could I bring myself to withdraw, could I control my rigid stump, or would I keep grinding?

I knew this as I'd known it before and always. I patted Isabel's forehead and sang that wretched anthem, that horrible doggerel about "guardians in the night." These were the only consoling rituals I could remember clearly enough to perform, now that the act was over, now that I'd hurt her, now that I'd failed to control the thing that called me away.

Above us shone the gleam of empty centuries. Eyes black and unblinking, always the narcotized eyes. Still disarranged from falling, the doll's cloth body canted to one side, promising to topple. Yet its face was aimed so precisely the head might have been mounted on a tripod. One bisque hand described the crack in the door, the other, Isabel's breast. *A doll's touch resonates with the caress of dead children*, I thought. Eyes gazed through me, their pupil, and slept through forever.

—Theodorus Laftsoglou Colquhoun
December 31, 1946

Notes from a Woman Soon to Be Divorced

Su Byron

DECEMBER

Endless South

I woke up and saw that it was winter. There were no birds, etc. Every piece of clothing inside my house was clean. Thank God. I looked into the mirror and saw that my eye was bright and black. Piercing. Wonderful. My lips were almost open. Beautiful. But my hands. Hands? Were very sad. Beating something. Like birds flown into their endless south and still trying to fly farther. Ridiculous. I noticed my heart seemed to be saying something. There is no winter. Am I awake? What was it saying? There were words on its lips. Entangled with the soap in my hand. Soap? I was trying to clean my wings. They were brown and bitter. I was old. It was winter. Try to overcome that. Pretend it is summer! The tulips, etc. Brown and bitter, my wings that I tried to clean. With white soap while my heart said something and I listened and heard nothing.

There Is No Waking While Things Like This Are Happening

They try to get the zebras to talk. That makes sense when you live out in the jungle. Because already the lions speak and the great giraffe sings, apparently. This is told to me by those who have struggled with wild things. Great warriors with pain splashed on their faces. One leans down over my body. (I have just been ripped apart by a lion.) Do you hear them speaking he says in another language. I hear them. It is song or something like words pasted together. Like a tight thing you would hold and never want to let go of. I notice my hand lying by the river. How beautiful! Try to wake up. Try! But the wild wind and the zebras and the warriors are singing. Their noise carries me up. There is no waking while things like this are happening.

Remember When We Loved Each Other?

To say I loved you would be like saying I need you to pick this sunflower
Or I wish you would please now come home to me even though it has been three years
To say that I am kind of dying here and getting old
Would be like saying
Help
What in hell happened to my face?
Remember when we loved each other?
Down by the water, etc. At any rate, let's turn the page
At this point the only thing left to talk about would be
How empty this cup is. This one I was drinking from.

These Were the Things I Was Trying to Say

I would not beg you but if I begged you would it make you come home?
Because I could get down on both knees.

There Is No Hell so Let's Talk About Something Else

My hands still look like the map of a child's planet
Thank god
Your hands are like a cow who has stopped moving in the field
Who has cried real tears
Who has cried real tears?

Our dead boy we folded in his suit
The policeman we handed over dollars to
The nun we gave real cake to chew
And to the strange waves we rode
We gave our drowning heads and hearts
That is to say, we drowned

There is no hell so let's talk about something else
The fields of people wandering

JANUARY

You Are My Very Own Truck That I Will Drive One Day into a Wall

In bed he asks me to spread my legs. His mouth open in an old man's pant. Belly touches mine but there is no jolt. I am thankfully drunk. Took codeine, too. He comes on my chest after he asks first. He has to ask! Later, I imagine a warrior coming from a northern country. Big arms slap me down. With his hand around my neck I pant. My brown eyes turn blue. This man pushes the truth out of me.

When he goes, I dream of someone else. My dog looks at me. I look back at him. It is true love.

Another Love Song

I thought his cock was bigger. It isn't. I must have been drunker last time. Now I take another swig and watch the clock. When he goes I will go out on the terrace and watch the waves turn into giant pirate ships. The pirates will wink up at me. I will wink back down at them. The biggest will spread his arms as if to invite me on board. I can see way down into the boat where a long wooden table is set with jugs of wine and whole birds being torn apart by men with open mouths.

I will go. I will go!

Love Song #34

From the moment we lie down together in bed to the moment when he asks if he can come on my breast, four minutes have passed. Why do I keep doing this?

Love Song #287

His car is broken down and he needs me to come get him. His chest hurts. His thumb hurts. He has a cold. He is coughing. He is worried. He is sad. He is angry. Ho hum. I am waiting for my boat now. Did not tell him about the ticket. Will take it to a sunny place where men wear ripped shirts and will rip me apart.

Love Song #965

Let me be your slave I told him. He pretended to understand but never brought it up again. Servant to king, I begged him. He talked about my tires. They needed to change. Tie me down, I pleaded. He asked for another cookie.

In the book I am going to buy at the store there will be a picture of a mighty king. All dolled up in royal garb. Long, thick legs waiting beneath all that velvet. He will demand that I crawl, inch my way up his thick fabric. Touch the purple, make him shiver. He may have to strike me down if I don't comply.

This king will never meet my boyfriend. I will keep them separate. The boyfriend is the one who will change my tires. The king will make me change his.

FEBRUARY

Facts

You force me to put my head underwater. I like that.
Tigers are not scared of us. You do not understand that.
We drive with your hands in shock.
Families pass by. Fever burns their cars apart.
God waves. A grocery store door hangs open. Your mouth is too dry.
The door opens. Not the door to your heart.

Heat Like an Ape Makes Itself Known in the Wee Hours of My Morning

There is no male around.
Only a sour memory of you leaning over me.
The neighbors were watching.
Your huge body.
My panting heart.
The way the dogs waited for the ending.
We each did our part.

Your pants wet in the car
As I leaned over the dashboard
North Carolina, South Carolina
The seas parted
You threw me on the engine hood
My small ass a light to passing cars

There is no male around
So I knit
Deep knots

MARCH

Promise

Wind instead of blood. In my heart gnaws a little mouth with tiny words that turn bigger as the day grows blacker. Stupid tongue. Waiting for a boat. Its very own train to its very own velvet corridor. Tonight my father is dying. I will not act differently. I will not kill myself. I will not laugh. I will not eat too much or too little. Or banish young mothers from my sight or kill my dog or beg my neighbor to take me to the hospital or give a blow job to my new boyfriend. Will there be a funeral? I'm not up for it.

Funeral

My father has not died yet but I am here remembering a great fever I once had. Wet rags turned to flames on my head. How I languished! There was a desert to die in back then. Poems not yet written. But the thing is . . . I thought they would be written. And so I came back to life. Great, grand life. Beady eyes always wanting to get cool. Some ice for my swollen throat. I am just sitting here waiting for them to call and tell me that my father has died. Then what? Then I will die. And all my brothers die. And you will die, too.

APRIL

Film

There is no time. My father did not die. His teeth are rotting and he drinks some coconut juice. His wife, from Puerto Rico, tells me about his body. It will be taken away by medical students. There will be no coffin or funeral. I should nod but I am thinking about trying to get into the bathroom so that I can take another drink from my bottle. The man I had to sleep with in order to even get here to visit my father is looking down at the rug. I spent $200 on a hotel last night. We made love four times. At one point he kneeled down on the wooden floor to wipe up candle wax I had spilled. His balls hung low from his 56-year-old loins. I shuddered. Age slams me into the wall over and over. The next morning there was nothing for me to eat at the breakfast table.

Love

The 56-year-old man has a stomachache. His tiny penis hangs down as he grabs his stomach and vomits. Or tries to vomit. Huge sounds from the bathroom. I make ginger tea in the kitchen and wish he were dead. How long will I have to wait to get back to my 26-year-old lover whom I knew 30 years ago? He was tall and his shoes were like boats. His young face will bury me.

Too Cold

How can I tell him that his 32-inch waist of which he is so proud disgusts me. Disgusts me! Fancy little girl primping. Bad breath. I need a big man with a bear's skin! Whose cave is littered with the bones of children! How can I tell this tiny man who loves me that I am sick to death of eating at the cheap pizza place? His little hand takes his little knife and cuts an onion in his salad. The waitress goes by with pins stuck in her nose. She smiles black teeth. A smirk? I am going to die! More wine. By my third, I am hurling rocks from my castle. His head bows under their hard weight. I can't help it! How I wish he would take me to the edge of the highway and abandon me. Just let me be!

MAY

Old Story

Expect big things in your heart
I yelled at you
Sorry
Stamp, stamp, stamp
The sound of my feet
Blue river
There is water and it is not stopping
Your hat is hanging from the branch
Your shoe has been eaten by the wolf
Bears turn nervously
One eye straight ahead
Do not look back
Their claws are something, aren't they?

Blue Hat in a Box

All through the years I thought of you. Through all of the wars. Through all of the brand-new washing machines and all of the old ones carried away by sad-faced men. They had hard times fitting these washing machines through my doors. Sweat poured off of them. Some of them sobbed. One asked me to phone his wife and tell her that he might never make it home. Because of this washing machine, I said? Others threw themselves at my feet and begged me to take a gun and shoot them. I would not. I stepped over them instead thinking all the time of you. Always of you.

JUNE

Kick-up-your-heels opera

There was a storm
Now it is over
Done
The table is set for one

One word

Forgive me

New Monsters

Plonsey/Horowitz/Bove/Adams/Looney

The New Monsters are a Bay Area combo lead by bassist Steve Horowitz (The Code International) and tenor sax "monster" Dan Plonsey (of Daniel Popsicle, and composer of Leave Me Alone, an opera with libretto by Harvey Pekar). Dan and Steve go back many years as both friends and collaborators; they toured together in 1999 in Steve's Mousetrap Quartet. Steve moved back to the Bay Area a few years ago and, when he heard the music Dan had been working on, "dragged him kicking and screaming" into the studio. They brought in Steve Adams (of ROVA Saxophone Quartet fame), Scott Looney and Jim Bove and worked the hell out of Dan's tunes. I've seen the Monsters play a number of times over the past few years, as they got their repertoire into shape; eventually, the pieces, once known only by numbers, were even given names. (Which always reminded me of that old joke: "86!" he shouted. "Hey, why didn't anyone laugh?" "You didn't tell it right.") Be sure to check out their eponymous new album (New Monsters, Positone).

I sat down with Dan Plonsey and Steve Horowitz to chat about the new record (that is, I was sitting down when I emailed them these questions; I can't really vouch for their bodily positions when they responded).

—B. Kold

SENSITIVE SKIN: So how did you guys meet?

STEVE: I think we first met at a Composers Cafeteria Meeting in the East Bay, in the early '90s. I had just come back up to the Bay Area from studying at Cal Arts. For me it was most certainly love at first sound.

DAN: Steve came along during the Cafeteria's final days, when an influx of composers who couldn't play instruments (and who couldn't compose either!) was forcing the founding members into a situation where we had to either abandon our egalitarian principles or disband the group. The Manufacturing of Humidifiers emerged from the Cafeteria, and when the horrible non-performing composers heard about it, they asked if they could write pieces for us. Almost demanded to. The answer was a resounding no. So Steve was sort of the guy I used to get out of a bad relationship.

SS: Steve says he heard your latest compositions and immediately thought they'd be best performed by a small combo, and that you had to be dragged "kicking and screaming into the studio to make a jazz record." Is this accurate? Do you hate jazz, or just going to the studio?

DAN: I don't hate studios, but I do hate jazz, and I suppose I sort of love kicking and screaming. The idea for the first bunch of pieces was to write something simpler that could be used by a smaller group than Daniel Popsicle (10–12 people), and to extend them through improvisation. So I'd just gotten finished with the idea of doing the pieces with 4–5 people, when along comes Steve. The thing is, when someone offers to help you present your music, and you see the possibility of it happening in a way that isn't entirely horrible, and you can continue to do it your own way too at the same time, you agree to do it. Plus I've gotten to kick and scream on a number of occasions. It's been pretty good in that regard.

SS: Originally these compositions were all referred to by numbers, instead of titles. Why'd you drop the numbers and go with traditional titles?

STEVE: We wanted to use the numbers, but Positone insisted on titles. They felt the numbers were too abstract. So Dan did a first run at the titles and then we sent them to the label to whittle them down. What we came up with was an interesting amalgam.

DAN: I was writing too many pieces to have time to think about titles, so I just numbered them. Like many composers, I've been seduced by the desire to be prolific, which is why the opus numbers seem attractive. But I actually have come up with many titles I like quite a bit. "My Socks Travel the Couch Line," "They're Sniffing Our Garbage," "Gargantuan Livestock Tended by Fools," "Twelve Different Boxes of Jello Have I," "Moving about, Humming, Still Our Flowers Are Blooming, Under the Old Portcullis." In 1980, I predicted that we were in for a "stupid decade" for music. Composers would write really clunky, misshapen, quotidian sorts of music and give them stupid, irreverent titles. I thought that the challenge would be to write the worst piece imaginable, and still have it sound good in an unexpected way. I was wildly wrong (except about the titles), but that's what I've been doing for 30 years.

SS: When you went into the studio, were you and Steve (and the rest of the band) on the same page, as far as what you wanted to accomplish, or did it take a bunch of live gigs for it to gel? Was there a lot of give and take between you and Steve and the rest of the band?

STEVE: We worked on the arrangements for quite a while and then did a series of live and loft sessions where we recorded everything and made a demo. After that we went into the studio and banged this album out in three days, no overdubs, all live in the same room!

DAN: We'd reached an agreement about a lot of the nuts and bolts: the tempos, the structure, who'd solo when, approximately how long things would go on, etc. Steve pretty much decided most of those things, but he checked with us. On another level, like most jazz bands that I know of, it's a collaboration. You let the other guys play the way they want to play, particularly in the improvisations. I can think of two occasions when I told someone that I wanted them to do something different (and they understood, and did). But as with all collaborations, sometimes you're amazed at the great thing someone's come up with, but other times you're kind of upset. And then you have to decide whether to say something. Certain things are beyond a player's control. And when the other players are as established as Steve, Steve, Scott and Jim are, it would be really insulting for me to ask them to be someone else. It's why I think so much jazz is just so bad: nobody wants to say anything, and the result is that there's no singular, strong vision.

SS: Did you have any moments of utter doubt, when you thought this would never work?

STEVE: I never felt that way about the music, never a moment of doubt, the music is so successful. As

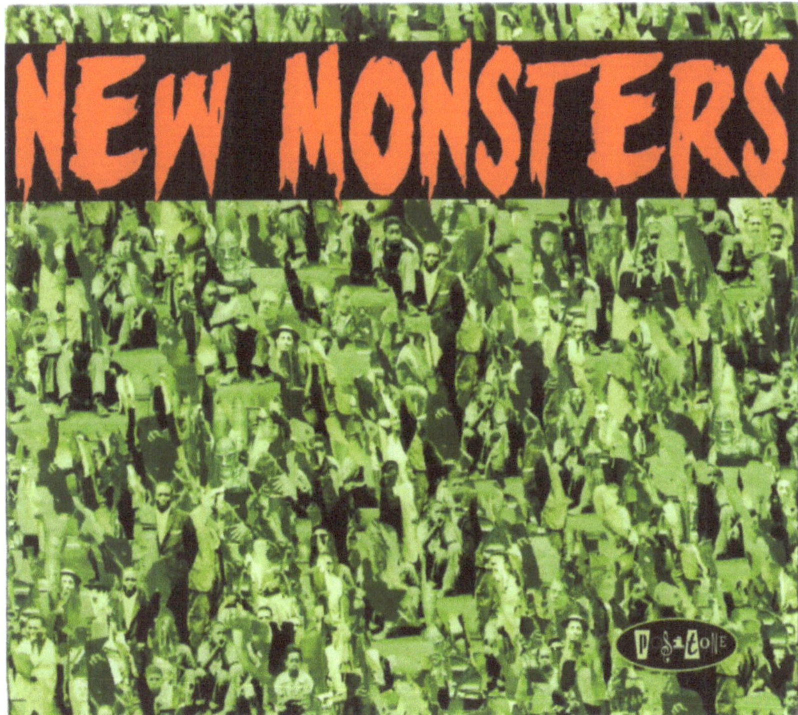

To listen, go here:
www.sensitiveskinmagazine.com/new-monsters

for Dan's mental health, that was another story, I kept telling him that this was going to be the album he wins a Grammy for. (I still think it will.)

DAN: I'm not sure it does work. I'm having fun doing it, but it's different from my own thing, where I have more control. I like music that's clunky. This is more smooth.

SS: You guys are both leaders. How was it trying to share the lead? Or did you? How did you divide responsibilities?

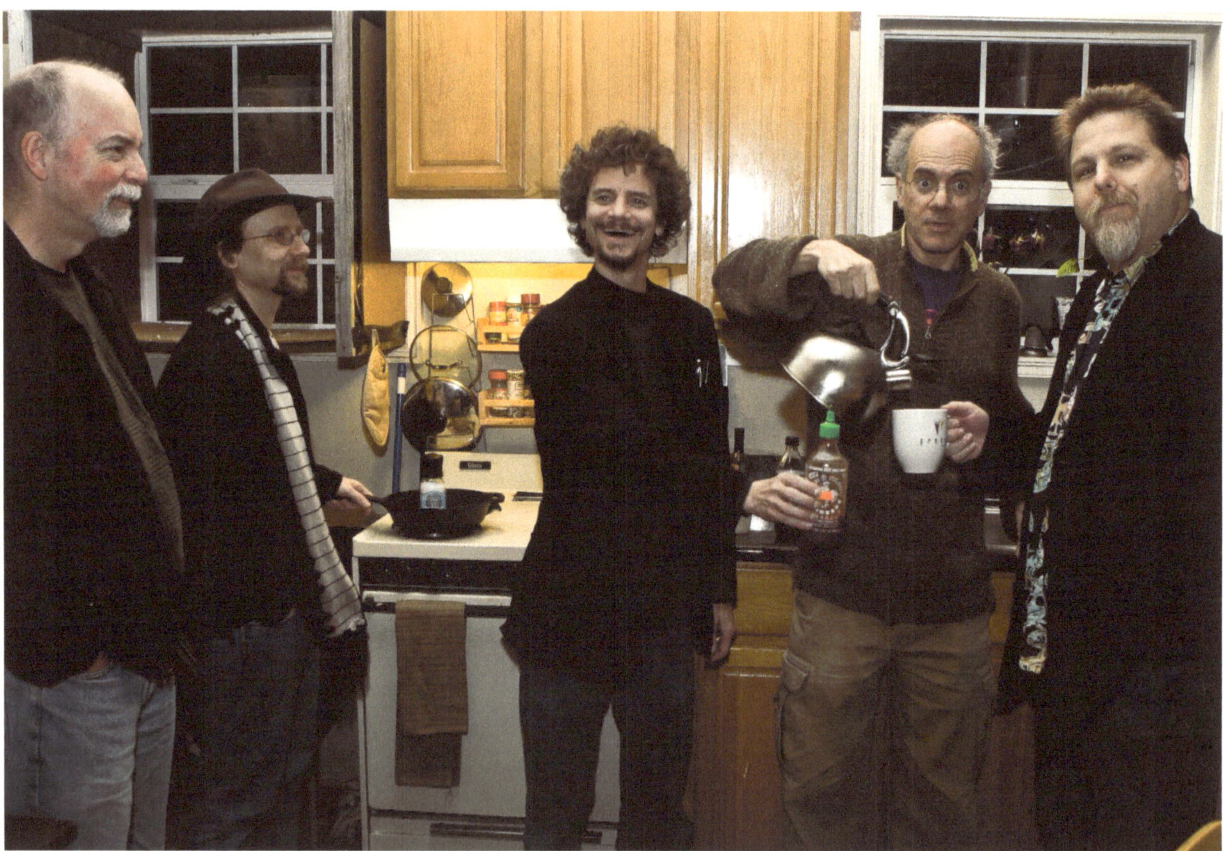

photograph by Jeff Spirer

STEVE: We have worked together a lot. This part seems to come easy, collaborating together I mean. I have the utmost respect for Dan and his music. I may push a little, but my goal is always to make sure he is happy with the music. Hands down, this is one of the best and most fun musical groups I have been in for a long time. I am having a blast playing with these guys

DAN: Well, the upside is that Steve does most of the work other than writing the tunes—coordinate schedules, get someone to record us, get a label to release it. And writing and playing are what I like to do. I get the best of both worlds in this band: a sideman's lack of worries and yet we're playing my music. Now all Steve has to do is find a major venue to present us and put together a world tour.

SS: Dan, I'm a huge Harvey Pekar fan. What was it like to work with him on the opera, *Leave Me Alone*? Did the experience inform your subsequent work? Or did you just want to get in bed and stay there for six months?

DAN: It was a very difficult process. I wish we could do it all over. We were planning to do it again, out here, in a full "composer's cut" version that would restore all the music, plus Harvey's original idea for the form. He basically wanted it to be a sort of *My Dinner with Andre,* just two guys talking about music, sitting in a cafe. I wanted Harvey to write a fictional story about a Cleveland musician (we're both from

Cleveland Heights) who is stuck there because of family, who struggles to get some compositions written and performed. But Harvey wouldn't do fiction. He wanted it to be about me, with me telling him about my music. So I'd send him things I'd written about music, and he'd say, "Sounds good, put it in." Harvey was very leery of opera. He didn't really accept that there was a reason for all the singing. Meanwhile, the producer had his own ideas—he wanted it to be high tech—and the director had yet another agenda. It was a collaboration where no one got what they wanted, and no one was good at talking it through. In my conversations with Harvey, he really only wanted to talk about things that had happened: musicians he liked, things people had done. Politics, sometimes. He said that as an artist, he was a "realist," and it wasn't until after it was over that I realized that one, there's no real possibility of "realism" in instrumental music, but two, my music comes very close to "realism." I don't edit much, I have no system, I just write down the music I'm humming. Harvey was a very important artist, and I wish I'd had more time with him. I wish we'd gotten to do the opera again. Because of lack of money and some other weirdness I can't get into here, it's unlikely that the recording or video will ever be released. It's a closed chapter, most likely. However, I'm still learning from what we did get to do.

SS: What are the future plans for the New Monsters? Do you plan on continuing to record more of Dan's compositions, or was this a one and done?

STEVE: Definitely not a one-off. Expect to see this group around a lot. More live playing, more recording.

DAN: I'm in it as long as I'm having fun, and as long as Steve is willing to do all the work!

SS: I think it's great you guys are making music like this—what has the response been so far? Do you ever wish you'd taken up a different musical genre than jazz—perhaps rock, hip-hop, or polka?

SH: The reviews for this disc are the best I have seen in years. Critics are saying some very flattering things. The press clippings have been very, very favorable. We've also been getting great responses from audiences at live gigs. This is a very entertaining and muscular band, just weird enough for the adventurous souls in the crowd, and melodic and conventional enough to make the average jazz listener very happy.

DAN: A handful of people like it. I think most people who have heard us like us. That's the way it is. At this point, after 33 years doing music that I've wanted to do, I'm expecting nothing more than the usual, which is: a few friends come to a show or two and say a couple of nice things, we play a few small gigs for 20 people, complain about it briefly, and then move on to the next project. But I never regret not having taken up idiomatic music. I'm glad I haven't. I've done my own music all this time and, because of my lack of success, nothing's interfered with my development. When you play idiomatic music, you are a servant to that music, and to the expectations of others. What I do wish, sometimes, is that life's obligations didn't keep me from practicing and studying more.

SS: I could probably take an educated guess at what some of your main musical influences are—Beefheart, Coltrane, Braxton, Sun Ra—but what are the some of your major non-musical influences?

STEVE: Kerouac, Dylan Thomas, William Burroughs, Robert Heinlein. I was a strange kid. I read *A Happy Death* over and over again in high school. It was right next to my copy of *Without Feathers*.

DAN: Science Fiction was big for me. In my formative years, I read only SF. Everything Philip K. Dick ever wrote. The idea that there are other worlds, other ways of being. It's therefore natural for me to want to invent my own music, with its own rules. Nowadays I read a lot of contemporary fiction. I like books that aren't about too much. I like Magnus Mills, Thomas Bernhard, Roberto Bolano, David Foster Wallace, Tao Lin. Of the painters I like the most, I think my music is most like the art of Henri Rousseau, de Chirico, and Rauschenberg. I think about Diebenkorn when I make arrangements: the way his lines are always thickened by other painted-over lines beneath. I also owe a lot to the dadaists, and to the abstract expressionists. I like drawing, and I'm planning to start painting.

SS: It's difficult making non-mainstream music in today's world. Or making any kind of art that's more difficult for the hoi polloi than, say, Thomas Kinkade (may he RIP). Who are some of your role models for swimming against the cultural tide, so to speak?

DAN: Charles Ives and Sun Ra both just did their thing in the face of indifference. They invented their own worlds, and brought us into them.

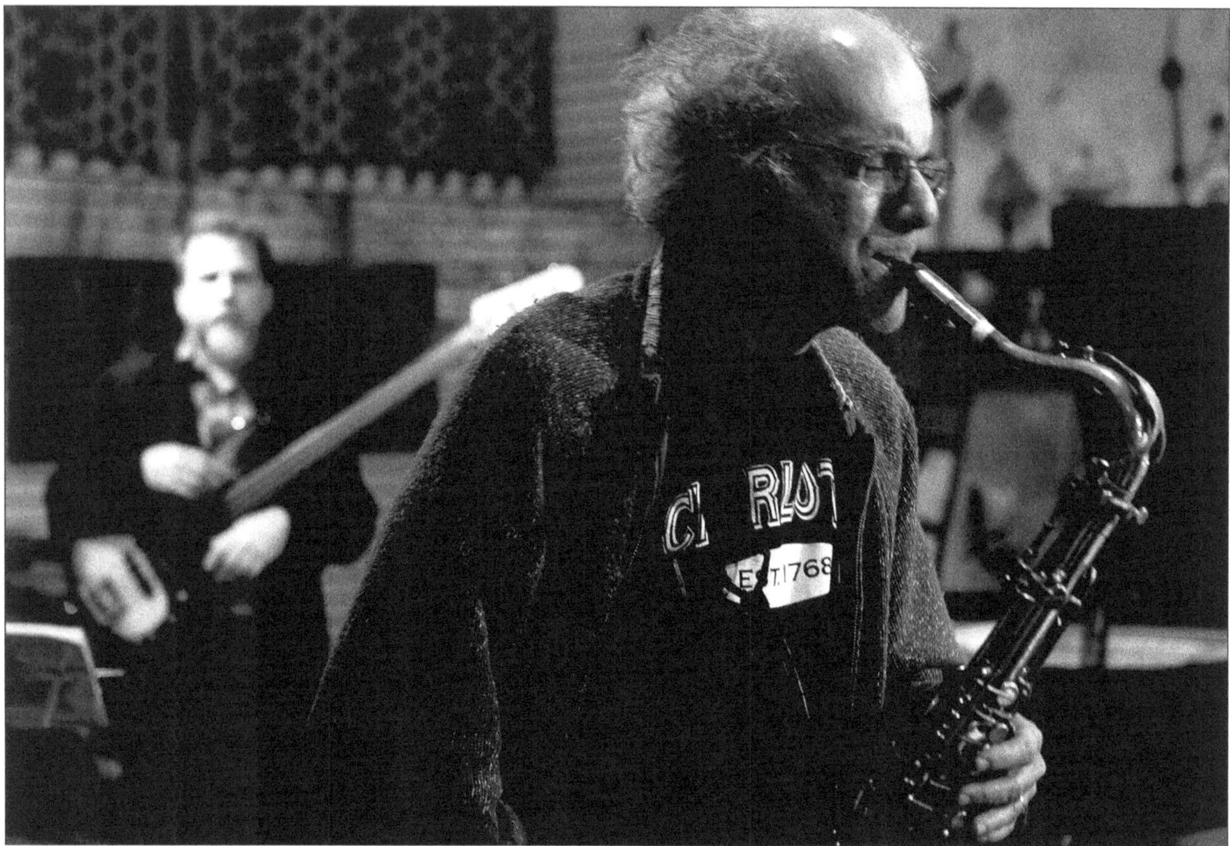

photograph by Jeff Spirer

STEVE: Yes, you have to make your own rules, you have to be your own dog. Zappa was a huge influence on me in terms of taking control of your career and being your own boss. In this day and age, it helps to have some entrepreneurial spirit. The playing field has been more than leveled out, it has been completely dug up. You have to take advantage of the new to get your music and message out there.

SS: Do you change your diet when you're in the recording process? Do you eat better or worse? Junk food or organic?

DAN: I have health issues which have forced me to eat fairly regularly, fairly healthily. I used to bring lots of pastries to a recording, but no more. However, if we're in Oakland and it's my project and I'm buying the food, it will be from Pho 84 most likely. Or from that Thai place near Myles Boisen's studio. Or that Cambodian place at 8th and Alice. Gotta have South-east Asian. I do think it's important to have enjoyable, inspiring food.

STEVE: I also have some health issues around food, strangely in fact, Dan and I have very similar issues, so I also try to stay on the straight and narrow and keep consistent with healthy eating. After all, I did work on *Super Size Me,* so junk food is out of the question!

SS: We've reached agreement! Excellent!

Guy Walks into a Bar circa 1997, Hollywood

Karen Lillis

SO THIS GUY WALKS INTO THE BAR LAST Thursday, and he sorta "lets it slip" that he's Lawnchair Larry. This older guy, you know? He says it to me right before I'm gonna tell him what he owes me for a light draft. I was looking at his face, trying to remember what Lawnchair Larry looked like. What year was that? Early '80s. I was looking at him for a while, I was thinking that maybe he looked like a guy who just lost privileges at his usual barstool. Never seen him before, but he's a regular somewhere, you know. Finally I said to him, "That'll be three bucks, sir."

Well, he stayed in the bar a while, several rounds, you know. But it was before happy hour, it was still pretty slow. The guy tried cozying up to a few girls when his drink was getting short, and he'd lean in and whisper something to them, and I'd see the look on their face, like, "Lawnchair WHA??" and they'd move away so he had to talk louder and he'd say "Lawnchair LARRY," and I couldn't help it, I'd start laughing. I kept having to pretend I was laughing at goddamn Johnny Fantastic's jokes. Poor Johnny starts smiling thinking that he's funnier than usual with those stupid gags. He even took the mousetrap out of his pocket. Eventually Larry left.

So happy hour came around and it was real busy, and I forgot about Larry for a while. But then Sophie came in. Right around seven-thirty or something, it was slow again. And as soon as I saw her, I remembered how much she loved Lawnchair Larry, so I started laughing again. And I tell her,

"You'll NEVER guess who the fuck came in today!" And Sophie's all, "Dweezil Zappa? Jon Spencer? Who?!" with those big eyes 'cause she's the last unjaded girl in Hollywood. And I scream "LAWNCHAIR LARRY!" and the two of us die laughing. I'm doubled over behind the bar, and Sophie's sprawled out ON the bar, and every time we catch our breath, Sophie says it again, "Lawn . . . chair . . . LAR-RY!" and we start laughing again. Until I have to tell her to stop, I'm at work.

But then Sophie doesn't let it go. I mean, we quit the laughing part, but every time one of the regulars comes in, she's all, "Minx, guess who came in today?" "Jake, guess who came in today?" "Mercury, d'ja hear who came in today?" The beardos came up to the bar, the rockabillies, the riot grrrls, the bike punks, the skaters, the Mexican goths, and she did the same thing every time. The thing I thought was funny about it was finding out who's from here. It was almost strictly down coastal lines. The people from California and the Southwest knew who Lawnchair Larry was, and the people from the East Coast had never heard of him. I mean mostly.

Sophie was really enjoying describing Lawnchair Larry to anyone who didn't know about him. She loves the part about him dropping the pellet gun, she works up to it real dramatic, you know? She makes it sound like he's not coming out of the clouds alive. But then a bunch of kids showed up who thought that Lawnchair Larry had died a few years ago, and some other kid at the bar said he'd heard that his death was just a rumor. Conor said he suicided for sure. "My mom went to high school with his sister," Conor said. He said Larry went to Vietnam after graduation and never got married, never got good with society, walked away and shot himself in the woods. For Conor, it all added up. But Sophie was convinced that he was the guy from earlier. "Maybe he faked his own suicide so that he could finally live down the fame," she said. Conor was being a hard ass: "So then why's he want to come into a random BAR telling everyone he's Lawnchair Larry?" "Well, 'cause his plan didn't work. He doesn't actually WANT to live it down—it's his life's dream! It's what he's got!"

Around the time Seth comes in for his pool game, Sophie got on a kick about the band name all over again. I thought we had finally decided on Boneless Skinless, but she starts on about wanting to name it Larry and the Lawnchairs. I really didn't want to fight about it, so I just served her another one and figured we'd talk about it when she was sober. Or better yet, just forget about it entirely. You know Sophie, sometimes she likes to say one phrase over and over all night, and then she never says it again. I thought I'd let this one play out like the rest of them.

That beach freak Lars has been stringing Sophie along for weeks. I don't know why she's so into him, but when he sat next to her at the bar, I didn't hear anything about Lawnchair Larry for the next hour. They were just talking low over their drinks, and Sophie kept chewing her ice and playing with her straw. Sophie was so quiet, I could hear Johnny telling Conor his oldest jokes: "Skeleton walks into a bar . . . ," and that one about the midgets and the prostitutes. Finally Lars gets up to use the payphone, and Sophie calls me over and whispers, "Crystal—I just threw up in my mouth." I gave her a seltzer with lime juice and told her to go gargle it in the bathroom.

A little later, Tony came up to the bar. Mistah Anthony fuggin' Balladucci, from Bensonhoist, Brooklyn. You've seen him, he's that hot short guy who plays bass for White Courtesy Telephone and drinks Jack-and-Cokes. Well, Tony and Sophie got into it over Lawnchair Larry. Tony had heard of Lawnchair Larry alright, but he told Sophie he thought he was stupid. He said Lawnchair Larry was about as interesting as a cat stuck in a tree. Not only that, he starts making it into this New York vs. LA thing, saying that if you want to see a real stunt, you've got to look at the guy who walked a tightrope between the Twin Towers of the World Trade Center. Sophie starts getting her panties into a bunch, but meanwhile Johnny Fantastic about lost his MIND when Tony explains that yeah, a guy walked a fucking tightrope between the towers back in the '70s, several times in a row, and he didn't even die. Johnny couldn't believe it. It was like his whole geek act went up in smoke in the space of one sentence.

But it keeps going from there, with Sophie and Tony throwing down these random reasons why LA is so punk rock and why New York will always rock harder, why LA is the city of the future and how LA isn't a city at all, and if that's true why did you come here, until I asked them to go somewhere and write the article for *LA Weekly* already because they're giving me a headache. So they took the debate over to the jukebox.

You know those gaffer guys who come in and drink Blackened Voodoo at the end of the bar? By one a.m. Sophie gets them to pick her up in a chair and act like she's Lawnchair Larry going up in the sky. Only it's more like the drunkest Jewish wedding you've ever been to, I knew they were going to pour her out of that chair for sure. And then Tony's there tightrope walking with the pool stick on the edge of the pool table, with his bandmates sitting on the other side of the table so it doesn't tip over. The gaffers are parading Sophie AROUND the pool table, and Sophie's telling Mercury to feed the jukebox for the Eyes and the Germs and the Bags and L7, while Tony gets Seth to play Television, Unsane, Boss Hog, "Chinese Rocks," and "I Wanna Be Sedated."

Tony said Lawnchair Larry was about as interesting as a cat stuck in a tree.

Right when Sophie thinks she's nailed the last word by getting most of the bar singing *OUR WHOLE FUCKIN LIFE IS A WRECK!*, something goes wrong at the pool table. I didn't see it, but Glen Vereen said that Jake got up from the band side of the table to get another drink, that tipped the table a little, and then Tony lost his balance and slipped off the edge, landed on a beer bottle. Before you know it, I'm calling the ambulance for the second time in a week.

And now, Sophie's over at Tony's place while he's stuck there with his leg in a cast. Yeah, she went to Los Feliz and got him some zines and soymilk and everything. I wouldn'ta figured them together, but why not, they're the same height. They seem kinda sweet on each other. Course, we'll see what the story is when Tony's mobile again.

Anyways. It got her mind off Lawnchair Larry in a hurry.

Photographs

Ruby Ray

In the 1980s, through the early '90s, I spent an awful lot of time travelling. Or maybe not travelling so much as running away. I was running away from this guy, this crazy guy who wanted to kill me. Finally, I realized he was me! Anyway, when I was going all the fuck over the place hither and yon without rhyme or reason, looking for places that either had good dope, or where you couldn't get any dope, I packed lightly, as any sensible traveller does (that and wore black clothing—it really is amazing how long you can go without washing black jeans.) But no matter where I wandered, I always carried a small library, as I was a budding author and needed inspiration (or grist for the mill, or just plain stuff to steal). A couple of books—large books—formed the core of my portable library: the two issues of *RE/Search* magazine featuring William S. Burroughs and J. G. Ballard, two of my greatest writing heroes (for some reason, most of my writer role models' last names began with the letter "B").

So what a pleasure it was to meet, all these years later, the person responsible for the iconic cover shot of the Burroughs edition, an image forever burned into the cathode ray tube of my mind's eye. Did I say ray? Yes, that's the photographer's name, Ruby Ray! It would be hard to overstate how pleased I am to present the following portfolio of Ruby's work, a small sampling of her documentation of the early days of punk, West Coast style.

—B. Kold

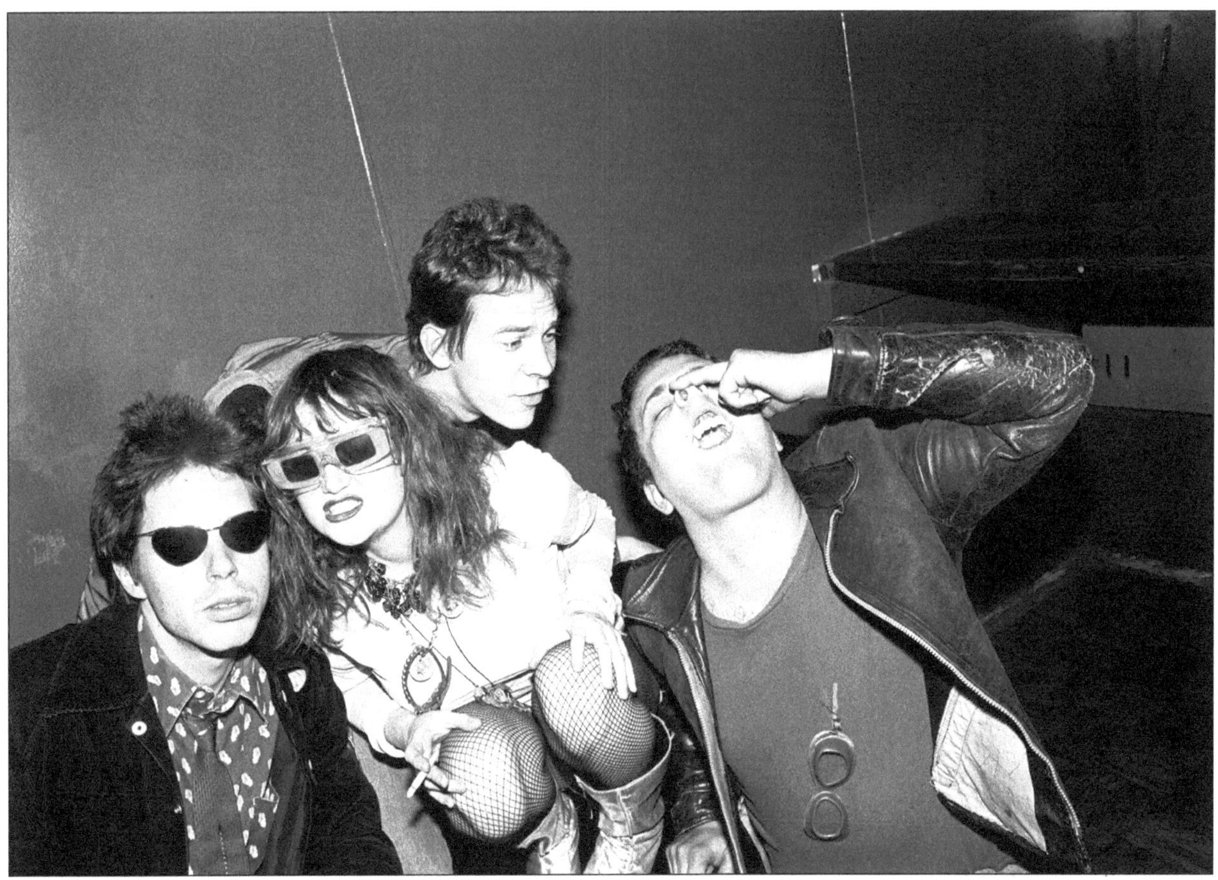

Welcome to LA, 1977: John Doe, Exene, Rand McNally, and Black Randy

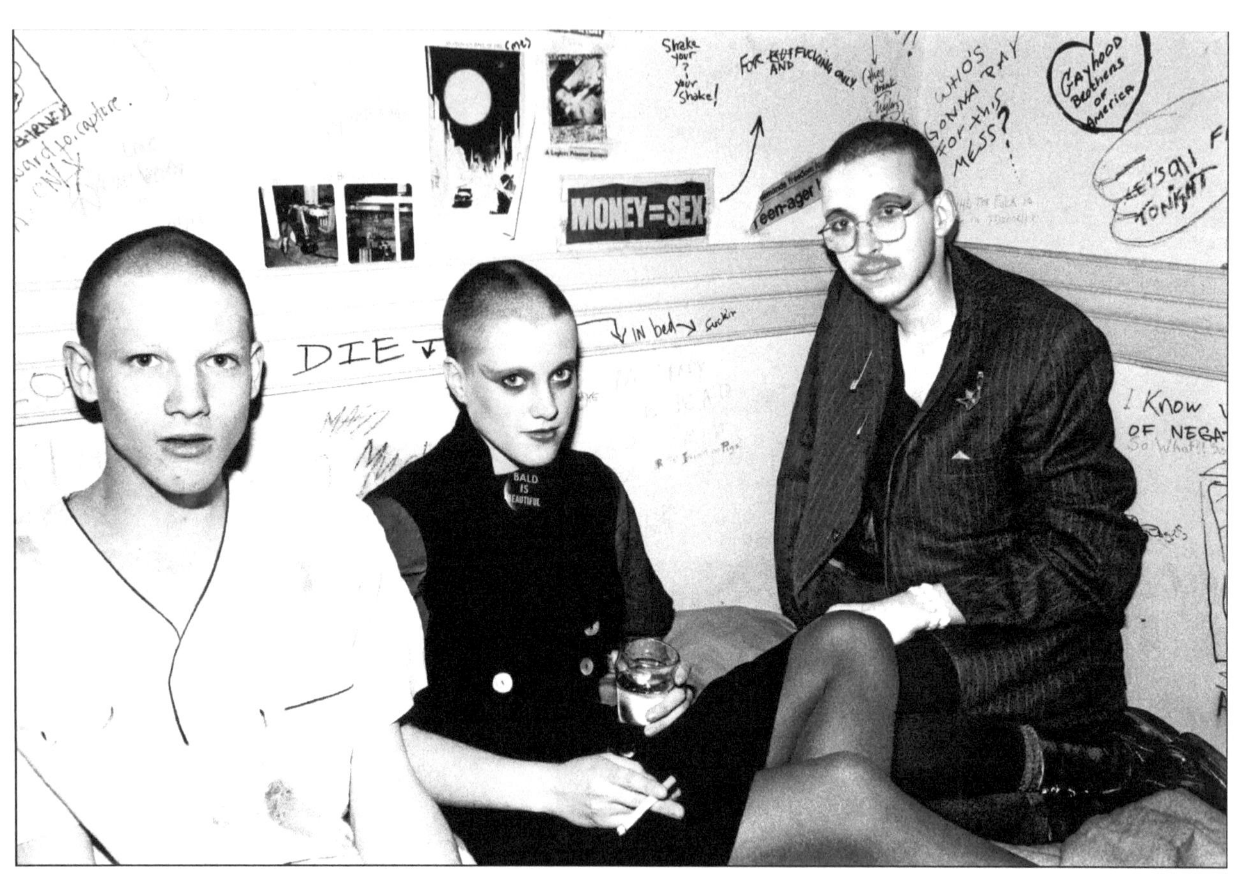

At Home with the Baldies, 1979: Bruce Loose, DieAnt, and Vince Deranged of New Youth

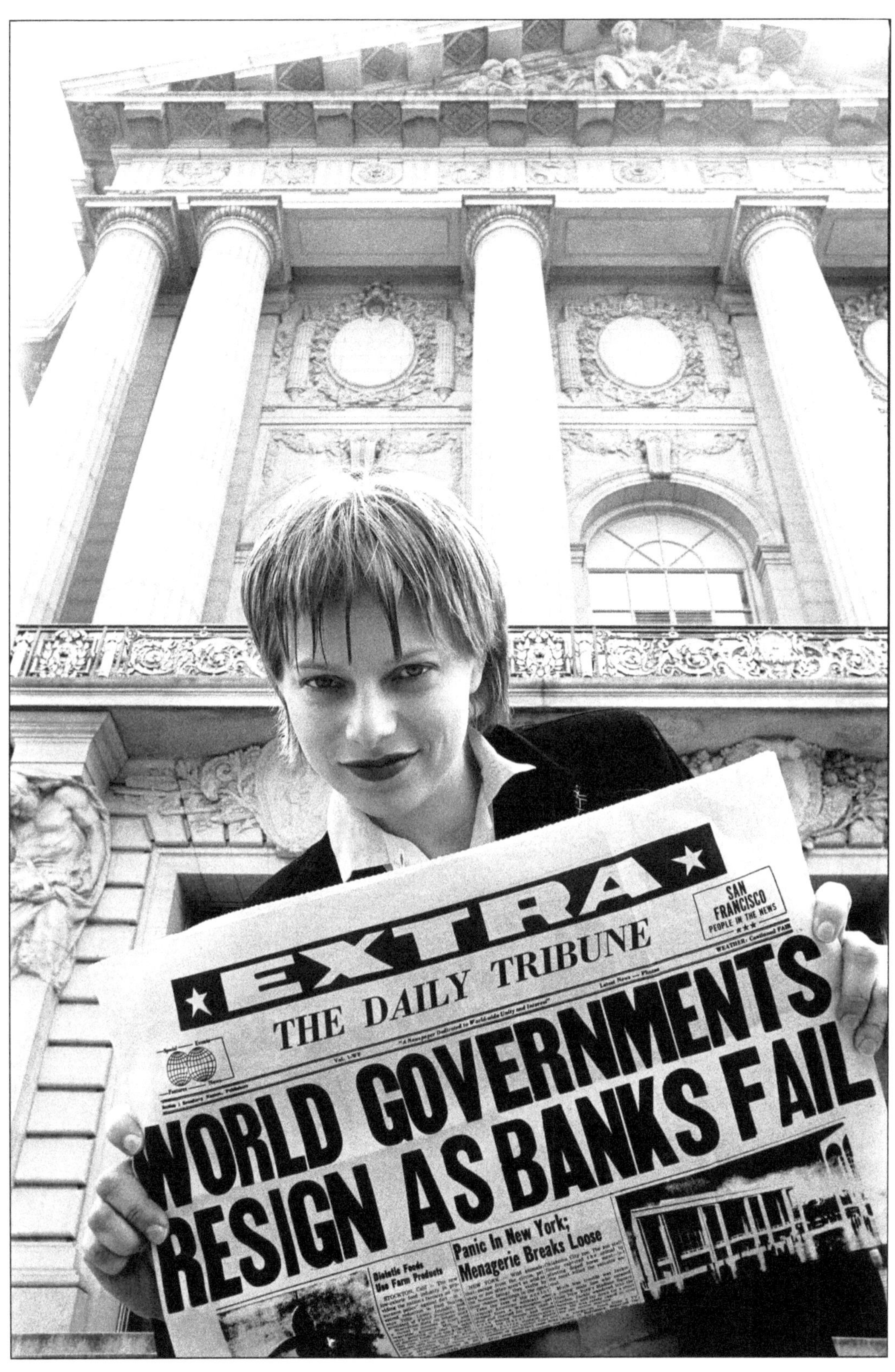

World Governments Resign, 1978: DeDe Troit of UXA

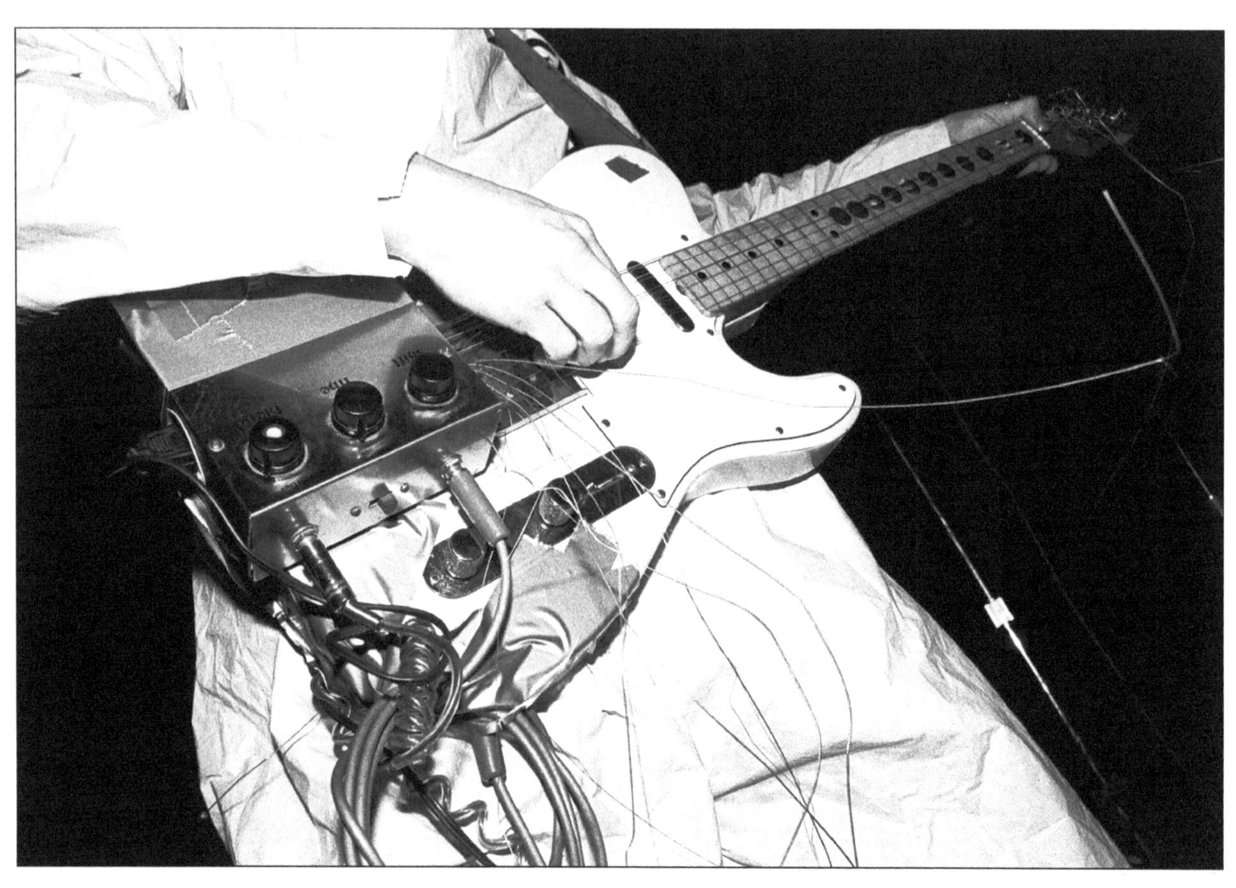

Devotar, 1977: Mark Mothersbaugh specialty

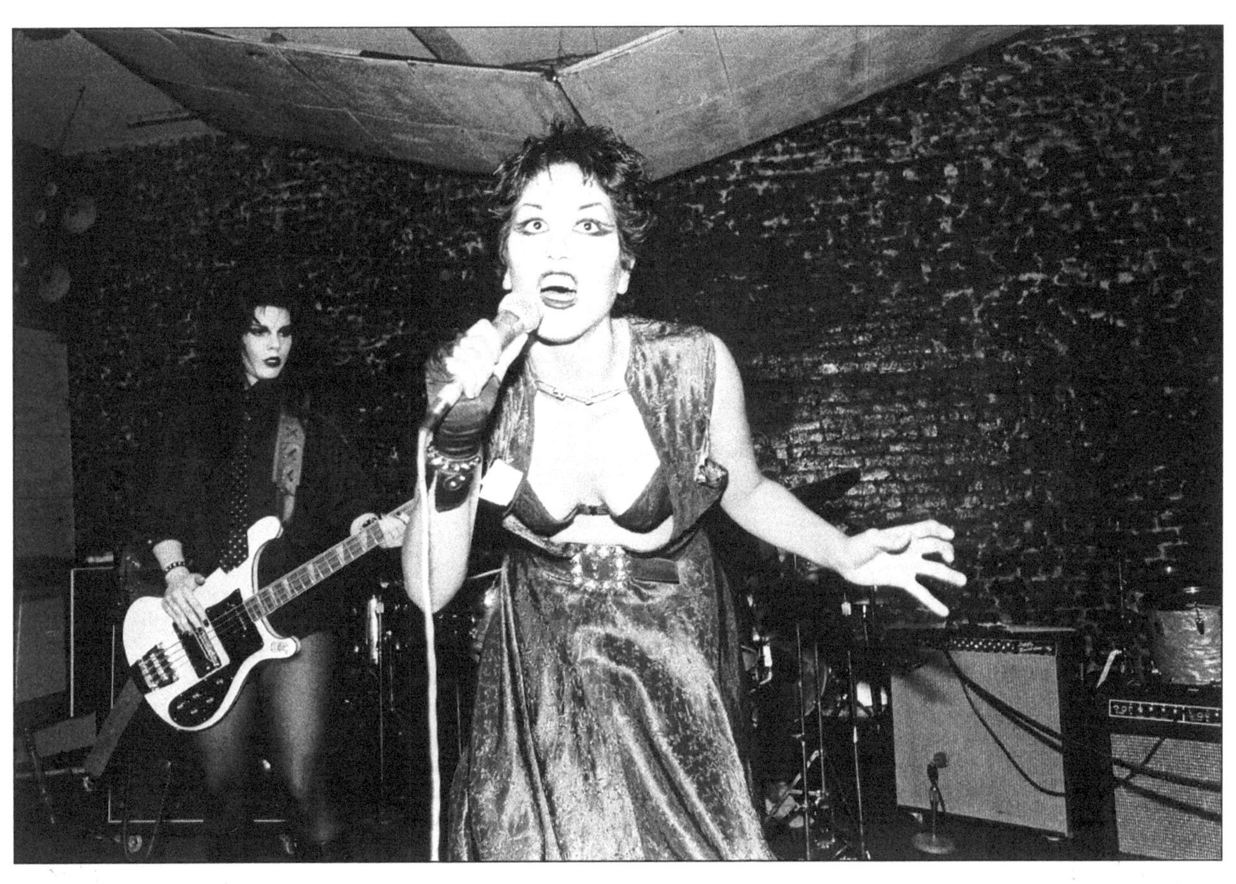

Pat and Alice Bag, 1978

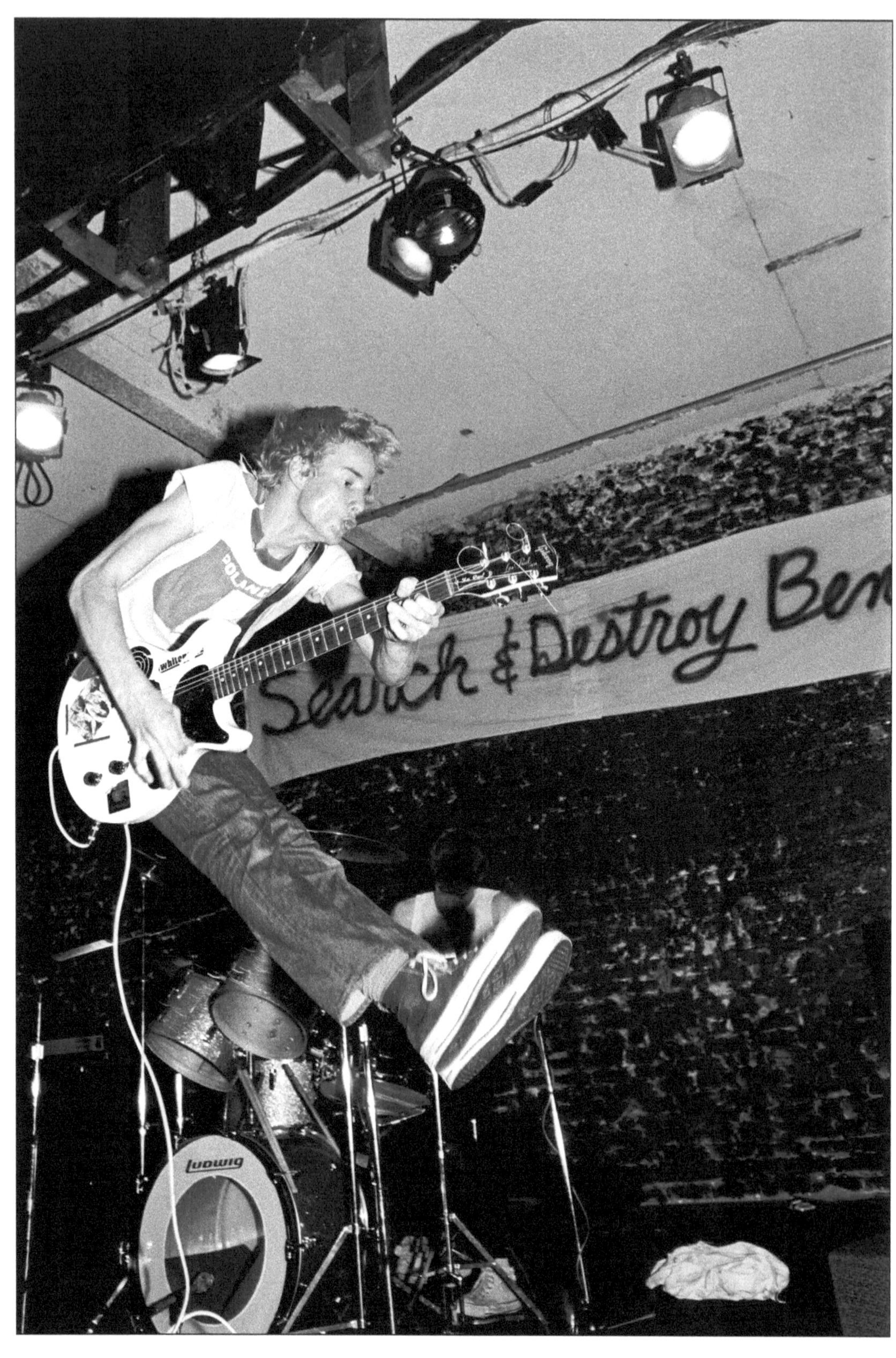

Chip Dil Goes Jackknife, 1978

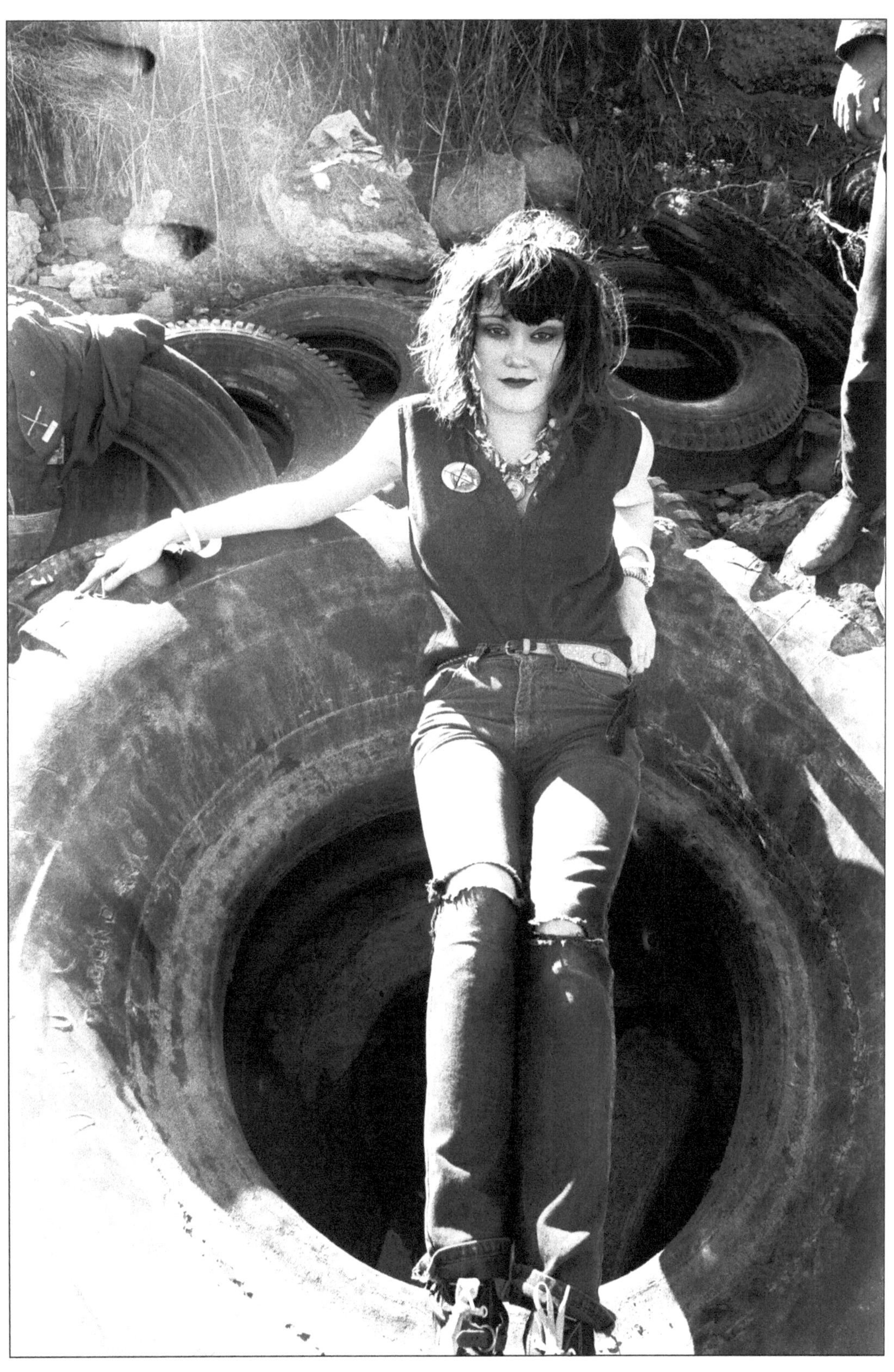

Exene at Tire Beach, 1978

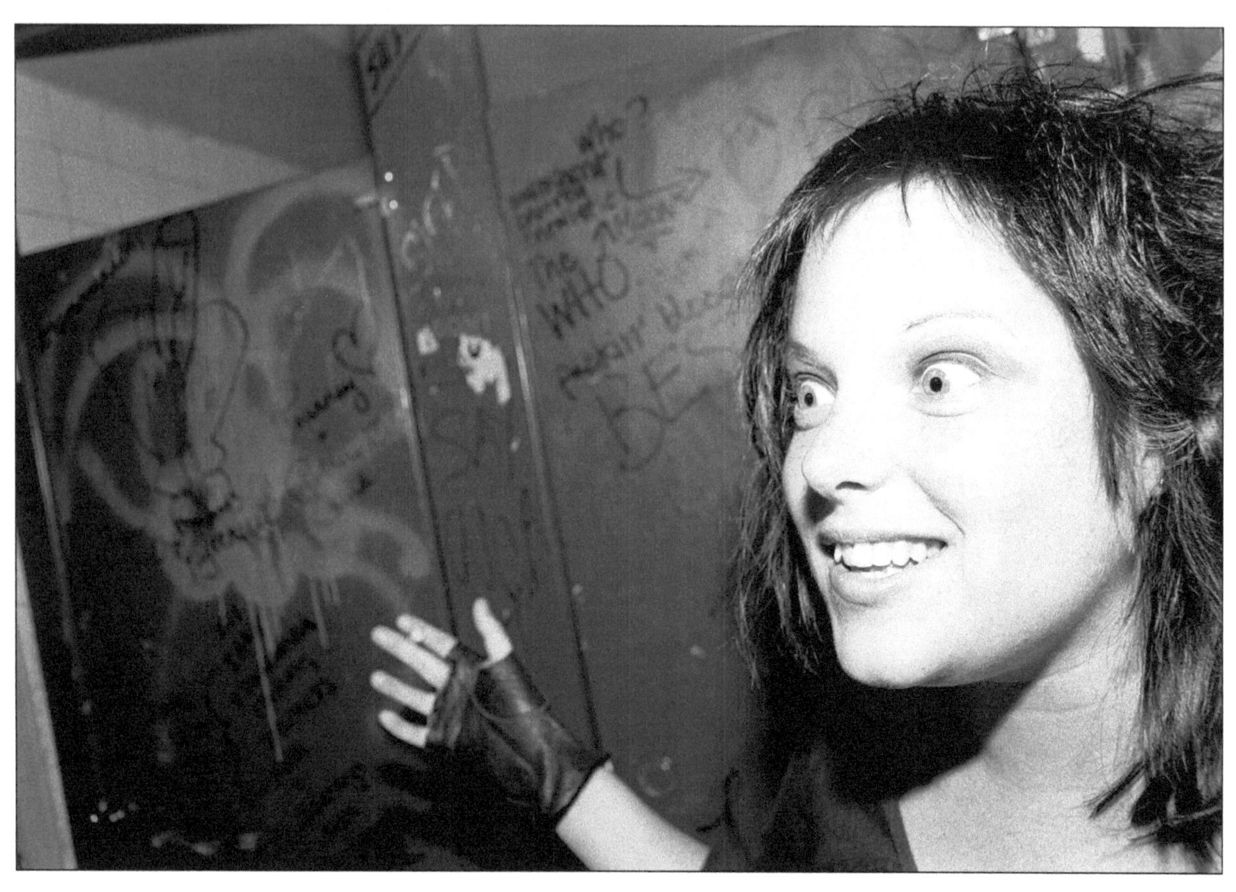

Sally in the Girls' Bathroom, 1978: Singer for the Mutants at the Mab

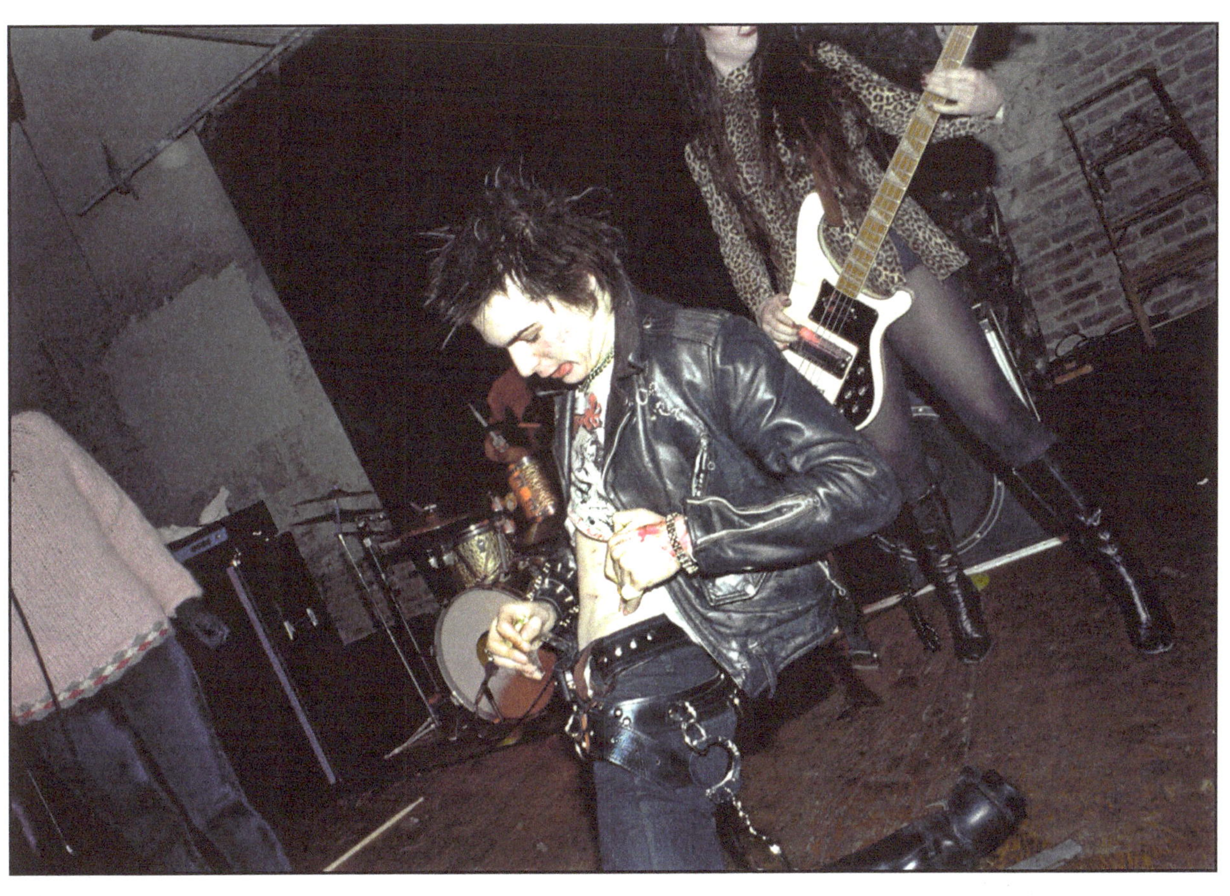

Sid Cuts Himself, 1978: At the Mab, the night after the Sex Pistols broke up

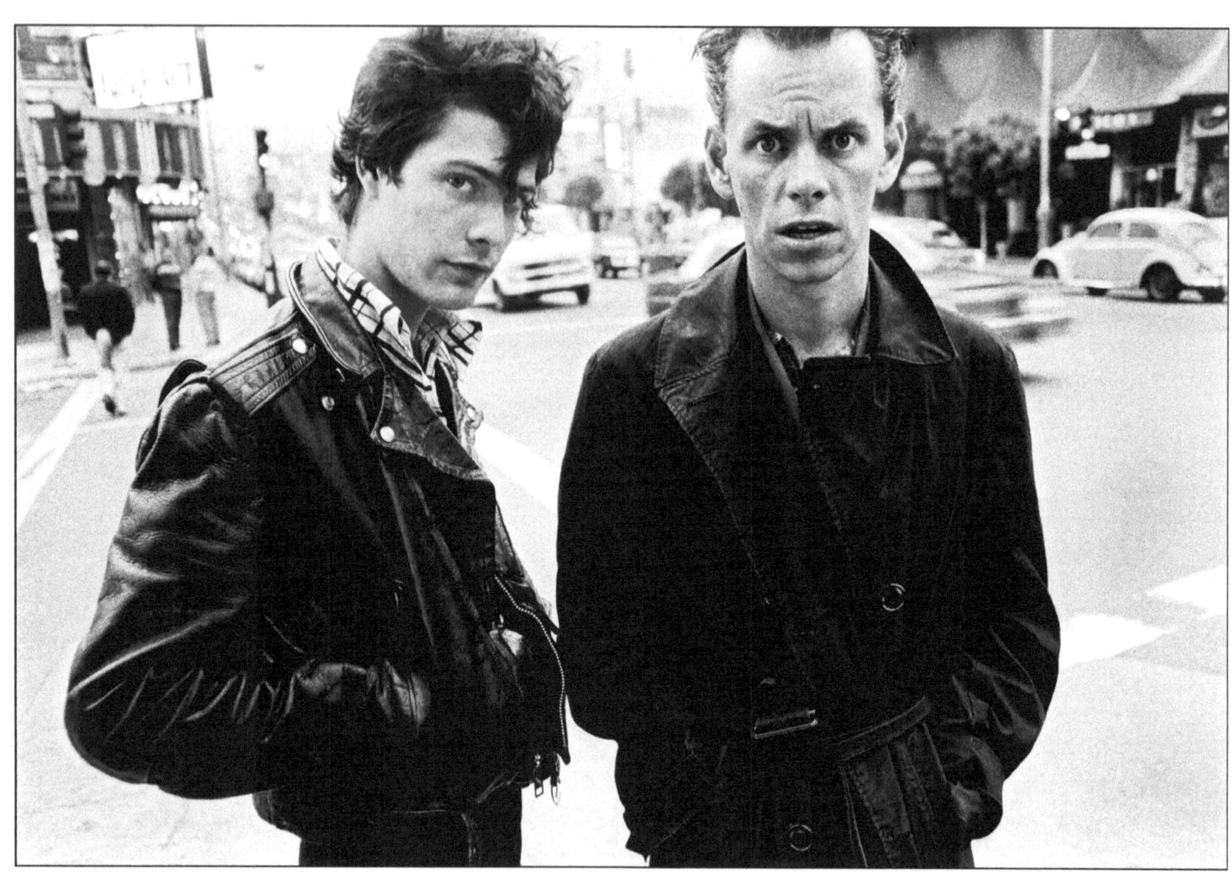

Screamers Paul Roessler and Tomata Du Plenty on Broadway, 1978

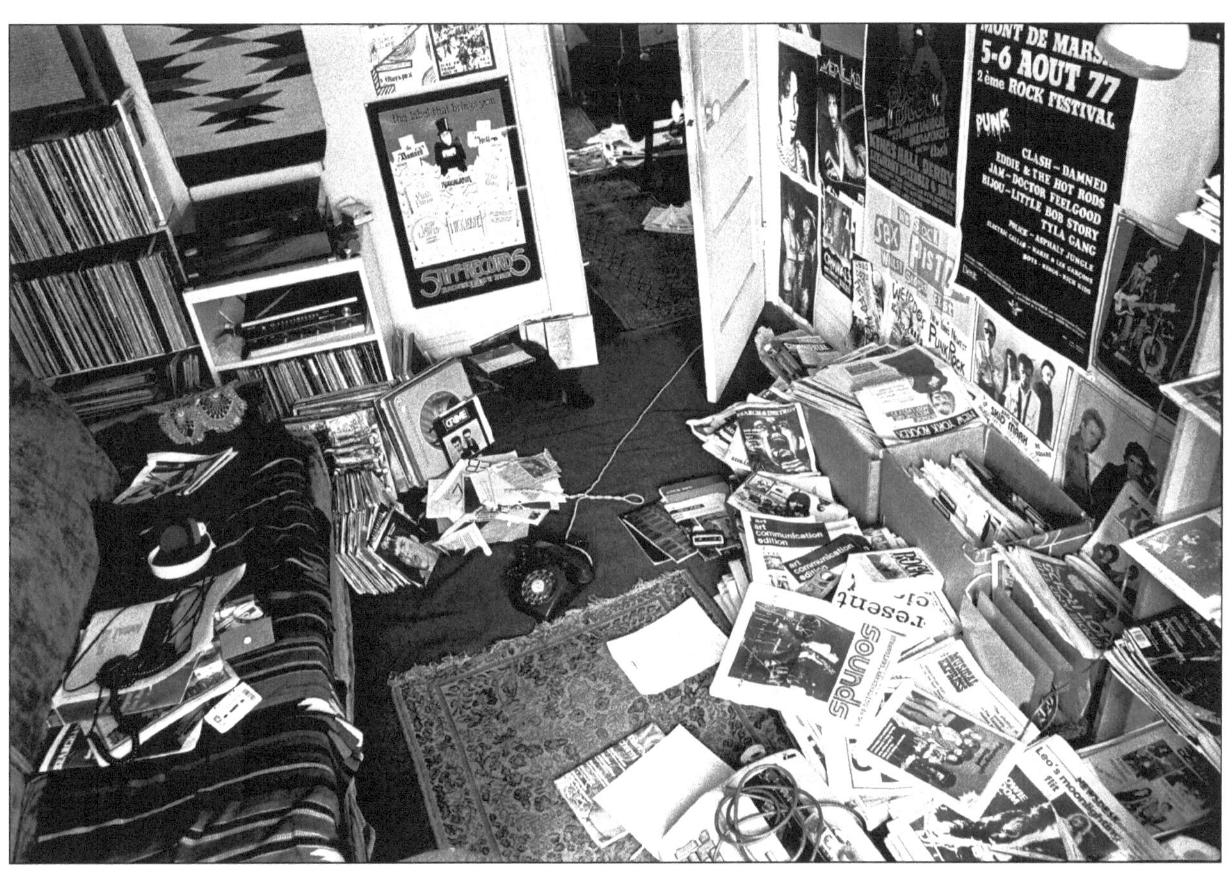

Headquarters, 1977: Vale's living room

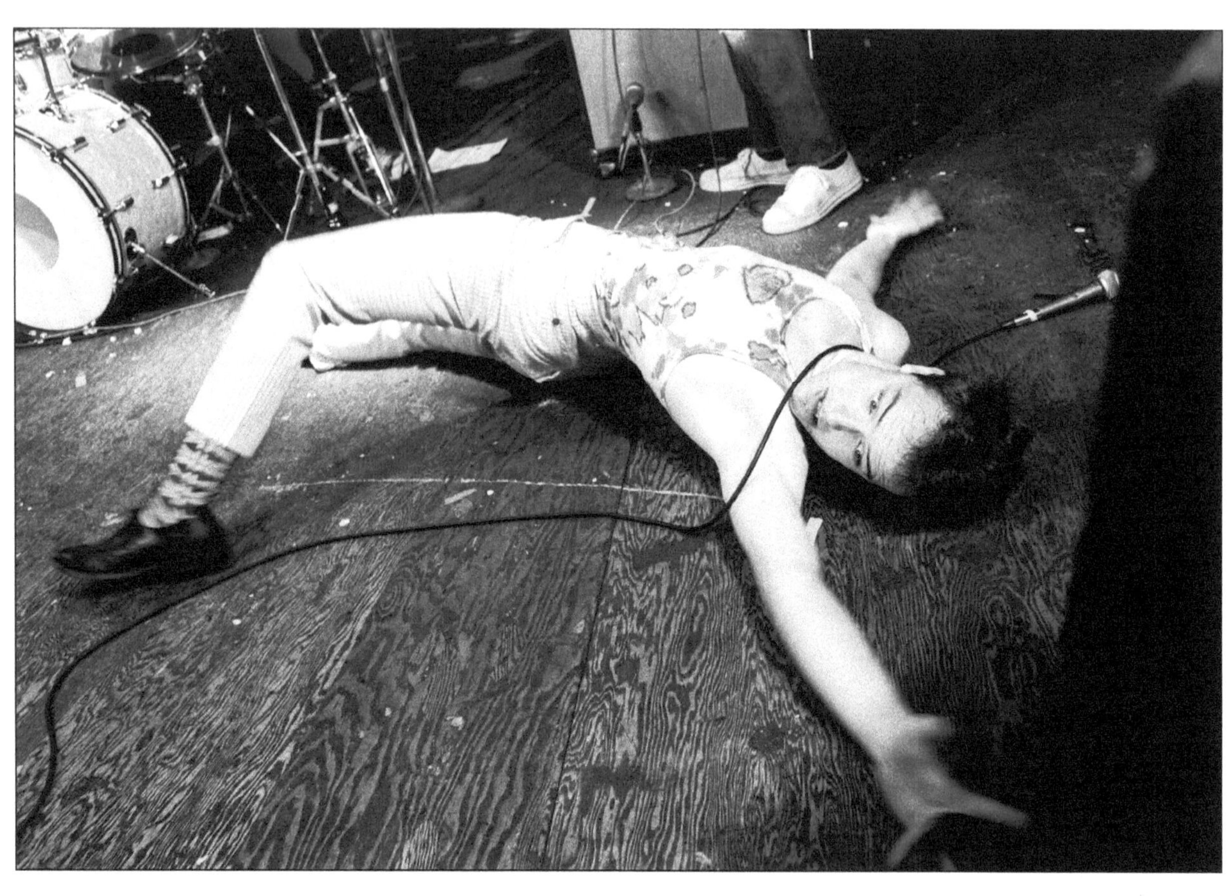

Slip and Slide Jello, 1978: At the Mabuhay

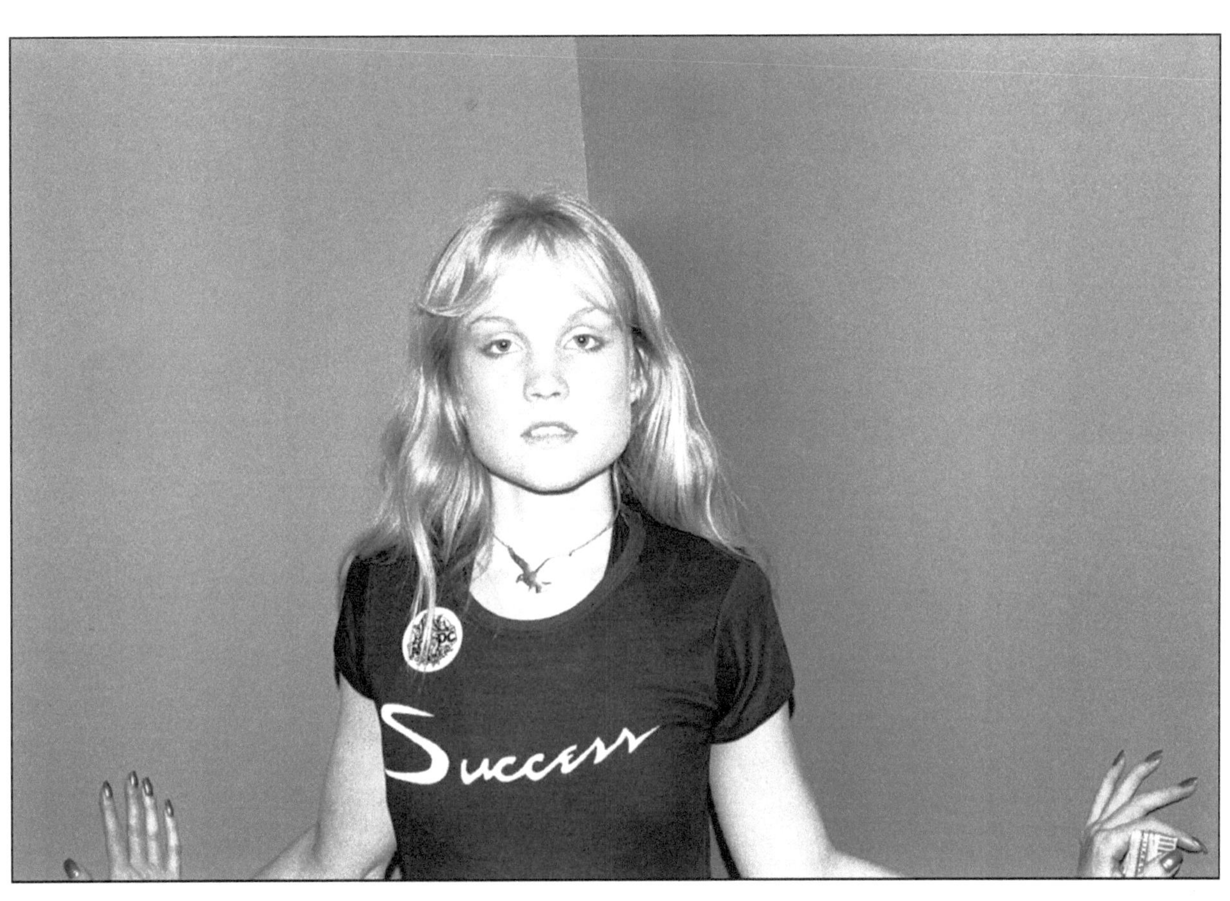

Success, 1977: Waitress at the Mabuhay, not impressed

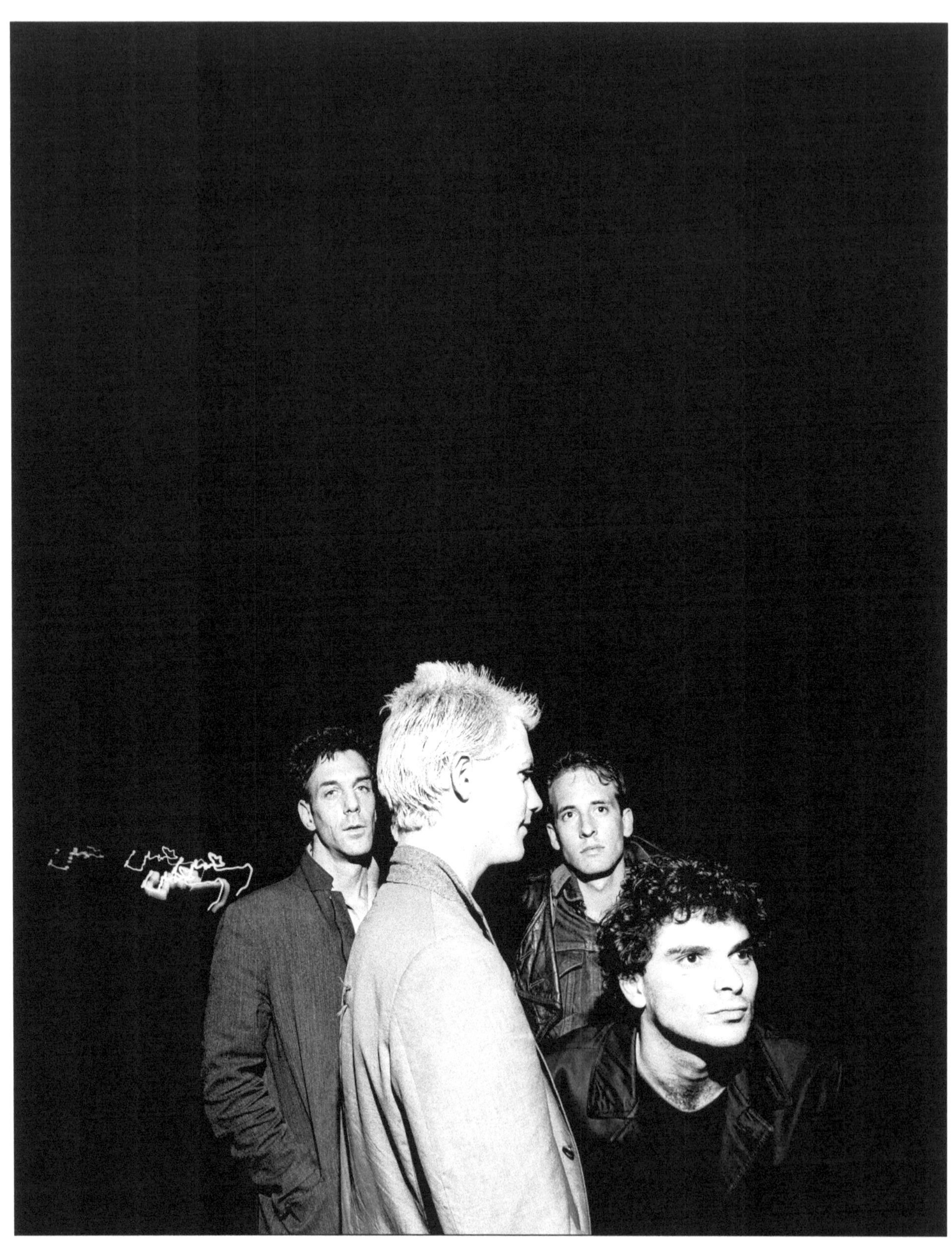

Flipper in the Dark, 1981

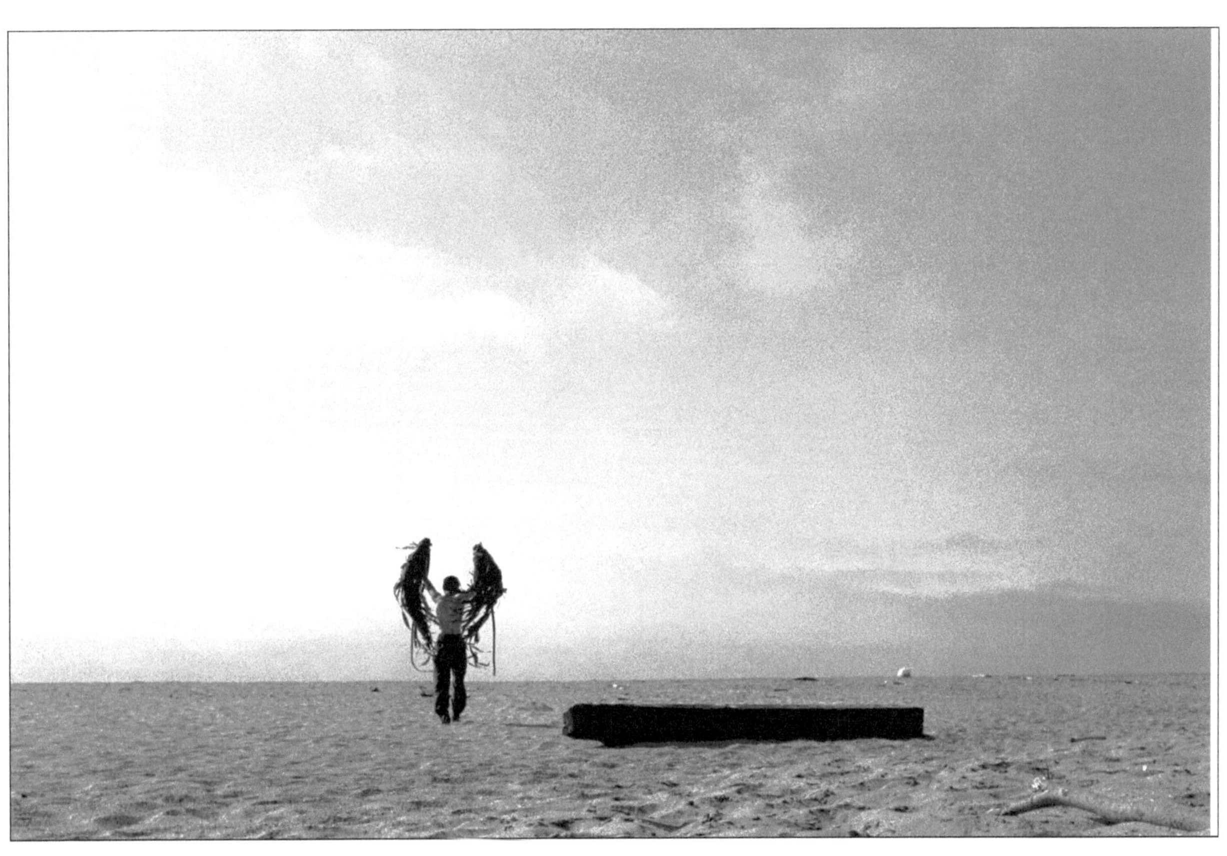

Avenging Angel, Monte Cazazza, 1981

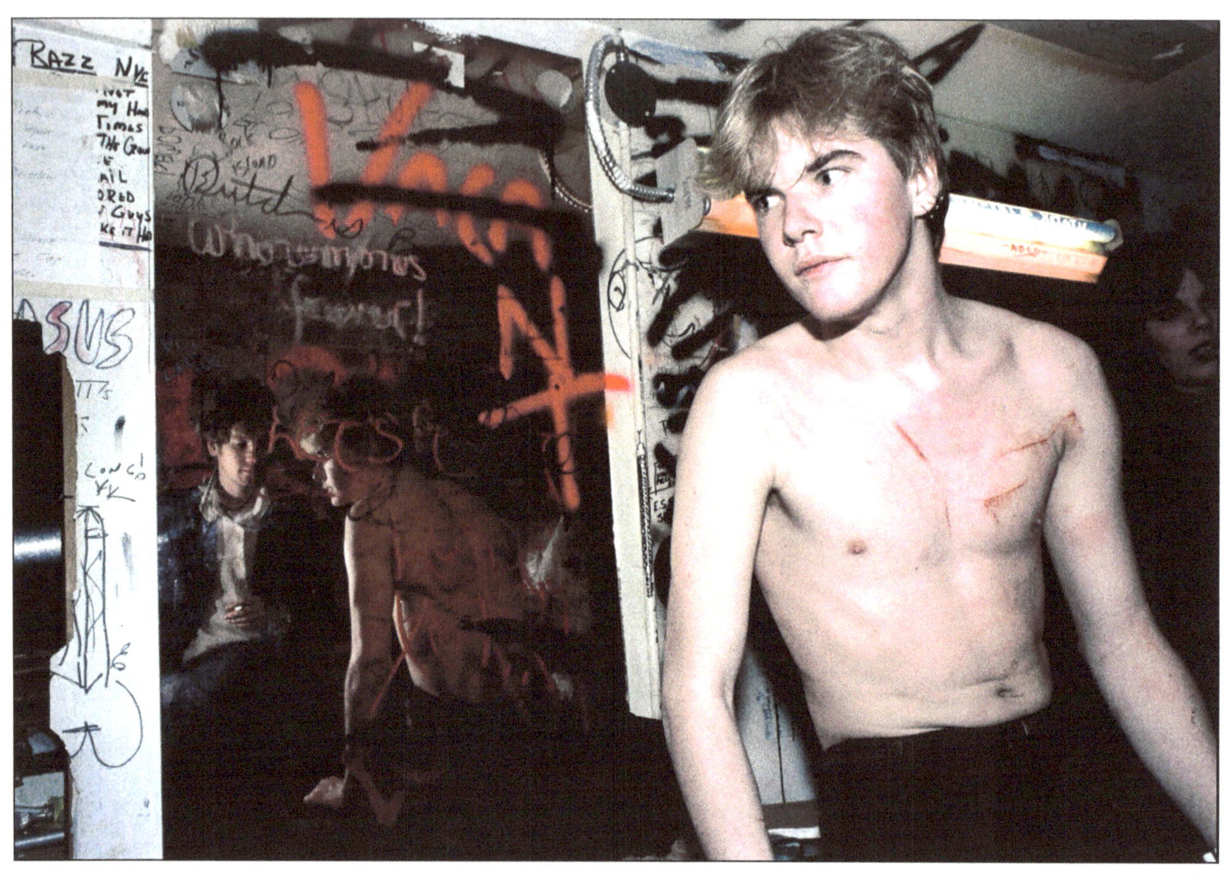

Darby Crash, Backstage, Cut Up, 1978: At the Mab, the night after the Sex Pistols broke up

How to Stop Smoking in 19,287 Seconds, Usama

Chavisa Woods

I ASKED NO QUESTIONS ABOUT ANYTHING. I JUST wanted to smoke cigarettes. Lots and lots of cigarettes.

I come back once a year to visit. I only stay a few days. I try not to ask too many questions. There's nothing I can do about the answers anyway. I'm only here five days a year. What can I do? I smoke a ton of cigarettes. I give some to my brothers. They can't always afford them. I can do that. I can almost always afford cigarettes and I can smoke cigarettes with my brothers.

I can also drink beer with them, and I can usually afford to buy them one dinner or one new outfit, depending on the mood of things. This visit, I bought them dinner at a Mexican restaurant in a strip mall: El Rancherito. Even though it was in a strip mall across the street from the Super WalMart, and even though El Rancherito is to Mexican what Green Day is to punk rock (people who don't know better think it is the real thing), it was owned and run by real Mexicans, and the food was very good. The restaurant provided endless chips, which my brothers liked, as well as ninety-nine-cent beer pitchers, also a big plus. My little-little and I polished off these ninety-nine-cent pitchers with no help from my big-little.

I have two little brothers. My little-little brother is smaller than my older little brother. My older little brother is big. He is my big-little brother. It was six o'clock. We'd just finished the authentic Mexican strip-mall food and two ninety-nine-cent beer pitchers, and I was getting ready to head to the car and to take them back to Big-little's place, when Big-little got a phone call from his cousin. My big-little brother has a cousin who's related neither to me nor to my little-little brother. His cousin is somewhere in between their two sizes. Big-little's mid-sized cousin is only related to Big-little and not related to me or Little-little on account of us all three having different fathers. I don't know who is the father of this mid-sized not-cousin of mine, but he sure looked like a kid who could use a dad when I met him.

The phone call consisted of Big-little looking ponderous and saying uh-huh three times, after which he hung up and informed Little-little that he wasn't going back to his own place because this cousin of his was there. Big-little was going to get his average-sized girlfriend to come take him somewhere else for the night.

My little-little brother had been planning on staying at my big-little brother's place that night, since he had no place else to stay, so he said he was going to need to get dropped off there anyway, Not-cousin or no Not-cousin. Little-little's stuff was at Big-little's and he had nowhere else to stay. What could he do?

We stood on the sidewalk of the strip mall waiting for Big-little's girlfriend. I took out three cigarettes. We smoked them. I didn't ask any questions. It was raining. We smoked under the awning until Big-little's girlfriend pulled up. He got in her mid-sized car. Little-little and I finished our cigarettes. We got into the car I was driving. Little-little took off his shirt and tossed it in the back seat with his other shirt. We drove on to Big-little's house where his, not our, cousin apparently was going to be, which made Big-little not want to be there, and I didn't know why. Not that I had asked.

It was dark. Dark in the country is really very dark. The stars are bright. Big-little's house is not really a house but a long, skinny trailer resting lopsided off a dirt road that comes off an old highway out on the edge of the woods. On the way there, Little-little told me that behind the trailer, through the woods, was a cornfield where this whacked-out kid is living in an abandoned shack, cooking meth. He knows this because he and his friend were riding bikes through the field the week before and the kid came out and started shooting at them. Little-little said he could smell the meth chemicals cooking even from several yards away. He knows what it smells like because he used to cook meth years ago before he realized just how bad of an idea that was.

He was riding bikes out there because he goes around the woods and all the surrounding areas tearing apart abandoned houses for scrap metal he sells at junkyards. He makes between fifty and two hundred dollars a week this way, depending. But he hurts himself a lot. As we pulled in alongside the muddy drive of the dark, now nearly invisible trailer, he was showing me a wound on his finger he had all wrapped up with duct tape from where he cut himself scrapping a few days before. I flipped the key off. He flipped the interior car light on and displayed for me a long, jagged scar than ran along the inside of his forearm. This happened two months ago when a copper pipe he was prying out of a wall sprung the wrong way and tore him open from just above his wrist to the inside of his elbow. Little-little, now twenty-three and still peachy keen, showed me this scar with his emblematic wiry enthusiasm, scrappy, scrapping his life away. When it happened, he told me proudly, he just stapled it together with Super Glue then wrapped it tight with duct tape and kept on scrapping. He's a scrapper. The wound had done something that sort of resembled healing, so he figured it was alright. He turned the light off, rolled up a pair of shoes inside his two shirts and asked if I wanted to come in for a second. I did want to come in. I wanted to smoke and I couldn't smoke in the car I was driving and it was raining outside.

We clopped up the wilting porch of the trailer where rotting furniture was rotting in the rain on the drooping, decaying wood. The porch was threatening to metamorphose into an organic life form, or perhaps just mold itself back into the wet ground. Maybe the porch would liquefy and become a moat around the trailer and you'd have to float on the couch to get across. Maybe even the couch would become an organic life form and give you a guided speaking tour of the trailer moat as it floated you up to the door.

For months, my brothers had been telling me about these green, floating, gaseous orbs they see coming out of the woods that they think are coming from UFOs landing out there. But I think it's more of a combination of mold, the meth kid cooking out in the field and also, last year the EPA cleaned off about fifteen miles' worth of toxic topsoil from this area. This was a prime county for asbestos factories in the seventies. The land is flat. It rains a lot. The toxic water seeps and sits. Oh well. Green, glowing orbs are a lot more fun to think of as alien life forms than all that other crap, especially if you're living with them. Especially if there's nothing you can do about them. What are you going to do? Try and communicate?

For months, my brothers had been telling me about these green, floating, gaseous orbs they see coming out of the woods that they think are coming from UFOs landing out there.

Little-little opened the door. Inside, the trailer was pitch-black and smelled of mold. I stepped into the wettish blackness. During the five-second count before the light was switched on, I painfully noted that we were not alone. In the not-so-distant darkness, I made out a small red light and something breathing uncomfortably next to it. From the red light, sounds were coming out, static broken by broken voices announcing numbers and positions.

Little-little turned on a lamp. A few feet away, sitting next to the TV was someone who I assumed was Big-little's cousin. He was a doughy boy, about twenty-one, dressed in a stretched-out white T-shirt and blue jeans. His face was as white as his shirt and his eyes glowed almost as red as the red light on the police scanner he held in his left hand. His right hand was holding on to the handle of a silver pistol, which he had pulled halfway out of his side pocket. "You guys scared the fuck out of me."

Little-little shook his head and hissed, then tossed his shirt-shoes bundle across the room like a Frisbee. "This is my sister," he said, pointing me out. I sat down on the damp couch, not the one on the porch but the one inside the trailer, and lit a cigarette. I asked my midsized not-cousin if he wanted one. He didn't want one. He shoved the pistol all the way back into his pocket and went over to the window, peeking through the slitted plastic blinds out into the total darkness of the muddy road and surrounding woods. He kept flipping the blinds open and closed. They made a clinking sound like plastic change, worthless and desperate to accomplish some impossible purchase, his freedom.

"No one's out there," Little-little told him as he rummaged through a pile of clothing on the floor and tried out about five different shirts, a couple of T-shirts and two long johns, one green-and-brown-cammo-patterned. I smoked my cigarette.

Not-cousin held the scanner up to his ear and listened to the sound of static and clicking. "It was you guys sitting out there with your lights on?" he asked, his red eyes dancing. I nodded and puffed. Little-little wanted a cigarette. I gave him a cigarette. He started smoking it. None of those shirts had worked, I guess. He was still shirtless. Those shirts were back on the floor, utter failures.

Little-little perched beside me on the arm of the damp couch, shirtless, barefooted and puffing. Not-cousin started pacing slowly. "Whatcha got?" Little-little asked him. He pulled the pistol out of his pocket and handed it over. Little-little flipped it around and made inspecting noises. The police scanner crackled. We all looked at it. Not-cousin waited and listened, then shook his head no. Little-little tossed the gun spinning in the air, then caught it. "I had one better than this just three weeks ago, a semiautomatic handgun," he told me. "It was an amazing weapon, but I had to bury it. Put 'er down!" he boomed. I smoked. Not-cousin paced.

"You buried it," I said, trying to make it more of an affirmation than a question. Questions wouldn't be a good thing. I've learned this over the years.

He handed the silver pistol back to Not-cousin. "Yeah, had to bury it back there."

"Ah, the gun's buried in the back yard here," I said, as a statement.

Not-cousin took his seat by the TV again. He was struggling very hard not to cry, so his face, instead of twitching or doing stuff people's faces do when they're upset, was unnaturally unmoving, pale around his glowing red eyes. He watched us talk, his head tilted sideways, swallowing hard between every few breaths, cupping the police scanner like a sick bird in his left hand.

"Yep, had to bury it. No good now, I'll bet. Probably full of mud." My cigarette was done. There was no arguing with it. It was gone. I put it out in an ashy soda can on the coffee table. "Sucks too, cause it was expensive."

"Well, yeah, semi-automatic," I said as if knowingly.

Little-little hopped off the couch and began boxing the air. "When I bought it, I knew it was stolen, but I didn't know *how* stolen."

"*How* stolen," I repeated, not as a question.

"I guess it was evidence for some shit that went down up in Chicago, and that's why those dudes that sold it to me were getting rid of it," he told me as he KO'd the invisible man. Number two came up to fight.

Not-cousin finally did something besides look desperate. He let out a moan and said, "That was dumb of you to buy that. They almost got you for that. They knew you had it. Came up here looking for it. It's a good thing they didn't have a warrant."

Little-little let his head go yessing. Fuck it. I lit another cigarette. Little-little put his out. Not-cousin had his own hidden away, menthols. He took one out and started smoking it, his fleshy lips quivering all around the butt. "I gotta get out of here. They've been here too many times."

"It's hot here," Little-little agreed. "But they never found nothing, and now I got my legal gun card, anyway." He magically produced a tan laminated card from his back pocket. He waved it around proudly while shadowboxing, and lo and behold, I saw the truth in the light. My scrappy, peachy-keen Little-little was now indeed the proud owner of a certified license stamped with approval by the very civilized government of the US of A and the great state of Illinois, attesting his god-given right to bear lethal firearms. Hallefallujah.

He shoved the card back in his pocket and hopped over to the other side of the room where a small hatchet lay next to the armchair. He picked up the hatchet and started hacking at the arm of the armchair. This obviously wasn't the first time he'd hacked at the arm of the armchair. It had some notches already hacked out of it. "Damn thing's falling apart," he hollered as a joke. "I picked up Uncle Tiny's axe the other day. I swear to god, sis, I just barely touched it. Damn thing fell apart. And that's what Tiny said, 'Put that down, boy,' as soon as I touched it, but it was already too late. He said that thing's been out there on that block for ten years, withstood wind and rain and storms—blood sweat and tears, I laid my little pinky on it and the wood handle crumbled right away." He took one last satisfying hack at the arm of the armchair, then dropped the hatchet to the floor. My second cigarette was nearing the end, but I was already thinking about the third. Little-little's eyes twinkled pain like a bad joke at me from across the room. "I guess I got the opposite of the golden touch. Everything I put my hands on crumbles to crap."

"Maybe if you didn't come at stuff with axes in your hand, it wouldn't do that," I said, dryly. He grinned big at this and flopped into the lap of the armchair.

All this was making Not-cousin more nervous. I put out my second cigarette and could already taste the infection beginning to form in the back of my throat. My glands were swollen, and my mouth had that metallic-taste skin it gets when it's sore. It made me cringe. I decided to wait a few minutes before I lit up a third smoke. But I didn't know what to do in the time between. There was nothing in my hands. My mouth was empty. I had no reason to be there anymore. I started seriously wondering what Not-cousin was doing there with a police scanner and a gun. I mean, I knew he was hiding out from the police. But in the absence of smoking, I couldn't help but think about things like *why*. Before I knew it, a question was coming out of my mouth. "What are you charged with?"

You know that look young boys get when they are being punished severely for something, and they think it's very unfair? You might see them, about nine years old and yay-high, hiccupping on a playground, nose running, slobber all over, Wiffle bat at their feet, the teacher asking, "*Did* you hit Georgy with the bat?" Then they let out a too-loud, quivering, "Yes! I did it. But! But! But!"

Well, that's pretty much what happened when I asked this question. He finally let his face go quivering and his eyes teared up and he blurted out his answer in that high, desperately pinched voice that one would expect to hear a kid use when he was admitting to hitting Georgy with a Wiffle bat. But what he said was, "Manslaughter two," in that voice, so it all had a different feel than the playground scene.

"Mhmm. Second-degree manslaughter," I repeated, trying to get back to statements.

"It's a bunch of bullshit," Little-little hollered from the lap of the hacked-up armchair. "They can't prove anything. They don't got proof of those texts. You threw your phone away, didn't you?"

"Yep."

"Where?"

"In the pond back there." Not-cousin pointed behind himself. He was referring to the small pond on the edge of Big-little's property. I started adding things up in my head. At the least, we had one *very* stolen semiautomatic handgun wanted as evidence in connection with "some shit that went down in Chicago," buried in the backyard, and one cell phone wanted as evidence for a manslaughter-two case sunk in the pond. The ground I was sitting on was fertile with evidence of crime. *Crime Garden*, I thought, and wondered what else one might be able to find beneath the toxic topsoil. I racked my brain for any incriminating paraphernalia I might have on my person, thinking this would be the best place ever to chuck it. I wanted to add something to the plot.

"They don't got shit," Little-little went on. "Sis, it's dumb. You got a cigarette?" I took one out. He held his hands up. I tossed it across the room. The cigarette flipped through the air like a slow-motion kung-fu ninja. Little-little leapt up like a spry cat and caught it, then sat back down in the lap of the hacked-up armchair. "Naw, they don't got nothing. Listen to this shit, Sis, and you tell me if you think it's right." Little-little lit up. My pack was already out, so what the hell, I lit up another one, too.

"Alright."

Little-little tilted his head back and blew smoke rings into the air. They hung around looking like flying saucers above him. "He was dating this girl for a while," Little-little told me, pointing at Not-cousin. "Then he met this other girl he liked better, and he started getting with her."

"I cheated on her," Not-cousin let out in a whimper, his neck already crooked for an execution.

"Right, but then he told his girlfriend the truth and broke up with her," Little-little continued. "She freaked out. She was only like, seventeen, and she had problems anyway. Really dude. She had problems."

Not-cousin's red eyes were sparkling in his doughy head. "I know," he cracked out in a whisper.

"Last week, his ex-girlfriend sent him all these text messages saying she was going to kill herself if he didn't come back to her. She said if he didn't come over right then, she was going to do it. And he didn't answer them or come back to her, and she killed herself."

"She killed herself," I said. "Wait a minute. You're saying she killed *herself*?"

"Hung herself," Little-little told me, acting out the noose-snapping motion with his hand in the air and his neck falling sideways.

"I never saw the texts before it happened," Not-cousin blurted out, his whole body becoming a pale quivering mess. "I swear I didn't see them." The police scanner crackled. He twitched, then fidgeted with the dial. We all got quiet, listening. It was hard to make out what they were saying. It was mostly numbers. I guess he was listening for his name.

I was becoming even more confused. "What does it matter if you saw them or not?" They didn't respond, but stared intently at the scanner. I kept on with my questions. "How are they charging you when they know she hung herself? They don't think you helped her hang herself, do they?" Now everything was a big question. Fuck. I sucked on my smoke.

Little-little jumped up and went to the window that looked over the backyard and the woods. "Shit, I think I see one. There it is. Come here." I got up and went to the window. I didn't see anything. "It was there for a second," Little-little told me.

I turned back to Not-cousin and repeated my question. "Do they think you helped her hang herself?"

Not-cousin was a young man who was trying too hard not to cry. He remained silent. Little-little spoke for him, keeping one eye out the window, watching for green, glowing alien orbs. "Sis, don't you get it? She hung herself because of him, and they're charging him with second-degree manslaughter." He sucked his cigarette and looked at me like I was stupid.

My cigarette was done, so I just lit up the next one on the end of that one. "That's not how manslaughter-two works," I said, my voice all jumpy, becoming exasperated.

Little-little let out a frustrated sigh. "There's some law that says if you get a message like that, or a phone call, where someone is threatening to kill themselves or someone else, or bomb something or shit, that you got to report it or you're responsible. It's like, 'If you see something, say something,' you know?"

I rolled my eyes. "Is it like a good Samaritan law?" I asked. "Ah." Little-little shrugged, pinched his cigarette out between his finger and thumb and went back to staring intently out the window. "Or maybe it's because of the Patriot Act?" Not-cousin turned the police scanner dial. Either way, it's bullshit," I told him. "They can't get you for that. There's no fucking way they have any real legal ground to stand on. No one is going to want you to go to jail for that, because that would set this crazy precedent that would make everyone around here liable for every crazy fuck who threatened anything."

For a moment a glimmer of hope sprinted across Not-cousin's red eyes. I even saw a hint of a smile light on his lips. “Ya think so?” he asked just above a whisper. But then everything went shitty again. He looked to the ground and shook his head no, answering his own question. “It don’t matter anyway. I broke my probation now, so they’re coming to put me up either way.”

“Probation. You were on probation?” He nodded. “For what?”

“Rape,” Little-little answered for him.

“Oh. Rape.” I put a period at the end of those words. I was still smoking my cigarette, but I wanted another one. I wanted ten another-ones. I wanted to line up all the cigarettes I could fit between my lips like overgrown teeth and set them on fire.

“*Statutory,*” Not-cousin added, chewing his cheek. “Damn man, statutory, always say *statutory* first, okay?”

“Whatever.” Little-little gave up his disappeared-green-orb watch for a minute to go to the kitchen and get a glass of water. “That was dumb, too. You want a drink Sis?” The dishes in and around the sink were piled up an extra foot above the cabinet level and looked like they hadn’t been washed in years, literally. They could accompany the talking couch in giving guided tours across the trailer moat. Put some suspenders on those dishes, they could have passed for tour guides.

“Nah. I’m good,” I replied.

“She was his girlfriend,” Little-little told me from the kitchen. “She was sixteen and he was nineteen. Her mom’s a Christian and all and didn’t like him. When she found out they’d been having sex, she called the cops on him.”

“What’s the age of consent in Illinois?”

“Seventeen.”

“Well at least this girl who killed herself wasn’t a statutory thing, too,” I said. Not-cousin nodded. Little-little came back with his glass of water and sat down next to me. “Still, you can beat this.” It felt weird telling him this, because I’m not the kind of lady who usually sides with convicted rapists wanted for manslaughter. “The longer you break your parole, the longer you have to serve,” I went on. “Your best bet is to turn yourself in and fight this. Have some people write letters to the paper outlining your case. Hell, call the ACLU. They might provide a free lawyer or at least get you some publicity. There’s no way people are going to support prosecution. No one wants to be liable for what their ex or what someone else *threatens* to do. I’ll bet he DA won’t touch it.”

They were both looking at me, very confused. They were looking at me like I was a floating green alien gas orb. Not-cousin shivered as if shaking off my incomprehensible statements. “I been to jail once already. Seven *months* was too long.” He swallowed hard and tensed his quivering jaw. “I ain’t going back. It don’t fuckin’ matter. One way or another, I ain’t going back.”

“Don’t you start talking like that! I swear to god, man. Don’t you fucking talk like that!” Little-little was on his feet suddenly, shouting. “Give me the gun! Dude, give me the gun!” Not-cousin swatted him away as he reached for it.

I watched them argue over the gun, continuing on with my cigarette chaingang. I knew why he was reacting this way. I knew what, “I’m not going to jail one way or another” meant, too. When Little-little was nineteen, he and some of his friends had a little meth lab set up for themselves, also out in the woods, but in a different woods. Four of them got busted. But not Little-little. He was lucky enough not to be around that day. That’s all. His best friend, who was also nineteen, got slammed with some serious time, several years in prison. Instead of going to prison though, that kid shot himself in the head.

His best friend, who was also nineteen, got slammed with some serious time, several years in prison. Instead of going to prison though, that kid shot himself in the head.

Little-little still talks about him and how grateful he was for the short time he was blessed to have known him. He hasn’t gone near the dragon since, no matter how broke he was.

I felt really dumb for everything I'd just said to them. What was I thinking? They kept arguing, like in a ballet in front of me. I tried to blow smoke rings, but failed. I thought about what a stupid little faggot I was; about my stupid little-art-fag clothes, and how I was talking at them with my faggoty, self-educated voice, telling them my faggoty New York ideas. I'm such a queer faggot, I was even thinking about Michel Foucault. I was thinking about how he said, "The guilty person is only one of the targets of punishment. Punishment is directed, above all, at others, at all the potentially guilty." I was thinking that, here and now, where I was, Michel couldn't have been wronger. There's always this faggoty debate about the three possible purposes of prisons being reform, punishment and/or dissuasion. I stared laughing, thinking about it. What do academics know?

Little-little hasn't been off probation for more than a few months at a time since he was thirteen. Every time he breaks any part of his probation, whether it's a ticket, a missed phone call, or a failure to report a change in address, he goes to jail. Every time he goes back to jail, he accumulates more fines and goes in longer than the time before. He's in his early twenties, and pretty soon, they're going to get him. He has a snake wrapped around his ankle, its tail is tied to an anvil, and he's hanging off a cliff. He spent the last five years of his childhood being illegal. He's spent the majority of his adult life being illegal. He's an illegal person. He's been marked as such, and as soon as they can, they will remove him. They will find whatever trumped-up reason to remove him for as long as possible. They will remove him.

And people will be glad. People will not be dissuaded. People will be relieved. He will not be reformed or punished, simply removed.

Keep America Clean. Please use provided containers.

Sometimes things are extremely simple.

I could tell Not-cousin was the same kind of case. He generally just seemed illegal. They both did. You could look at them and tell. They were illegal people. Eventually they would be removed.

Little-little finally had possession of the gun and was walking it down the hallway that led to the bedroom. He was putting the gun to bed. The gun was real sleepy and had started fussing. But when he got it in there, it went down easy as cold, hard steel.

I tried another smoke ring. It failed. Not-cousin went back to flipping the switch on the police scanner. Finally, some words came out of me that didn't sound like stupid, gay New York words. "You need a plan. You got a plan?" He shrugged. Little-little came back in, then went through to the kitchen and searched around the fridge for a beer. "Maybe," I tried, "you should leave Lebanon. There are only three thousand people here. If you just drive for fifteen minutes, you'll be two towns away. They have different cops, cops who might not be looking for you so hard, cops who might not even know you."

"You think so?" he croaked out.

Not-cousin isn't the brightest bulb. "They just want to get rid of you," I told him. "If you can, leave the state. But at least, you have to leave the town. If you don't want them to find you, at least get out of town."

Little-little went back to the window and sipped his beer. "Yeah, dude. They did find you here the last time."

"Ummmm" came out of my mouth like a long frog. I should really leave soon, before the swat team bursts in, I thought.

But it's hard to leave, sometimes. I know that. This is the kind of place where people just stay, and stay, and stay. This place has staying power. The staying power had installed itself in Not-cousin's mind like an invisible electric shock line around a chicken coop. He hadn't received the shocks in quite a while, because he didn't even remember to try to cross the line. It was not an option. If I hadn't been such a weird faggot, I might not have ever tried too hard, either. I was shoved repeatedly over the shock line at a young age. I was a chick that got shoved. At the time, it seemed like an awful happening, being ostracized for my strange plumage. Sitting there though, I knew my feathers of faggotry were my privilege.

I shook my fancy feathers and extinguished a cigarette. Not-cousin's eyes met mine, glimmering. "Your brother said you live in New York. Is that true?"

I nodded. My feathers were too big. They were

going to knock things over. They were going to put someone's eye out if I wasn't careful.

"New York *City*?"

"Yeah."

"Oh." Something was trying like hell to get out of his throat, but it was banging into something else down there, and making all kinds of weird noises. "How are you . . . well, I mean, how are you going back?"

Goddamnit. My fancy feathers drooped. My fancy feathers got all wet with shame and sorrow. My fancy feathers were impotent. They couldn't let me take anyone. They didn't really fly. They just looked nice. I wanted to fold them up and hide them beneath my ridiculous sequined vest. "A plane. I'm sorry."

"Right, right." He nodded. "How much does that cost?"

I just shook my head, no, solemnly. The words, *A plane. I'm sorry,* bounced around my skull. Two clean sentences. Complete sentences. Heavy, cold sculpted sentences. A plane. I'm sorry. Four words, two periods making up a real pair.

"It don't matter. It's a extradition state anyway," he told me, letting me off the hook.

"Fuck! Fuck! Fuck! Look Sis. There they are! Fuck! Quick, come here." Little-little was losing it by the window. Not-cousin and I both hopped up and took a place beside him. He pointed. "There they are. See them?" I didn't see anything. "Wait." Little-little flipped the light off. The three of us stood in the total darkness of the trailer listening to the mixed static of the police scanner, staring out the window. It was really very dark out there. The stars were trying to peek out through the mist leftover from the rain. One could vaguely make out the silhouette of the forest line. "See? Right there," Little-little pressed. I scanned the trees' edge. As my eyes adjusted to the darkness, something became startlingly clear. Little-little might be crazy like a fox, but he wasn't bat-shit crazy. Or maybe we all were.

There, bouncing along the forest's edge, radiant as extracted souls, were two glowing, green balls of gaseous light. But they didn't move like gas. They were balls that bounced, as if moving of their own internal agency. They bounced up and down like Gummi Bears. They bounced into and off of each other. They bounced back and forth and around and around like a children's song. They did all of this very slowly and unself-consciously, as if they were absolutely real and would have been surprised if you told them that their existence was serious problem for humanity, for logic, science and all that.

They bounced around for a good minute and a half, then they bounced back into the forest, totally out of sight. "What'd I tell ya? What'd I tell ya? That's what we saw the other day, isn't it?"

"Yep." Not-cousin nodded yes.

Little-little turned the light back on. "Hot damn Sis! You saw 'em?"

I nodded yes.

"Come on." He started going through the pile of shirts again. "Let's go out there and find 'em."

"Ummmmmmmmm." Another long frog. "Yeah. I gotta get going." I picked up my bag, threw it over my shoulder, and headed to the door. Little-little followed skipping behind me.

"You can't go. Not after what you just saw," he said, insistently.

"Yeahhhh. I gotta get going." I nodded and made an unfortunate face. "I'll call you tomorrow." He was totally stunned. But what could I do? I wasn't going out into the crime garden to hunt semi-intelligent glowing green orbs, with the possibility hanging over my head of a SWAT team breaking in any minute. I could deal with one of those things individually. Not all of them. Something in me had absolutely shut down. I wasn't cut out for that. That just wasn't my idea of a good night. I was supposed to meet an old high-school friend at a bar at ten, anyway. I searched for some way to make things normal, to make things right. "Here. Take this. Keep it." I reached into my bag, retrieved an unopened pack of cigarettes, and pressed it, like a talisman, into Little-little's hand. "Call you tomorrow," I told him. "Good luck," I told Not-cousin. "Be careful," I told them both.

I SPED DOWN the pitch-dark, winding country roads. These roads were burned into my head like a map of crisscrossing scars. My mind was racing over several thoughts. I was thinking about how I probably look rich to my brother. I was thinking how broke I was in Brooklyn. I was thinking that if I changed my plane ticket and stayed a few months, I could probably help keep Not-cousin out of serving outrageous amounts of jail time over an outrageous charge. I was thinking that, even if was I was pretty broke, I had language and they didn't. I was thinking about Pygmalion. I was thinking this would be madness on my part to stay and try to help them, because eventually, they both would do something else to land themselves in the slammer no matter how many marbles I shoved into their mouths, no matter how many times they repeated *The rain in Spain.* I moved away for a reason, I reminded myself. This place kills people, I reminded myself. I slowed at an unlighted railroad track and remembered that those same tracks had taken two of my uncles. One of them was a suicide. He just laid his head down there on the cold steel one night and let an iron giant take care of the rest. The other uncle was working on the tracks and fell over from a heart attack and hit his head on a spike. He was a few months away from retirement, but was already too old for that kind of work. I was thinking about how much sad death, murder and suicide I had seen there in the southern border of the rural Midwest, and how little I had seen since moving to a big city. I was thinking how ironic that seemed. But amid all these thoughts was one glaring thought that kept screaming at me that I was trying not to pay attention to. *What the fucking hell were those green, glowing orbs that bounced around like Gummi Bears, seeming to move of their own agency?* This was not a good thought for driving down an empty country road at night. I flipped the doors to lock and turned on the radio, then pressed the pedal to sixty.

It took a moment for the news to register. It was repeating for a while before I really heard it. I was turning onto the lit road of an actual town and could see my destination, "Chubby's Bar–Serving Spirits for More than Forty Years," just beyond the stop sign, when the news knocked five times, hard, on the cognizant part of my brain and I let it step inside.

Hello, nice to meet you, Osama Bin Laden is dead. *Come in. Have a seat. Or not. Shuffle around a while. You seem a bit unsettled.*

I pulled into Chubby's parking lot and turned off the car along with the repeating news.

The bar was permanently stuck in late seventies, in the best way. Everything was black leather and red paint. A mirror made up the wall behind the bar, reflecting bottles of spirits. Smoke hung in the air, although it's no longer legal to smoke inside in Illinois. Chubby's owner was a real rebel. The three people sitting inside hushed and turned as I entered. They stared at me blankly. Not quite like I was a green gaseous alien orb, but as if watching to see if I might turn into one. I guess they weren't used to seeing chicks in ties and vests with psychobilly faux-hawks around there. Weird little faggot, I was. The staring lasted and lasted, even as I perched myself on a bar stool and tried to act casual, just a person wanting a drink in a bar. The staring went on. "Can I get a whiskey, neat with a seltzer back?"

They weren't used to seeing chicks in ties and vests with psychobilly faux-hawks around there.

The female bartender, who was now standing in front of me, stared even harder. "Huh? What did you say?"

"A whiskey with nothing in it and a soda water, a seltzer, separate," I tried again.

"You just want me to pour you whisky in a cup?" she said, angrily.

"Just like if you would do it on the rocks, but without the ice," I said timidly, almost as a question. This wasn't helping at all. I thought it was the simplest thing I could have ordered. Apparently, it was an alien libation. An old man in ball cap and overalls nursed a Budweiser in the far corner. At a table near him, an old woman sat twirling a straw in a Coca-Cola can with what appeared to be the Bible open beside it. They were both still staring at me too. "However you usually do it, is fine," I kept on.

"I don't never do nothing like any of that. You

want *soda* (pause) *water*? You want that alone in a different glass? I don't have any of that. I might have some tonic in the back. You want that?"

I didn't give a shit about any of this. I just wanted to know if Osama Bin Laden was really dead. But I had totally pissed off this bartender, and I didn't know how to un-piss her off. She looked like everybody's aunt. She was in her late thirties with clean, short blonde hair, and generally appeared to be a legal, sane, normal person. But boy had my drink selection pissed her off.

"It's fine. I'll just take a whiskey and a regular water." She filled up a glass of water and sat it in front of me, clangingly. Then she got a pint glass and headed for the whiskey. "Oh that's, yeah. Um. That's too big. I mean," I tried to make it a joke, "I can't hold my liquor that good. Ha! Not that I'm a drunk, but. . . ."

She paused, holding the whiskey and pint glass, glaring at me. "How big a cup *do* you want?" I pointed to a regular tumbler. If it's possible to point with embarrassment, that's what I did. She grabbed the tumbler and slammed it down in front of me. "Why don't you just tell me when." She started pouring. I told her when. She stopped. I got out my wallet. She stepped back and chewed her bottom lip, staring at the glass, then shook her head. "I don't know how much to charge for that," she said aggressively, as if for asking me for an answer. I heard the old man *hmph* loudly in my direction. Then, thank god, the door opened behind me, and my old buddy from my teenage years, Janey, stepped in.

"Hey there," she squealed, smiling the bright, perpetual smile of the kind of optimistic lady who can

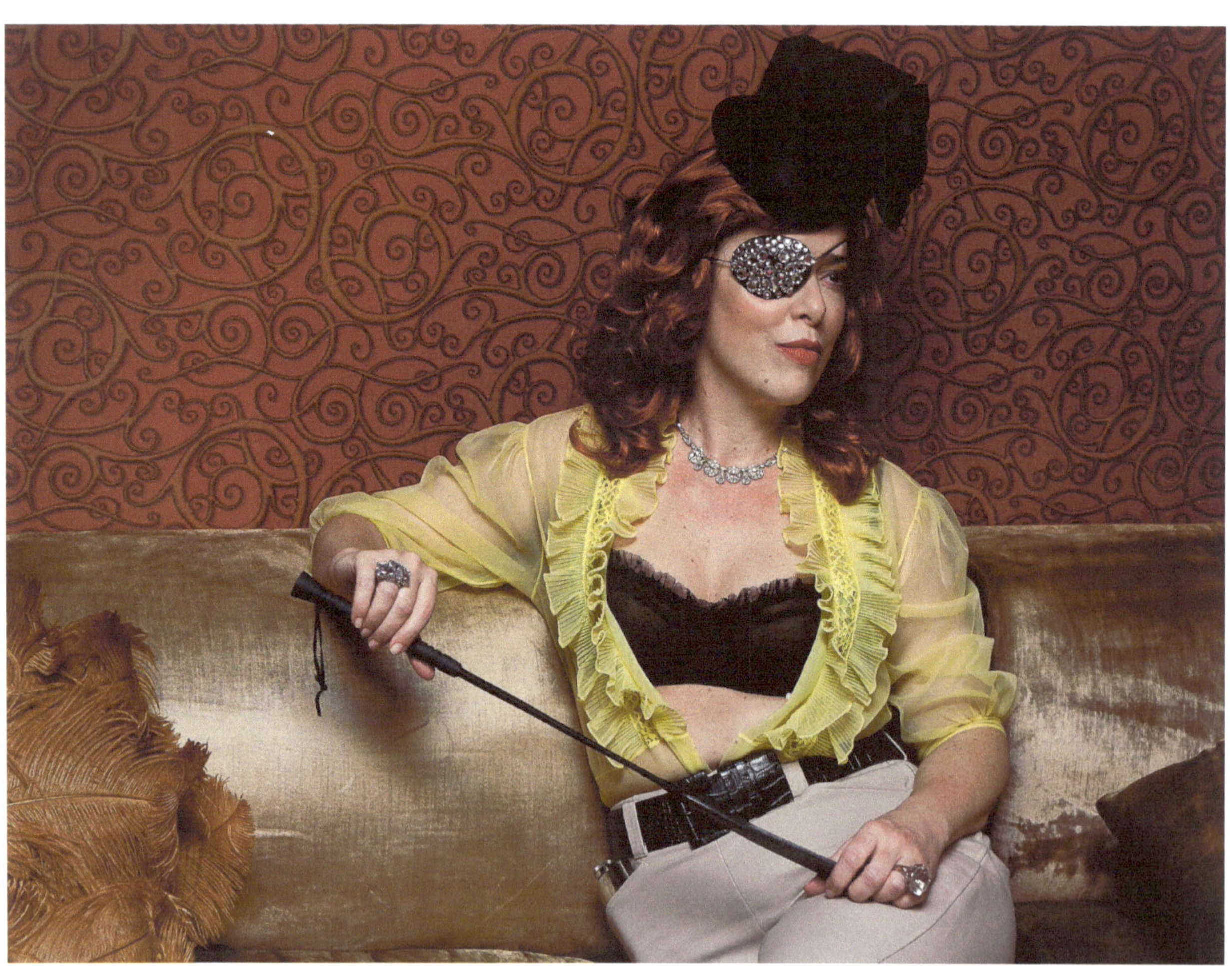

Aristocrat, photograph by Jeff Spirer

bounce into any bar in the southern, rural Midwest without everyone turning to stare at her. She hugged me and sat her pleasantly plump self down next to me. "Hey there. How you doing in here?" she asked the bartender.

"Just fine. What can I get you to drink?" the bartender asked, still suspicious, but seeming to thaw.

"I'll have a hot cherry bomb, if it's not too much trouble," Janey chirped.

"Coming right up," the bartender chirped back, very happy about knowing what someone meant again. She then proceeded to mix cayenne pepper, lime, bitters, vodka and Red Bull in a pint glass, topping off the concoction with two cherries and a straw. Easy as pie. Hot cherry bomb. Sure. Why not? "That'll be four dollars."

Really? I thought. *Are these people fucking with me?*

She eyed my drink, friendlier now. It was like magic. I had a translator. "I guess yours'll be three-fifty. That sound fair?"

"Fine by me." I laid my money on the bar and took out my cigarettes. "You can smoke in here," I told Janey. She smiled and nodded. I lit up and sipped my whiskey. I wasn't being stared down anymore and could finally pay attention to something besides my drink order. The television above the bar showed what appeared to be hundreds of frat boys waving American flags. The bartender noticed me watching.

"They got him. Can you believe it?"

"I just heard. Just before I came in."

"Where've you been?" Janey asked. "It happened hours ago."

"I'll turn it up." The bartender went to the TV and turned the volume up. The news anchors just kept repeating, "Osama Bin Laden is dead," in slightly different ways each time. Sometimes they said, "Osama Bin Laden has been taken out." Sometimes they said, "Osama Bin Laden was successfully killed by Seal Team Six," and sometimes they said, "Barak Obama is dead, I'm sorry I mean . . . Osama. . . ." It was Fox News they were watching. Everyone in the bar was staring intently at the screen but no one seemed very happy about it. They looked much happier in New York City, where the world's largest and most morbid tailgate party had suddenly erupted at Ground Zero. I read the words scrolling across the bottom of the screen. *Usama Bin Laden is Dead.*

I *hmphed.* "Jesus, they're spelling it wrong."

Bin Laden's face popped up like a Hungry Hungry Hippo. Then the thin, wrinkled old lady with the Coke popped up like a Hungry Hungry Hippo as well, right up off her bar stool and growled, "Yer dead now, motherfucker. We gotcha, motherfuckerrrrrrr!"

"Calm down, Iris," The bartender smacked the bar counter. Iris went back into the pond.

"I really like this place," Janey chirped. "It's weird." She smiled big and giggled. "I'll have to come back." She looked around herself. "It's like another world in here." Janey grew up two towns away in a slightly bigger town. Chubby's was my hometown bar.

"Barak Obama has successfully killed Usama Bin Laden," the news anchor said.

"*Obama* didn't kill him," the old man at the bar muttered at no one and everyone. "The *Seals* killed him." He looked disgusted, like he'd just vomited a bit in his mouth. "*O*bama," he sneered. "Hmph."

"I'm glad he's dead, anyway. We can all rest a little easier now," the bartender told us.

"What's your name?" Janey asked sweetly.

"Donna."

Janey introduced herself and me to Donna the bartender.

"Where are you from?" Donna asked.

"She lives in New York City now," Janey told her proudly. I guess that question was mostly directed at me.

"New York City? Well then, you must be more excited about this than anyone," Donna told me.

I kept watching the TV. "They're spelling it wrong," I repeated. "Look."

Donna turned and looked. "Well, how bout that? They're spelling *Osama* with a *U.* Is that an alternate way or something?"

"I don't think so."

"Usama Bin Laden is dead," the news anchor repeated. And I couldn't help but notice, she was pronouncing it by the new spelling. I extinguished my cigarette in the black ashtray.

"I don't think it's a mistake," I told them. Janey smiled big at me. "It's on purpose, see, it's USA-m-a.

They're doing it on purpose. They're renaming him as if he's now property of the USA. Get it? USA-m-a."

"I'm not really a political person," Janey said, shrugging and smiling. But Donna was listening and looking incredulously at the screen.

"That *is* weird," she concurred.

"I haven't seen you in years. Tell me everything," Janey said, changing the subject.

"I've had about enough of that myself." Donna muted the TV and headed over to the jukebox. In a minute, Travis Tritt was serenading us.

"Tell me all about New York City." Janey smiled big, and her perfect eye makeup sparkled. "I want to know everything. I want to live vicariously through you." She leaned toward me excitedly. Her elbow bumped a cup that was sitting next to the ashtray. It fell over, spilling out a wad of cash and some change. I thought it was a tip jar, but as I replaced it to its original position, I read the words scrawled on the side in black marker; "Donation's for Chastity's funeral."

Janey and I stared at it. Her smile fell down so hard it scraped its knees and looked like it might not be skipping around again for a while. I grimaced. "Oh. That's depressing." I slid the funeral donation jar far away, out of sight and mind. I lit up another cigarette. When I exhaled, a noise came from my chest that sounded like Satan's dog with a throat infection. I started coughing.

Janey recoiled. "That sounds *really* bad. Are you okay?" I banged on my chest with my fist. It felt like I had an alien gestating in there. It was doing somersaults, practicing for the Alien Olympics, or maybe for the moment it might decide to burst through my chest. And I didn't have Sigourney Weaver around or anything. I gasped for breath, hunched over and grabbed Janey's wrist. She jumped.

"Listen Janey, forget about New York City. I don't even remember New York City. There's something weird happening around here," I whispered, and took up my desperate coughing again.

Janey stiffened. I held tighter. "What do you mean?" she asked, her voice shaking with confusion.

"I saw these things. These green things. I was out in the woods tonight, with this kid who's wanted for manslaughter," I whispered. Janey's eyes got big and her eyebrows got all twisty. "It's only second-degree. It's nothing. Forget it. Like I was saying, I saw these things . . ." Janey was looking at me like I was crazy. I tried to figure how to proceed. Someone touched my shoulder, softly tapping.

I turned to find Iris staring at me, nearly nose to nose. The wrinkles around her eyes looked like a dried-up beach. "Can we help you?" Janey asked, trying to keep it cool.

Iris's thin lips moved. "The time is coming."

"I'm sorry?" Janey came back. I let go of her wrist and swiveled around on my stool. My chest growled. Iris took a pamphlet out of her Bible and handed it to me. On the front was a picture of the sky and what seemed to be silhouettes of people floating up into the clouds. There were words printed in a very kitschy font across the blue sky: "But What if It IS True?"

"Iris! I told ya." Donna was coming out of the ladies' room. "I told ya, Iris," she hollered. "You can sit in here, but you gotta leave people alone."

"It's coming," Iris informed us, nodding ominously and sidestepping toward the door as Donna made her way toward her. "It's coming. Prepare yourself."

"You gotta get now," Donna said, taking her by the arm. They walked out together.

I gasped and something in me growled louder. "Weird shit has been happening all night. I'm telling you. There's something going on." My level of paranoid desperation startled even me. I began to worry I might be losing my mind.

Janey patted me on the shoulder and shook her head. "Calm down, hon. She's just a crazy old woman. Every bar has one."

She picked up my cigarette from the ashtray and started to put it out, but I snatched it from her and nearly shouted, "I'm not done smoking that!" The beast in me growled too. It was an unearthly double growl. Janey laid her hands squarely on the bar and stiffened defensively, eyeing me from the side.

Donna came back in, "Sorry about that, girls. She does that all the time."

"It's fine," Janey assured her, trying to get her smile back up off the sidewalk, but it was all wobbly. Donna went and sat at a booth far away from us and read the paper. The old man in the ball cap was still there at the other end of the bar, smoking and drinking, occasionally muttering at the screen. Silently, ten-hundred million frat boys waved American flags, their bulbous lips chanting *USA* like a birth cry as they held their glittering girlfriends up on their broad, white shoulders, above the streaming words, "Usama Bin Laden Is Dead."

"I hear you've been doing really good in New York. You just had a book published. How's that going?" She was trying so hard, poor thing.

The beast and me sucked down my cigarette loudly. "Yeah. I had a book published. It's going great. I got an award. Listen, Janey, have you ever seen any, like, green orbs in the woods around here?"

Her face did a little dance. I realized, as I watched her face go from the twist to the two-step, that she was scared of me. She hadn't seen me in three years. How was she to know I wasn't totally bonkers? Luckily, she'd known me as a kid, so she was also concerned for me. She inhaled deeply and straightened herself. "Okay." That word was like a reset button. "You saw something? Okay." Still resetting.

I nodded. "Yeah. I definitely saw something. Have you heard of anyone seeing—I know it sounds weird—but green floating balls?"

"Can I have one?" I nodded and handed her a cigarette. "People *have* said they've seen things around here." She put the cigarette to her lips. I lit it. She sucked on it lightly, then picked up her drink and took a big sip from the straw. That thing could have been a chocolate milkshake the way she drank it right then. "I've only heard about silver saucers. Not green balls. Who knows. I've never seen anything like that. But I hear a lot of things. Farmers have always seen things. You know that." She shrugged. "We made fun of them. *You* made fun of them. I think they're a little crazy. Maybe it's sun stroke. But I don't know." She looked up at the light, pondering. The alien beast in my chest gnawed at the end of my cigarette. "I did used to see this dead Indian in the field behind my house when I was little. My dad saw him a few times too. I've told you about that. You remember? The Indian ghost?"

I nodded. "That's right. I remember those stories. I thought you might just be trying to scare us though. It was real?"

She sat her drink down. "I think so. I know what I saw." We silently contemplated the existence of other worlds. "It's hard to tell though." Her hand shook slightly as she ashed the cherry. "Some things are a little fuzzy since the electro-shock therapy."

"The what?"

"Oh I didn't tell you about that?" Her blonde hair was perfectly cut in a bob. Her makeup was clean and shining. Her mouth always held a slight smile, even as she said those awful words. "It was nothing," she said, shaking her head, shrugging it off. "I just had a bad few months a couple of years ago. They did the electro-shock therapy, and it really helped. It's just that now, some of my memories are a little fuzzy." I was looking worried at *her* now. Where the hell was I? What alternate universe had I fallen into? Apparently you can go home again, but maybe you just shouldn't. "No, it's fine," she told me, reassuringly. "I got my degree. I have a great job, a nice house, a new boyfriend. I'm really happy."

She did look fine. She looked better than me. It all sounded just great except for the electro-shock therapy part. "I didn't even know they still did that." I said.

"Sometimes they do," she chirped, and smiled, lifting her glass to toast. Toast what? I had no idea. But I toasted back.

The old man at the end of the bar muttered something and raised his beer bottle. Donna came over to get him another. She asked me if I wanted another one of the same. I told her I did. She poured it easy as pie.

"Fuck the country, and fuck this country too," I said, lifting my glass for my own toast. Donna was already at the other end of the bar getting the old man a beer, but I didn't give a damn if she could hear me. Janey shuddered though. She didn't toast back. "Sorry, it's just been a really intense night. I'm an asshole." Her drink was almost gone and she wasn't ordering another. She had a look on her face like she wanted to get out.

"It's okay," she said, patting my hand. "I know you always hated it here. What the hell happened tonight? Did you say something about manslaughter?"

I shook my head no. "Yeah. It doesn't make any sense. This kid is hiding out from the police. He's wanted for second-degree manslaughter. He's staying at my brother's place. My big-little brother. He's my brother's cousin. He's not my cousin. He's my not-cousin." I laughed out loud.

"You know what, I'll have another one too." She held up her glass. She was intrigued. Donna came over and started mixing the weird concoction. "What did you mean, it doesn't make any sense?"

I gulped down the top third of my new whiskey and lit up another smoke. I like to smoke when I tell stories. "I don't see how anyone could call it manslaughter of any degree. He had this girlfriend, and he cheated on her, broke up with her, whatever. She was like, seventeen. She started sending him messages saying that if he didn't come over, she was going to kill herself. And he didn't and she—" The story was broken off by the sound of glass breaking on the old cracked floor, like a broken heart breaking over something long-before broken.

Donna's hands were cupped in midair like they were still holding cups and mixers, but they weren't. Her face was as pale as yesterday's ghost, her eyes intense, watery and her lips barely parted.

She looked at me like she wanted to kill me, but more than before. She wanted to spit on me, and tar-and-feather me, and ride me out on a rail. "You talking about Chastity?"

"God, I hope not." My cigarette fell out of my fingers onto the bar. I felt very sorry. Sorry was writing itself all over me, but I don't think Donna saw it. She stepped back slowly. The glass made broken glass noises as she did so.

She leaned back on the counter and looked from me to Janey. "I'm the one who found that girl's body. You think it's a joke, a funny story?"

My alien started screaming.

Janey watched us, frozen. She eyed me eyeing Donna.

Donna walked over and picked up Chastity's funeral donation cup like it was a sick baby. She sat it between us. "Why'd you move this? Didn't want to look at it?"

"I had no idea" came out of my mouth in a croaking whisper. "I didn't mean to . . ." How the hell was I supposed to know? I was twenty miles away from where it happened. There were only two other people in the bar. What were the fucking chances?

Donna tapped the cup." I helped raise that girl. She my best friend's baby. Then she got in with that no-good, lowlife bum." She shoved the cup forward. "Feel like making a donation, New York?"

"Wait a minute," Janey laid her hands flat on the table. "How do you know she's even talking about the same person? Let's calm down. She didn't know her. She just met this guy who told her . . ."

"Shhhh," I hissed.

Donna did not like this. "Who told her what?" she demanded, stepping closer. "*Where'd* she meet this guy? You know where that bum is?"

Everything was like a bad train coming off a bad track right at my head. I started hacking up a storm. I couldn't breath suddenly. It sounded like a herd of alien hell-puppies. Without moving from where she stood, Donna grabbed the cayenne pepper next to Janey's drink and dumped some in my whiskey. Then she took my cigarette that was burning up her bar and dropped it in my water.

"Drink that," she told me, referring to the newly cayenned whiskey. "It'll loosen up your chest." Was she trying to kill me? "Go ahead. You're getting a little green around the edges," she pressed.

What the hell. I picked it up and gulped it down. It burned everything. I gasped and sputtered. My chest rattled then settled. My beast did feel freer, but I didn't know if that was a good thing. I smacked my lips and rubbed my eyes. "Damn!"

"You want some water?" Donna asked. I nodded yes. She nodded yes back. She didn't get me any water.

"I found her body and those texting messages. I showed them to the cops, 'cause I felt like they were like, her suicide note, you know?" Donna didn't look like she was going to cry. Her jaw was stiff and square. She was a toughie. My eyes were tearing up though, bright red, I'm sure, and my throat and mouth burned like hell. I kept swallowing. Donna tapped the funeral donation jar. I took out my wallet, produced a twenty and dropped it in. She nodded, turned around and swiveled back with a glass of water for me. I drank the entire glass in five gulps. "What'd you say your name was, again?" I just shook my head no. She looked to Janey. "You have any ideer where he's hiding?"

Janey picked up her purse and took me by the shoulder. Childhood friends can almost always be counted on in a pinch. "I'm sorry. I think we'd better get going now." I felt half alive. Janey helped me along my way. The old man at the bar was just staring at us trying to figure out what was going on. Donna's pursed lips quivered a bit, like Not-cousin's earlier that night. "It ain't right what happened. They're gonna find him with or without you," Donna kept on as we backed out the door. "We just want some answers," she hollered. The door shut behind us.

I wheezed all the way to the car. "I see what you mean about having a weird night," Janey said, propping me against the hood as she unlocked the passenger door. "I'm driving you to where you're staying. You're not in good shape."

My throat felt like an atomic bomb went off in a sandpaper factory. "What are the fucking chances?" I bellowed out. "That was weird. Don't you think that was weird?" She nodded and half smiled at how horribly obvious the answer to my question was. I bent over and hacked. Something big moved in me. "Yes," she told me, searching for her keys. "That was one of the weirdest nights I've ever had. I just want us to get out of here. That was awful."

"It's too much of a coincidence," I kept on. "What the fuck is happening? It's like they planted her in there."

"They?"

I pounded on my chest, then balanced with my hands on my knees, groaning and beginning to convulse. "I don't know what I mean," I coughed out. "It just feels like someone is engineering everything."

"This is a small county, that's all."

"No. This is just too much. If I wrote this, no one would believe it." I let myself go into a coughing fit for a second and regained my breath. "*I* can't even believe it. Can you?"

The passenger door was open. Janey was standing next to it, staring at me with the most awful look on her face, her keys held tightly in her hands. "You look really bad. You look . . . green."

"What?" I hung my head over the black tar and coughed again. A little piece of mucus flew out of my mouth, landing on the ground in front of me. Janey stepped back.Something rattled inside of me. I felt like I was going to explode. The mucus was green and slimy, reflecting the light from the bar sign. My chest heaved. I covered my mouth with my hand and took off running, doubled over, thinking I was going to vomit. That fucking cayenne whiskey bitch did me in. I made it around to the back of the building. Holding onto the brick wall with one hand, the other on the dumpster, I let myself go with the reverent acquiescence of a drunken vomiter who has no choice but to let the void grab hold of her and show her how to make something out of nothing.

But what was coming out wasn't coming from my stomach. That thing in my chest, it was shaking itself free. It rumbled and screeched and pushed forward. My mouth wrenched itself open as wide as it could go. I felt a giant ball of slimy gum, slug like, birthing itself through my facial orifice. It wiggled, elongated and squeezed, reducing itself like a rodent sliding through an impossible opening. It just kept coming out. I moaned loudly. I pounded the wall and heaved. It finally landed on the ground in front of me with a horrible plop.

I fell back on my ass and stared at it. It did not stare back. It didn't have eyes. It wiggled up against the wall and squealed. The thing was green, like a miniature version of the Blob, green and slimy. I moaned again. It started having some kind of seizure. Green slime and mucus, and I guess my infected snot, was flying off of it. As it shook itself free of my infected bronchitis placenta, it became visibly lighter and its glowing grew brighter. It began to become beautiful, and it began to ascend.

It was a little wobbly at first, like a baby bird trying out its first feathers, but soon enough, it was going up, above the roof of the bar, my very own green glowing orb floating up there above the trees in that beautiful dark and twinkling country sky. I heard

Janey scream. A few counts later, I heard the sound of her engine revving and the screeching of tires against pavement.

I watched my orb for a good while. It was just hovering there, about forty feet directly above me. Then, over the trees and the little houses, I saw another green form rising. It was faint at first, but it quickly grew clearer. The green light was a very familiar shape. I squinted. It kept approaching at about the same height as my glowing green orb. I cocked my head. It was that goddamned moldy couch. I heard voices. That goddamned couch was glowing green and flying around above the town. On either side of the couch were two more green glowing orbs. That couch and its two green orbs flew up right next to my green orb and parked. The muffled voices revealed their faces. Little-little poked his head over the side of the glowing couch, his feet dangling off the end. "Aw hell," he shouted. "Lookie there. It's my sister."

Not-cousin poked his head over the other side. "Hey there. You got one too!" he hollered, not as a question. "How do we lower this thing?" I heard him ask Little-little.

"Going down," I heard a heard voice say. The voice was deep and goofy like a children's-cartoon character.

The couch and the orbs descended. I rose to my feet. Little-little sat on the glowing green couch hovering a few feet above the ground. The three glowing orbs bounced off each other sweetly, as a greeting. Little-little smiled his peachy-keen smile at me. He still hadn't found a shirt he liked, I guess. "Hey Sis. We went into the woods and we found these fucking things. They're great. I think maybe they were ours already."

I nodded, understanding

"You coming?"

I looked around myself. "Where are you going?"

"We're heading to a non-extradition state," Not-cousin told me proudly.

"Nah, I'm voting for Mexico," Little-little came back.

The couch shivered. "All aboard that's coming aboard," the couch said.

The green orbs started circling. Not-cousin and Little-little held out their hands. I put my hands in theirs. They pulled me up, seating me in between them. Little-little looked so happy. "I sure am stoked you're coming with us, Sis. I miss ya, you know?" I put my arm around him. He laid his head on my shoulder, like he always used to do when he was a kid. The green orbs spun faster around the couch, beginning the ascension once more.

We hit about seventy feet and started flying like condors, the towns streaking past far below. The clouds were clearing. The stars were coming out, twinkling brighter. There's nothing like a country sky. "To your left, notice Central Point, home of the Redhawks. In the 1930s Central Point was a booming mecca for traveling businessmen and tradespeople, as the railroad provided the perfect midpoint for those traveling from Chicago to the southern states. The town to your right is Little Egypt, and we will be coming upon Cairo soon, home of the Fighting Pharaohs, known for the largest man-made lake in the country." That couch had turned out to be a world-class tour guide after all.

I laid my head on top of Little-little. Not-cousin watched the green orbs circling us, with amazement.

"East or west?" Little-little asked.

"I don't care."

"We can drop you off in New York first, if you want," Little-little told me. "Did you hear they got Osama? We heard it on the scanner."

I nodded. "Yep. I heard."

"Maybe we should go to Ground Zero," Not-cousin suggested. "There's a huge fucking party there."

"In this thing? They'd shoot us down. Forget about New York. New York doesn't exist. It doesn't even have a sky."

Little-little took a pack of cigarettes out of his pocket. "I'm glad you said that. Still, I'd like to see it sometime. Big Apple." He offered me one.

"Give me the pack," I said. He gave me the pack. I chucked it over the side and watched it spiral down to the cornfields of Central Point. "I think we've had enough." Little-little nodded and chucked his last smoke over the side, too.

"West it is," he said.

"West it is," the couch answered. The three spinning green orbs twisted around, heading west.

Two Poems

William Lessard

Paul Kelly

First time I saw you
you were riding
a stolen motorcycle
down the middle
of our baseball field,
the cops in hot pursuit.
Last time I saw you
you were fat and ugly
and fixing elevators downtown
when you weren't getting loaded
at the local bar.
What happened between
I can only call age,
too many fights, too much drugs,
one-too-many trips to jail.
And when I heard
that you had been killed,
shot down at a pay phone
on the avenue
by some Jamaicans you had screwed
in a deal,
I have to admit I was relieved.
I'm a selfish guy, perhaps,
but it was nice to have you back
the way I wanted to remember you.
I never told you this, I was never
really your friend,
but you should know that
all those years growing up,
I admired you from afar.
You were so alive,
you had so much guts.
You were everything I wanted
to be—and still are:
The coolest guy in the neighborhood.
Blond curls blowing shoulder-high,
the lights of a corner truck going red,
as you gun the throttle,
and grin.

My Father's Rubbers

It was the day after the funeral.
My mother and I went out back to search his car,
a 1988 Caddy Cimaron with bent driver-side wiper,
parked at an angle on the grass.
We didn't say it; it was probably due to years
of my grandmother's conspiracy theories,
but we had visions of bundles of cash
hidden under the floor mats.
We looked and looked.
At first we turned up nothing:
a few empty packs of cigarettes,
gold-lettered matchbooks
from restaurants he never took us to,
phone numbers with no names attached
written on ripped slips of paper,
an open bottle of Canadian Club
with peeled label,
a cassette of Mozart's *Requiem*
conducted by Leonard Bernstein.
So much for finding treasure, I thought,
when, just about to go back inside to watch *A Christmas Story,*
I found something:
Tucked in the pouch behind the passenger's seat,
my father's rubbers.
Not the ones for your feet—
the other kind.
My mother didn't see them, thank God;
I jammed them in my pocket
when she wasn't looking.
Later that night, after she had gone to bed,
I took them out beneath the plastic sunflower kitchen clock,
its petals flecked with grease.
I stared and stared at the box, its bright-blue coloring,
its bright-white writing, its hastily torn-off top.
I thought about him, age 56, lying straight in the coffin,
a sense of peace filling my chest,
joy (almost),
a thankfulness that before he left this world
he left me a gift—this one useful lesson:
We don't break the rules; we are broken by them.

Medium

Jennifer Adams

THE NOTICE WAS SMALL, A HALF-SHEET OF paper tucked, unauthorized, into the frame of the subway map.

"Mrs. Taylor and she says DON'T GIVE UP."

Elizabeth leaned closer, oblivious to the discomfort she was causing the woman slouched in the seat in front of her, rubbing her eyes and yawning through her morning commute.

"She tells you all before you utter a word. She can bring the spirit of release and control to your every affair and dealing. . . ." Illness could be cured, evil eyes and lurking dangers revealed. Satisfaction was doubly guaranteed. "See her in the morning, *be happy at night*. CALL FOR APPOINTMENT."

Elizabeth reached up and tugged the slip free from the metal frame. It stuck, and one small corner tore off, but the paper was hers. Her hand shook as she held it up and read it again.

Jake had been gone for nearly three years, and she thought she was over him. She no longer woke up in the night with wet cheeks, and it had been months since she felt the grip of a panic attack squeezing out her breath when she saw any man in the street who resembled him. This was good; he was fairly ordinary looking, and it happened often.

But neither could she say she wasn't still in love with him. Since he was gone, and since he was never coming back to her, she had tried to move on. Recently, she'd even begun to date again, feeling the rush of years pressing on her, weary of sleeping alone every night. She didn't want to be alone, always.

She'd met a few men with whom she could sleep, and did, with some satisfaction, but they weren't Jake, and she was strangely happy to give each a perfunctory kiss and close the door behind him the next morning.

Every time she though of Jake, who wore socks in bed, who left half-full cans of Dr. Pepper all over her apartment, with whom she was just beginning to really, really fall in love when he was killed so unexpectedly, her heart swelled and constricted at the same time and a lump filled her throat.

At work, she slid the paper into the top drawer of her desk. She looked at it surreptitiously throughout the day, pushing her chair back a few inches, crossing her too-thick legs in their tights, her feet in flats, and squinting into the drawer as though looking for her green highlighter or a binder clip which was somehow eluding her amid the litter of salt packets and chopsticks and large-size paperclips, bent into uselessness for some forgotten reason.

She chewed the inside of her lower lip as she entered columns of numbers into a spreadsheet, biting until her lip bled, and she sucked at the wound, savoring the metallic saltiness. She appeared to be typing, but her fingers hit few keys. She pondered, instead. Mrs. Taylor. Solver of riddles, finder of lost property, dowser of love. The flyer made many promises: Bringer of miracles. It could happen. If love can be stolen by an icy day and a cross-town bus, could it not be restored, or at least soothed, by a person like Mrs. Taylor?

When things have become so bad they defy belief, belief becomes a loose thing, malleable enough to permit dreams and wishes you know shouldn't come true.

At three-thirty, she picked up the phone and dialed the number: 718. Boroughs, of course. The Bronx, maybe. Flatbush? Maybe there were such things as fortunetellers in the East Village once, but no more, surely. But before the other line began to ring, she tapped the button and hung up.

Five minutes later, she dialed again, and this time, a rich, smooth voice answered.

"Yes."

"Mrs. Taylor, please. I'd like to make an appointment."

"You called! That's brave, dear. You made it in two tries."

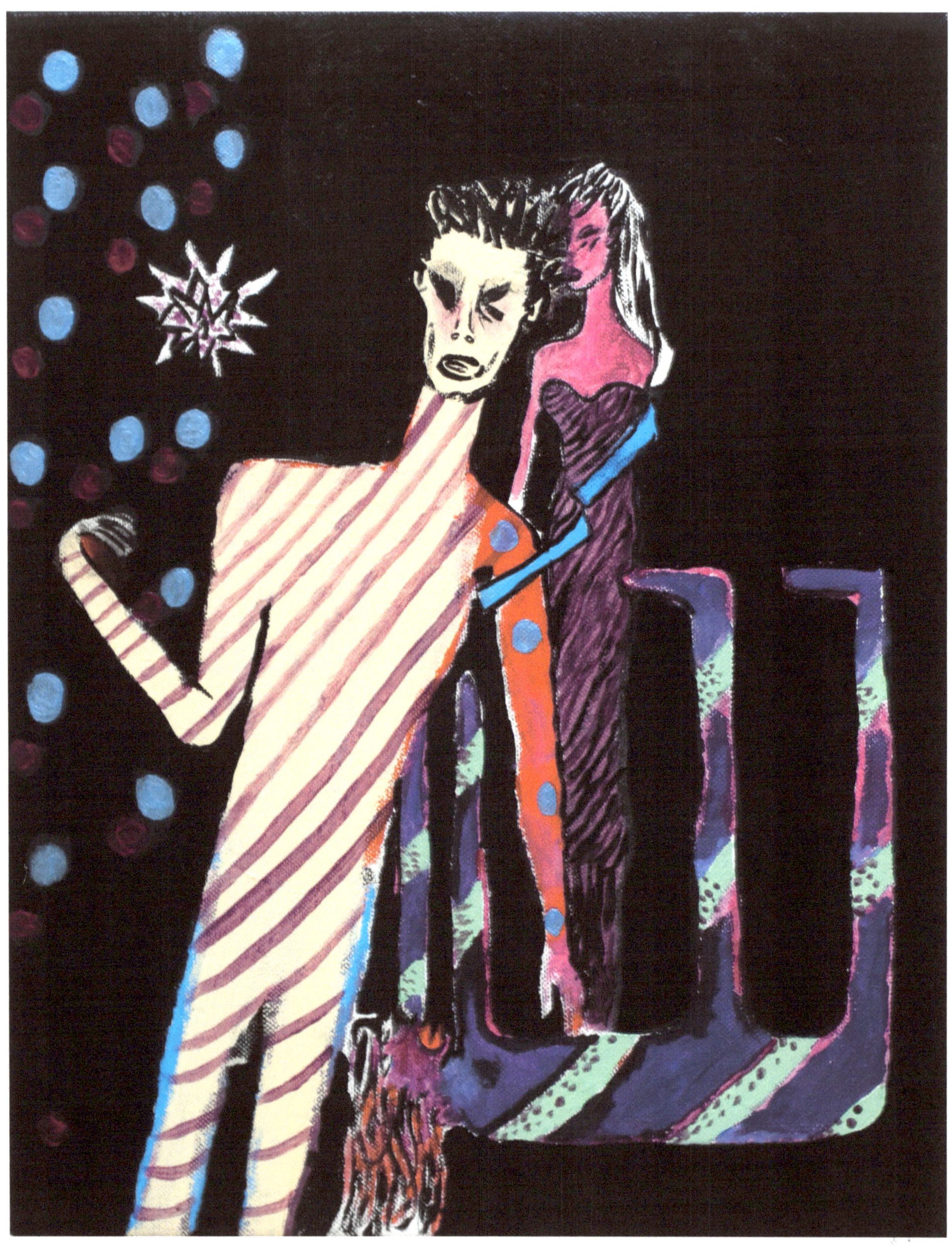

Blown, acrylic on canvas, by David West

Elizabeth paused, nervous, her hands now slick with sweat. She felt a drop slide down her stomach, over the soft rolls of flesh, down toward her waistband.

"I'd like to make an appointment." she repeated, trying to sound business-like. The voice chuckled.

"Of course, dear. Nights? You're working." Elizabeth frowned at the phone, already guessing so much about her, and guessing right. "Tomorrow night." The voice chuckled again.

MRS. TAYLOR'S HOME was not in a colorful, smoky, vibrantly ethnic neighborhood in the Bronx, nor in a forgotten, decrepit, rent-controlled ancient tenement in Hell's Kitchen. Instead, she lived in Queens. Elizabeth rode the Q train all the way out to the end, to a block of thirty-year-old houses and eighty-year-old apartment buildings. BMWs and Mercedes nosed out of slanted driveways, but piles of garbage bags accumulated behind white-painted garden gates. TVs flashed blue behind front windows as the darkness drew in. There was nothing menacing, nor even mysterious, in this neighborhood.

"When they go, you know, they sometimes wish they could say something to us if they didn't get to say goodbye." Elizabeth nodded, the tears streaming down her face. "Sometimes I can find them, if they're nearby. I can try, if you want me to."

Mrs. Taylor's house was architecturally sacrilegious, a regrettable concoction of cinderblock inset with panels of rough stone, and a second story balcony of that white-painted, overly-curly wrought metal. 1-B was the garden apartment, sharing the ground floor with the owner's precious single-car garage. Her rooms were small, but bright and clean. Red curtains obscured the front bay windows, and the door to the back kitchen was shut tight. The window was open, and Elizabeth felt the sweet, moist spring air, which smelled of humidity. This wasn't home, didn't feel anything like New York.

Mrs. Taylor seated Elizabeth across from her at a small, square black table Elizabeth was pretty sure had come from Ikea. Mrs. Taylor herself was a surprise. Slim, very elegant, with the shoulders of a dancer, she wore a sleek red wrap dress and deep green polish on her gleaming brown toes. Her hair was a mass of tight braids, frosted with silver around her temples, majestic as a crown. Her skin was plushly creamy, her eyes huge, depthless black, set in a web of fine wrinkles.

Her voice was rich-tipped, lush, deeper, tilting higher and lower with each word, musical but jazzy, syncopated, but unaccented. She was too vivid, and Elizabeth remembered why she was here, and her heart did that shrink-grow-shrink that hurt so much and happened so often.

Mrs. Taylor seated herself across from Elizabeth on a matching black-slatted chair (it was from Ikea, she knew so) and smiled warmly.

"The fee, my dear. You pay now, and everyone pays the same. Ninety dollars."

Elizabeth thought hard. She had that much, but it meant she'd have to go to the cash machine again to get through the week. She figured it might be forty-five. That didn't matter. She dug into her tote and pulled out her wallet. She snapped it open and her checkbook slid out, bouncing off her round thigh and onto the floor. She leaned over too far to reach it, her fingertips barely brushing it, nudging it further away, the moment stretching out into agonies of embarrassment. Out of the corner of her eye, she caught Mrs. Taylor's slight shake of the head, her downward-cast eyes. Elizabeth blushed even deeper. She hadn't meant to write a check, she wasn't asking. She didn't even know why she carried the checkbook—she only used it once a month, to pay her rent.

At last she leaned down by that extra fraction, grabbed the checkbook, and jammed it back into her overstuffed bag. She snapped open the billfold and counted out four twenties and a ten. Mrs. Taylor palmed them and they disappeared.

She sighed deeply, smiled, and took Elizabeth's hands. She shut her eyes, not squeezing them tight, but resting them, closed as if in sleep.

Elizabeth took a breath to speak, and Mrs. Taylor hushed her.

"You don't need to speak. You wait for me."

Long moments passed. Cars passed on the street outside. Mrs. Taylor sighed some more, and Elizabeth began to feel silly, began to feel she'd been had. She tried not to squirm, resisting the urge to pull her hands back.

"Sit still." Mrs. Taylor spoke without opening her eyes. "You're here about a man." Her voice held assurance, but Elizabeth realized the conclusion was an obvious one. Why else would she be there? She did not reply.

"That's okay. You don't have to tell me what I know." She paused. "He left. Left forever. He passed."

The lump in Elizabeth's throat swelled beyond bearability, and her eyes filled with tears. She breathed a gasp, a sob. Mrs. Taylor stroked her hand.

"When they go, you know, they sometimes wish they could say something to us if they didn't get to say goodbye." Elizabeth nodded, the tears streaming down her face. "Sometimes I can find them, if they're nearby. I can try, if you want me to." She nodded again, choked out words through a throat thick with tears.

"Yes, please." Mrs. Taylor sat, very calm, while Elizabeth breathed herself back into control. Mrs. Taylor let go of Elizabeth's hands, placed hers flat on the table. The room filled with silence, and a cool breeze rushed in through the window, blowing the red curtains out into the room. Mrs. Taylor frowned, lines creasing her smooth forehead.

"He says, 'did you get the dock?'" Dock? No, Doc. Dr. Pepper. He asked her that, when he came over, to see if she'd remembered to buy it for him. She always did, and there was, even now, a six-pack at the back of her nearly-empty refrigerator. She shook, her whole body trembling, but she said nothing. Mrs. Taylor went on.

"He says, 'How are you doing?'" Elizabeth opened her dry, dry mouth.

"Um. Okay. Not great. I miss him." Fat tears spilled down her cheeks.

"He says, 'It's good here. So, thanks for saying hi. Be good.'" Elizabeth waited. After a long moment, Mrs. Taylor moved her hands and took a deep breath, her eyes open now. Elizabeth stared at her through her swollen eyes, breathing as quietly as she could through a stuffy nose.

"What else did he say?"

"That was all."

"How can that be all?"

"That was all." Elizabeth's bafflement shifted to anger.

"No, that isn't all. What else did he say?"

"Sometimes they don't have much to say. They're in another place now. They don't seem to spend as much time thinking about us as we think they do. As we want them to. They've moved away."

"But I've spent three years missing him, trying to get over him, and all he can say is, 'Be good?'" Mrs. Taylor sat back in her chair, eyes turned sharply on Elizabeth.

"They move away. They are gone. You can think back on what he was like when he was here, and compare that with what he said to you now. How does it fit?"

"Fit? It doesn't fit. It doesn't fit at all. We were in love." Her voice was thick and clogged with tears, growing louder in her anger. She knew she sounded like a child remonstrating with a punishment, trying to reason with an unreasonable force. "We were in love." But as she sat, tears drying on her face, feeling salty and twisted and wretched, she remembered, clearly, the last few days and weeks of her time with him. He was noncommittal, even evasive. He came over, drank half his Dr. Pepper, put his feet up, and watched a game on her TV. He fell asleep right after he came, and then woke up and went home an hour later, blaming an early morning meeting. That last night she sat up, unable to sleep, worried then about what now was clear. She may have been in love, but he was not, and his death only forestalled what was now happening. She was being dumped, blown off, let down easily, even from beyond the grave.

The Battle of Skinner Butte

Ray Jicha

Moving north from San Francisco I slept on the beach near Arcata then made my way to Eugene where I got dropped off around 10:00 p.m. I found a little downtown bar, ordered a draft to pay for the stool and washed down the last of my speed. I had work to do. I started with the bartender.

"I just hitchhiked up from San Francisco the last couple of days."

"No kidding. How'd it go?"

"Pretty good. I slept on the beach last night."

"What brings you to Eugene?"

"I don't know. I heard good things about it. I heard Ken Kesey lives here. I loved *The Electric Kool-Aid Acid Test*."I see now that I lost him right there, though his reaction, returning his attention to his glassware, was more subtle than my approach.

"Yes, he's got a farm outside of town."

I waited until it became clear no more information was forthcoming. "Oh, yeah? Huh."

I let it drop. What was I going to do, ask for a ride up there?

I spent the next couple of hours trying to convince everyone I was a funky fellow traveler deserving of their shelter—it had worked before—but tonight I tapped a dry well. The best I could get were directions to an all-night diner and a park to sleep in called Skinner Butte. It came time to go.

Out on the street everything went quiet as I slow-walked it toward the diner but I kept my ears open just in case. I paused at some park benches to cinch up my bootlaces and get a long-sleeved shirt out of my backpack. A man strumming an acoustic guitar rounded the far corner. Sensing opportunity I fished out my harmonica and honked to call him over. He spoke first.

"Do you want to play?"

Uh-oh. "I don't know too much." *That's putting a smiley face on it.*

"That's all right. We'll find something."

"This harmonica's in G. If that helps." It didn't help me any. I didn't know what "in G" meant.

"Well, how about if I just do a little blues shuffle," he started to strum, "and you jump in anywhere. Don't worry about the notes. Just play what you feel."

"Right." *Play what you feel. Play what you feel.* I repeated it over to myself as I tried to get psyched up. I tried swaying to the rhythm like Ray Charles, put the harmonica to my mouth, *play what you feel,* and blew. What I felt was humiliation and remorse because I did not know how to play. That's pretty much how it sounded too. He wilted visibly in the corner of my eye, and stopped strumming.

"Can I see that for a minute?"

I handed it over.

"Maybe I can show you what I'm talking about."

He then played a lovely blues, pulling and bending notes, seemingly without effort. I gave up on the harmonica.

"Can I try the guitar?"

"Sure." He crossed it to my lap.

"I know a couple of chords." *Why do I keep talking?* As he played I carefully bent my fingers to form an E chord, then an A. I played one for a few seconds, then the other. After a couple of laps I was able to make the transition rhythmically. He fell in playing a melody against my chords. After a few bars I got brave and tried to play a D. I stumbled and lost the beat, but laughed at myself as he smiled and nodded, indicating I was on the right track. We went back around for another pass. Eventually I was able to incorporate the D into the song and he began to play with more force. *Look at me. I'm jamming!*

The simple riff grew tiresome after a few minutes and we let it drift away. We smoked a cigarette and I asked if he knew any good places to stay.

"They're not too friendly to street people around here, but there's a park up the hill about a half mile, Skinner Butte. Nobody will mess with you in there."

Street people? "Yeah, I heard about that. I heard there was an all-night diner nearby too."

"That's on the way to the park."

We lingered for a few minutes, not saying much, then wished each other luck and parted ways. I walked as far as the diner, not yet resigned to the park. I thought I might meet someone or at least pick up some information. Maybe I could stay up all night. The speed still held.

The over-lit restaurant made me squint at first but I found my way to a booth, set my pack upright on the seat across from me as if it were my dinner companion, and took a look around. There were signs everywhere. "We Reserve the Right to Refuse Service to ANYONE," "Restrooms for CUSTOMERS ONLY," and affixed to the wall in every booth, "NO SLEEPING!"

"You can't keep that here."

It was the waitress. She meant my pack. I looked confused so she pointed to a sign near the front that I had missed: "NO Backpacks Allowed in Seating Area."

"Where am I supposed to put it?"

"You can sit it on one of the chairs by the door."

"Can I get stuff out of it?"

She said yes and I complied with the regulation. I took out my reading and writing materials and went back to my seat more puzzled than put off.

My good behavior had earned me a glass of water and a menu from the waitress. I ordered a cup of coffee and a side of fries. I couldn't figure out what was with the gestapo tactics. I noticed the rules seemed to have been designed specifically to thwart me.

You're being paranoid.

I looked at the clock above the door.

One-fifty. It'll get light around six o'clock. It looked like a mile or two back to I-5. I could start walking around five o'clock. Three hours? I can do that, if this speed holds up. I figured I could sleep in the car that picked me up if I didn't figure something better first.

"One refill on the coffee." The waitress again, as she poured.

I would have to stall. I nursed my second cup, ate my fries one at a time, asked for more water. I read and wrote and consulted my maps.

"No sleeping." My head snapped up. "If you put your head down again I'll have to ask you to leave."

I looked at the clock: three-ten. I looked around. There were only two couples in the restaurant, sitting far away. I looked at the empty cup on the table in front of me.

This hurts. "Can I please have another cup of coffee? And some water?"

I went to the bathroom and washed my face. I felt like a wrung washcloth. When I returned to my table the coffee and water were there but they did not help. When it became clear that I would not last I saved myself the humiliation of getting asked to leave and inquired at the register about the park.

"Skinner Butte, right up the hill."

"And it's OK to sleep there?"

"People do it all the time."

All the time? Really?

As I lifted my pack from its seat by the door I looked at the signs again.

A lot of people like me must have come through here. I wish I could find some.

See, in the sleepy southern town I came from I was a freak, a hippy, almost alone. I thought if I could just get out West I'd find something, be welcomed into some fold, but there wasn't any fold: it was 1985; the only hippies were thirty-five years old and either hopelessly burnt out or starting organic juice companies. To the people in this town I was a tired cliché—a cliché without money, and in the eighties money talked and bullshit walked to Skinner Butte.

Outside I started up the street towards the park. Beyond the restaurant the street grew dark and empty. A small pickup drove by and disappeared around the next bend. The hill got steeper. I could see the lights of the park a couple hundred yards ahead. A set of headlights came down the street towards me. It looked like the same truck that just passed me.

I'm not sure. Adrenalin.

Less than a minute passed before I heard a vehicle

coming up behind me. Its engine had a familiar pitch. I went taut. It passed me.

Same truck. No mistake now.

I quickened my pace. The park was still a hundred yards away; the hill got steeper. *I don't know what's happening but it's not good. Don't run. Not yet.* I only saw one silhouette in the truck the last time it passed me, *even odds unless he has a gun. He probably has a gun. If I can get to the park I can get away from the road so he can't drive up on me. Don't run. Don't look scared.*

I was about twenty yards from the park when I heard the revving of the engine as it built from around the bend ahead. The headlights pinned me when they came back by and I tried to avoid direct eye contact until I passed into their penumbra. The truck passed by at only a few feet away but did not slow down. I saw the face of my pursuer at this time. Hideous thing, bloated and white, with eyes the color of piss, the tendrils of its wet moustache obscuring a lipless, croaking gorge. It looked at me, malignantly.

That's it. This motherfucker is after me. Here's the park. Run!

War drums pounded through me as I took off like *The Naked Prey* down the slope, across the parking lot, grass, and a pathway lit by orange lights, toward a line of trees and the dark shadows beyond. I had cinched my pack as tight as it would go so it would not toss and break my stride. I saw an opening in the trees and ran through it. The path dropped quickly and once down a few feet I threw myself to the ground and crawled back up to see.

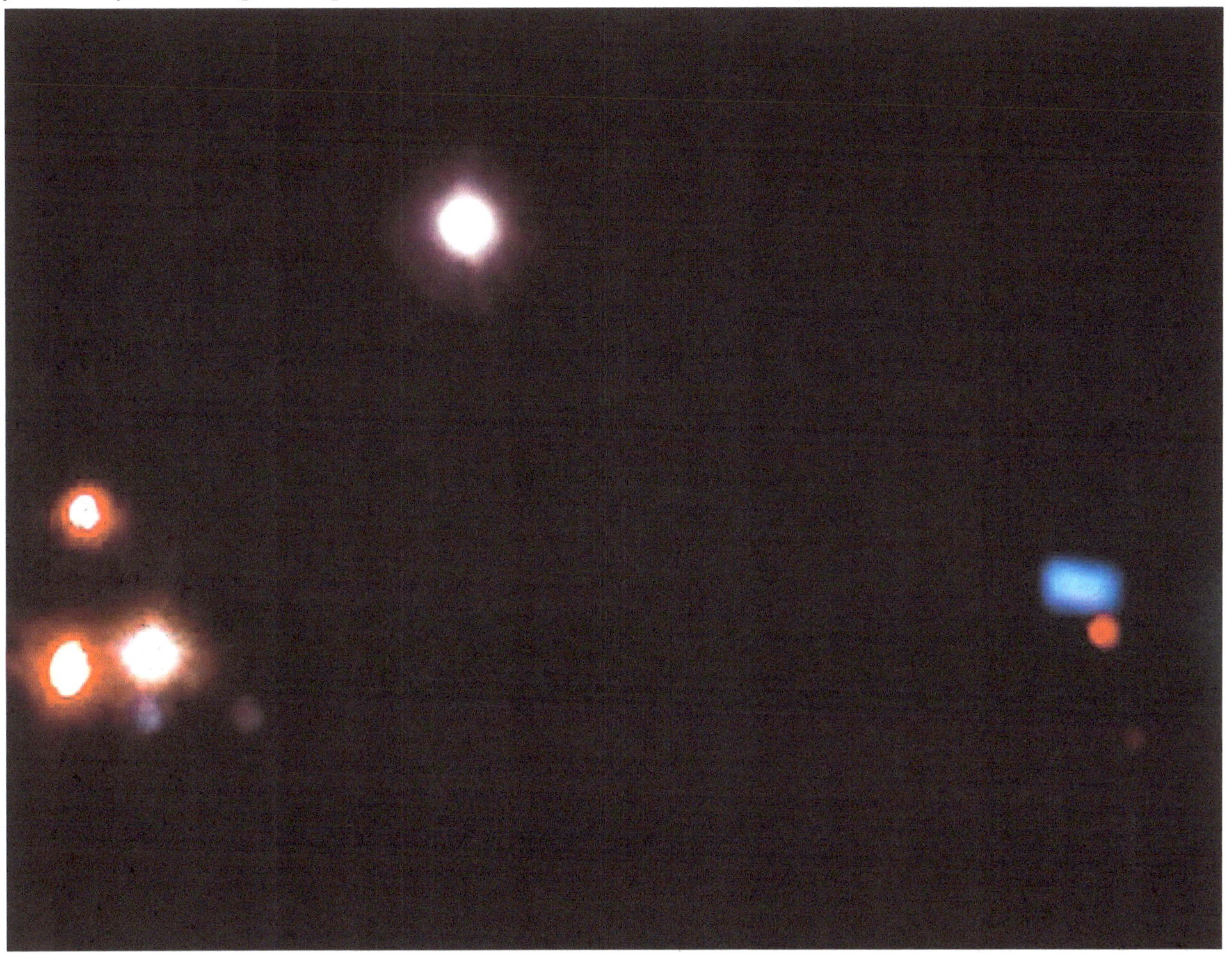

***From Darkness to Light*, photograph by Kym Ghee**

Though I had stopped, my sweat, acrid as a race riot, kept running into my eyes. My heart skittered like a chicken with its head cut off. My exhalations sounded like storms at sea.

G*et ahold of yourself. He probably won't follow you*

in here. Jesus Christ, he's right there! The monster had driven into the parking lot from an entrance further on and cruised down close to the edge of the grass while he scanned the tree line.

He's fucking looking right at me! Those orange lights are shining right on my face!

I crouched back down and tried to listen. *I can't hear anything but my own breath!* I looked again, keeping as low as I could, terrified that the truck would stop, and saw it turn out of the parking lot where I had entered and drive away toward town. *He's probably going to get help.*

I turned and slid down the path another fifteen feet to the point where it flattened out and stopped. I was hemmed in by a river, which I could see here and there in the moonlight.

He probably knows I'm trapped.

Another path ran at right angles to the one I'd come down and paralleled the river. I turned right and trotted gingerly as my eyes adjusted to the dark.

This should take me below the park entrance. Then he can only come from one direction. Unless this is how they planned it. He's probably got the park mapped out. They probably knew I'd run this way. It might be an ambush. With me crashing around down there they could hear me coming but I couldn't hear them. *Find a place to hide where they can't sneak up on you.*

I moved along more carefully for another few yards until I found a bare spot under some bushes and wedged myself into it with my back to the river. I tried not to move. I tried not to breathe. As I strained to inhale only through my nose, my chest jerked and seized. The heat I had generated while running now built up around me into a fetid, invisible chrysalis. I could have swum through my own sweat.

But I had bigger problems. The men were back. I heard at least one car engine, maybe two. *They're pulling into the parking lot.* I heard car doors and voices. *How many? I can't tell. More than one.*

I reached around, unzipped my pack and slipped my hand inside. I groped with my fingertips until I felt the leather of the hunting knife sheath.

Keep an eye out for movement.

I stopped to take a few breaths. I opened my mouth wide to exhale without sound.

There! I think that's a flashlight. Oh shit. Oh shit!

I pulled out the knife, a six-inch, carbon-steel, full-tang straight blade that I carried, at some legal risk, against just this eventuality. It felt reassuringly stout. I held it in front of me with both hands with my elbows resting on my knees. I sat on my pack with my weight forward over the balls of my feet. I looked up and down the trail in front of me. I couldn't see more than a few feet in either direction.

I saw the beam of a flashlight swinging back and forth along the treeline at the top of the trail. The men talked quietly to each other so that I would not hear.

Maybe they'll go the wrong way. If they come this way, use the knife. Stab someone? No, as a threat. What if they have guns? Then it won't matter. They probably have guns. They know exactly what they're doing.

I looked back the other way only to see another flashlight beam at the top of what must have been the other trail they knew about. I could hear them stepping on the leaves and twigs.

How many are there? Too many to fight. They're not taking any chances. They're walking right to me. They must have known I'd try to hide right here. It's like they're herding goats to slaughter. I heard them whispering signals. I saw their lights and shadows moving. I heard their footsteps falling all around me. *Here they come . . .*

An hour passed, maybe more. The flashlights came no closer, the voices got no louder. My heartbeat and breathing slowed down. I stopped sweating. I began to reevaluate my situation.

If they were there wouldn't they have got here by now, or moved or something? Now it looked like the flashlights might just have been the orange lights of the park. The movement came from the tree branches in front of them, swayed by the breeze that rustled the leaves to sound like voices and footfalls to me. That guy was definitely following me, though. I didn't make that up. Jesus, did I imagine all the rest? All those mushrooms and the first hallucination I have is of some guy trying to kill me. That speed is making me crazy. I suddenly felt very tired. I guess I have been up for a long time. I gave up the fight soon after and fell asleep on the bare ground with my knife still in my hand.

Some Poems

Les Bridges

Stuck on a Runway

Thunderheads loom over Dallas.
Stranded planes mill
like nervous, 100-ton cattle,
blood streaks across silver flanks.

185 strangers and I marinate
inside metal sausage as promises
of departure go unmet,
hours leak toward infinity.
Squatted on concrete,
civilization evaporates.
Soon the killing of the
stewardesses will begin.

Engine Block in Empty Lot

From long-gone Ford,
grey-metal V-8,
streaked with rust,
squats solid as
tackle anchoring
line of Detroit Lions.
Patch of black
testifes where oil
escaped worn engine,
reentered earth.
Shards of beer bottles
stud chained-off lot,
become emeralds when
fired by sun that
sneaks in,
thin as a crackhead,
over Third Street tenements.
Next door, poets prattle
of pain and pleasure
on Nuyorican stage,
never coming close to
sweet petroleum thunder
that once came pounding
from these dead pistons.

Me and My Answering Machine

Burst through door,
kick the cat,
hustle into bedroom
to your pulsing red kisses.
Know you care,
somebody cares, if it's only
a bond salesman from Shearsons
or landlord 'cause I'm late
with the rent check again.

When I'm home, you step
between me and them,
grab intruders on third ring,
ask them with phony cheerfulness
to check in after the tone,
the tone that sounds
like an EMS truck hurtling along
on another terror mission.

Sometimes, though, you're like
all these other slime buckets.
Can't trust you to deliver
when I feel it slipping away.
When I'm looking for her call
after battling guys with razor
blades on their elbows,
when, below my cold blue bedroom,
it's the midnight of howling
firetrucks and foraging crackheads
and bad dreams hammer
spikes through my eyes,
and the sheets are a sweaty shroud,
and your buttons aren't glowing,
and your bell isn't ringing,
and I'm doomed to be alone
through another empty New York night.

Schizophrenic

Two weeks before 14th birthday,
flowers that could be seen
dancing in her azure eyes
turned to base metal.
Soot enveloped her brain.

She took kitchen knife
to her paintings, canvas
peeling back onto itself like
pared apple skin. Four years,
23 paintings, dead in an hour.

These were paintings that
had made her mother, the painter,
and her father, the doctor,
sure she was destined
for the Art Institute and then
Whitney, Guggenheim, Castelli.

Her hair turned to straw.
Her eyes became the blank blue
that precedes videotape.
Specialists came, stared, whispered.
Fear tugged her mother to gin,
her father into arms of his nurse.

Thorazine mugs patients in
hospital, red-brick island
surrounded by muscular oaks.
In parking lot,
three black Mercedes
hunch on manicured gravel.
Blue-hatted drivers slouch through
Daily News as parents dispose of cakes,
flowers,
duty.

Sick Lazy Fuck

Mark McCawley

"If you look a dog in the eye too intently, it may recite an astounding poem to you. You might have been mad for a long time and have realized it only at that moment."
—Jean Genet, *Funeral Rites*

SICK. LAZY. FUCK.
Three small words.
Like "Get a Life."
Or "Sick of You."
Or "I'm Moving On."
Or "You Should, Too."
Simple words.
Like "I Hate You."
Or "I Never Really Loved You."
Or "I Never Did."
Or "Thank God We Never Had Children."

But those three small words, they cut the deepest. The first two, like the blade of a double-edged knife. The last one, the handle she stuck in with a twist. Three words: three exclamation points ending the sentence that was our marriage.

* * *

I WAS TERRIBLY nervous, agitated, desperate. Found it impossible to think, to concentrate, beyond those three small words that wound like a tight spring in my head. I stared at the television screen for hours, days, I don't know how long. Three, four, five? I can't be sure. Even when I shut my eyes, I could still see those flickering images: people in furious flights, flashes of intense emotion, distorted faces or faces expressing nothing at all. Brief words, news of death, more destruction, daily struggles, the entire spectrum of human experience and behavior, alongside the latest antacid and haemorrhoidal cream. And always, her face. Those three words.

I had become periodically insane, with long intervals of horrible sanity, during which time all I wanted, all I wished for, was to fall asleep, drift off into a beer-fueled oblivion. The blue light from the television illuminated the small flat, now seemingly larger for its emptiness. The room looked exactly as I felt: empty. Hollowed out. No matter how much I drank, I couldn't get rid of that feeling, nor could I erase those three words from my mind. Strange how we only really notice things by their absence. A Renoir print, a china cabinet, a coffee table, a person. Now it was only my easy chair, the TV, the coffee table and me. She took the rest.

I couldn't remember the last time I had reached R.E.M sleep. Insomnia was relentless. It all seemed absurdly cruel. The same thoughts ricocheted about my mind like shrapnel, sometimes not even thoughts at all, and always about her, about us. It was like I was obsessed, addicted. And I was going through really bad withdrawal.

After four, five days of little or no sleep, I began to hallucinate. Tiny bugs. Faces popping out of the television, out of the walls, then disappearing. Quite disconcerting. Sometimes it was as if my eyeballs were functioning independently of each other, and the longer I remained awake, the worse it got. All I wanted to do was to sleep, to get out of my exhausted body, my burnt-out mind, for eight or ten hours of uninterrupted unconsciousness.

Then the idea came to me.

How my earliest, most pleasurable memories were of being in warm moist places. I went to the bathroom and ran the bath. Without undressing, I stepped into the water, sat in the tub. But the tub wasn't big enough. When I tried to bend my legs to fit inside, my knees stuck out of the water. When I tried to submerge them, my chest stuck out. It seemed hopeless. No matter what I tried, some part of my body was always exposed to the air. Then the water cooled down. I added more hot water, yet that cooled as well. Frustrated, I twisted the hot water faucet and left it running. That did the trick. I laid back, victorious. The tub filled to the brim and began spilling onto the bathroom floor.

Almost immediately, I could feel my body getting lighter. The water made me feel warm and safe, like a baby in a womb. At some point, I had no sensation whatsoever. It was as though I were floating weightless in a universe of pure peace and tranquility, interrupted only by a faint and distant knocking which I ignored. I chuckled as I watched the tiles around the tub change colors, from white to orange to yellow to copper to magenta. An entire kaleidoscope of colors, mixing and blending and bleeding into each other.

Then the knocking returned again, much louder and closer this time. An immense thud, followed by a crash, then footsteps. Several people were standing above me. They all seemed very angry. One of them was the building manager, Louise. She was really livid about something. Someone turned off the faucet and pulled the plug in the tub, and the water began sinking away. This made me very angry. I attempted to turn the water back on, but several people grabbed me and yanked me out of the tub and onto the floor. I'd never felt so cold before in my life. Strange hands kept grabbing me, touching me, I don't know how many. Their fingers felt like icicles as they cut off my shirt and jeans. I remember one icicle in my backside before everything went suddenly black.

* * *

There was a burning sensation in my right arm, and it hurt when I tried to move it. I glanced down to see a long transparent worm snaking up my arm, then disappearing into the crook of my elbow. A progression of white uniforms fluttered in and out of the room as if out of the walls themselves. The room had the distinct odor of disinfectant. I wasn't sure where I was or even how I had gotten there. I felt hands touching me, fingers probing. Strange faces glanced down at me, conversing with one another as though I wasn't even there. Some people stood around as if waiting for something to happen, something bizarre or violent. All of them spoke in hurried tones about blood samples for this or that test. They filled up vials with my blood. I was poked and prodded, yanked and tugged. At some point I tried to say something. Someone abruptly rolled me over onto my side and stabbed my ass with something sharp.

After four, five days of little or no sleep I began to hallucinate. Tiny bugs. Faces popping out of the television, out of the walls, then disappearing. Quite disconcerting.

There was a strange taste in the back of my throat. I dozed off.

When I reawakened, a woman in a white uniform was sitting in a chair beside my hospital bed. Her lips were smeared with bright red lipstick. Her blonde hair was pulled tightly into a bun at the back of her head which made the skin on her face look taut and unreal, as though the bones were suddenly going to poke out through her thin, extremely white translucent skin. She was reading a paperback. On the cover was a large man with a mane of flowing hair and a bare chest and impossibly long arms holding a petite woman. I couldn't tell if the woman on the cover was trying to get away from the man. I watched the crimson-lipped woman's lips move as she read. I thought I might get sick. My throat felt raw. It felt as though I hadn't swallowed anything for days.

* * *

It was like a bad dream. Or some kind of sick joke. At least that's how I recall those first few days in Metro-Mercy Hospital's psychiatric security ward—the wing reserved for those patients deemed a danger to themselves or to others. Most new patients spent at least couple of days there for observation. It was the only ward in the hospital with a locked door. The lock was electronically controlled from inside the nursing station. Its constant shrill was a reminder that I was an inmate here, considered dangerous, if only to myself. I still had no idea what crime I had committed.

There were usually no more than ten patients on the security ward at any time. I had only counted six. Most were completely sedated and numb as zombies. Their reddened, bloodshot eyes, staring out into nothing. Was this how I looked, I wondered? Probably. There didn't seem to be any mirrors in the security wing. And what magazines there were had had their dates blackened out, and any violent imagery removed altogether. Of course it didn't matter. It was impossible to read with all the drugs they had us on. Even if I managed to read a passage or two, I soon forgot what I had read.

There was nothing to do on the security ward but watch TV, await the outcome of our daily early morning visitations with the Chief of Psychiatry, Dr. Soza, and wait to be transferred to the regular psychiatric ward. During those consultations, none of us were allowed back in our rooms except to sleep. We were brought to a central common area where everyone could easily be observed by the nursing staff. The nursing station itself resembled a kind of fortress. Sheets of Plexiglass rose up from the station's counter to the ceiling and completely encompassed the station, except for a two-part Plexiglass entrance door, the bottom of which was constantly closed. On the top half of the door was a sign written in large bold letters: "No Patients Beyond This Point." The staff inside always looked nervous, as if half-expecting something to occur, something violent. If someone strolled too close to the nursing station, a voice would boom through the intercom: "Please stand back. Someone will assist you."

There were two long couches and several padded chairs in the common area surrounding the sole TV which sat on a shelf high on the wall, out of reach. The nursing station had the only remote. It was constantly tuned to a public television station. No one ever thought of asking to change the channel. The programs were mostly documentaries about wildlife, the environment and air pollution, in the afternoon, and game shows in the early evening. Nothing remarkable. I suppose it didn't matter, since very little of it registered anyhow. I could barely concentrate long enough to finish a cigarette, which we were allowed to smoke once an hour if we had been admitted with them. Patients were constantly bumming them, or got suddenly friendly when you lit up. Never seen so many people so eager to share someone's secondhand smoke.

We were never left alone, not even to piss. Who knew what could occur in that time? If anyone had to go to the toilet, they had to be escorted, one at a time, one after the other, by a member of the staff. The large quantities of watered-down coffee, combined with the drugs they had us on, meant all too often that more than one of us had to go at the same time. We would rock back and forth waiting for our turn. Sometimes someone didn't quite make it. Long trails of urine and brown-yellowish blobs were scattered along the entrance to the facilities.

We were always within their sight. They sat beside our beds at night, waited for us just outside the washrooms, a step or two behind us at all times. Although I had this overwhelming desire to be left alone, I was never left by myself for more than a minute during those first few days. A nurse or an orderly was constantly nearby. A person can do a lot of damage in sixty seconds, I suppose, if they set their mind to it.

I was spending too much time taking a dump, and my nurse had already poked her head inside the room twice to see what I was doing. Maybe I was attempting to drown myself in the toilet. It only takes a tablespoon of water to drown oneself, or so say the experts on drowning. I was in the middle of wiping my ass when she poked her head inside for the third time.

"Almost done, pet?"

"Look for yourself," I said, holding out the wad of

soiled tissue for her inspection.

She winced and abruptly turned away. I dropped the wad into the toilet. For some reason I didn't flush it. Then I washed my hands. I figured she'd think twice before poking her head in on me again.

* * *

THE CHIEF OF Psychiatry, Doctor Soza, conducted his rounds between ten and eleven in the morning. During that hour, all patients had to remain in their rooms while Soza and his posse of interns interviewed patient after patient. I'd been in the security ward for two days, though it seemed longer. Since my arrival, I anticipated his daily morning visits with a distinct sense of dread.

Soza was the type of anti-human that made you feel worse by just being in the same room with him. Each conversation left me wanting to scream because I knew I was powerless against him. He controlled my fate and was the sole determiner of the length of my internment.

I sat on the edge of the hospital bed while he and his posse stood across the room from me. He was scanning a folder. Whenever I moved, or scratched my head, his posse would scribble on notepads they

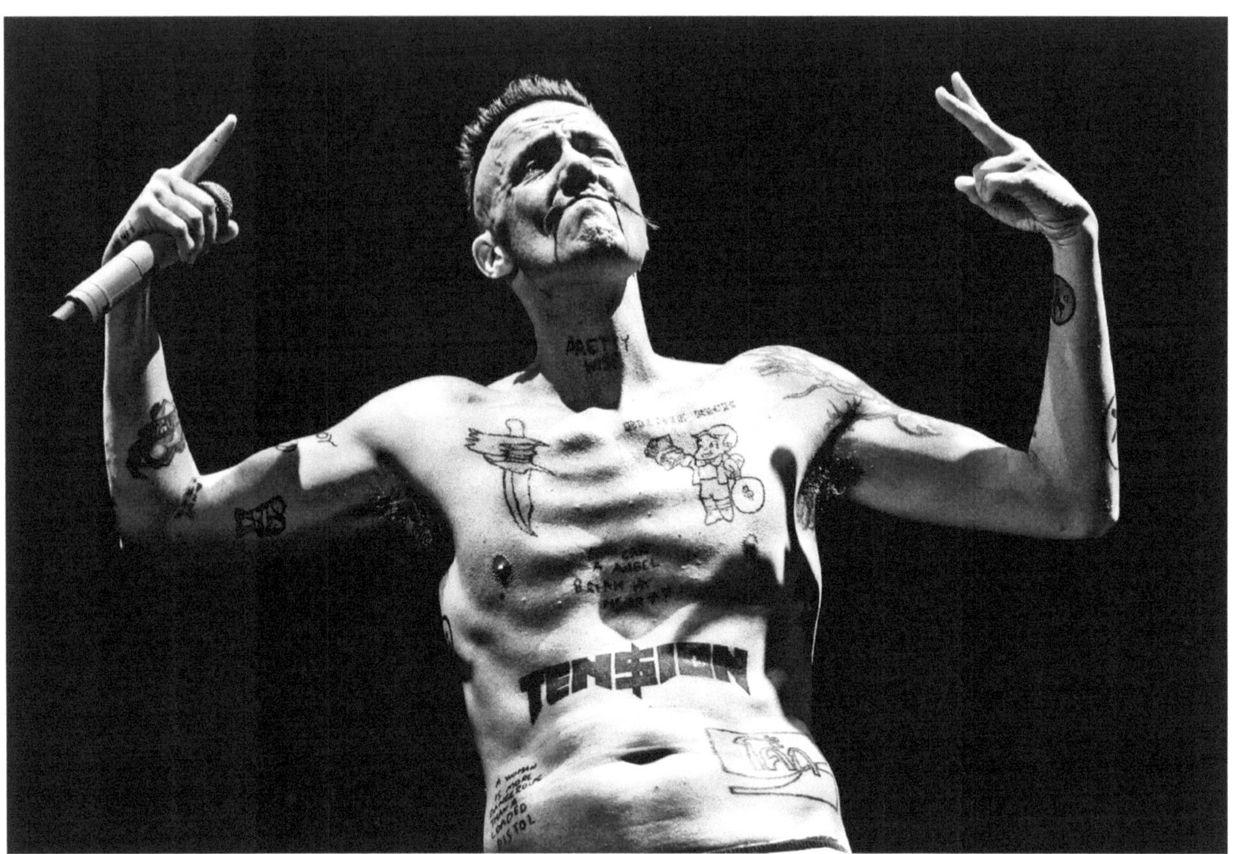

photograph by Charlie Homo

were constantly carrying.

"So, how are we doing today?" he asked in that monotone voice of his, not looking up at me as he spoke.

"Okay, I guess." The posse scribbled.

"Just okay?" he asked, without inflection. He still hadn't looked up at me. He appeared to be attempting to match the name on the file with the person in the room with him. I wondered if this happened very often. Mixing up patients, mixing up medications.

"Well, maybe more than just okay." I said. "I'm

feeling much better than I did yesterday." I was lying. In fact, since my arrival, I had felt an increasing sense of anxiety building inside of me. I figured it was due to lack of personal control.

"I was hoping I might be moved to the regular ward. Then I could have regular visitors, maybe even a day pass." Soza looked up from his file folder. His left eyebrow rose and curled.

"Yesterday we talked about the incident that brought you to Metro Mercy." He was pointing at something in the file folder. "Do you have any more thoughts about it today?"

"I'm not sure. . . . I mean, some of it makes sense to me . . . but some of it still makes no sense at all. It's like a dream, sort of, like I'm looking at somebody else's life. . . ." Shit. I knew I shouldn't have said that last bit the instant it came out of my mouth.

"Hmmm . . . what do you think it means, like you're looking at someone else's life?" he asked, scribbling something new into the file folder. His posse mimicked his scribble. "Did you feel as though your life is not your own but someone else's?"

"Like whose?" I was confused. The posse looked first at me, then to Soza. They seemed confused, too.

"Why don't you tell me?" he replied. The posse looked at Soza and then at me.

"I think, I mean, I don't know. I don't think I was trying to hurt myself. I wasn't thinking about suicide. . . ."

"What makes you think you weren't thinking about suicide?" Soza asked.

I thought about this for a while. Soza began clicking the end of his pen.

"I figure if I was trying to kill myself, I'd attempt something a little less painful than scalding myself to death," I said, then added, "Can someone actually scald themselves to death?"

"You'd be surprised what people are capable of," Soza said. "There's always a first time for everything. Have you thought of taking your own life very often?"

"I don't think so . . . I mean, I don't know. I'm not sure what I'm thinking. It's all so confusing," I confessed. Fucking bastard could convince a rock it was a blade of grass.

"I can see we've accomplished a lot today," Soza said, first glancing at his wristwatch, then dropping his pen into the left breast pocket of his white lab coat. He closed the file in his other hand.

"We'll talk again tomorrow morning."

* * *

FOR DAYS, I'D felt a vague sense of anxiety building up inside of me as if my nerves were being tugged and pulled taut. I had a corrosive sensation in the pit of my stomach, a muscular tension stretching across my chest and up the back of my neck, like my skin was wrapped too tightly.

I winced at every sound and felt the hospital tilt whenever I stood up. I staggered as I walked, moving as if some outside force was drawing me.

Then this vague sense became a feverish state. I sensed motives in the mundane, hidden purposes beneath the surface. I was sure that the doctors and nurses could read my thoughts. I knew the evil night nurse was poisoning me, so I refused to eat, or even fill out the menu.

She brought in a tray of food anyway. The food looked synthetic, inedible. "If you don't start eating," she threatened, "you'll be fed intravenously, whether you like it or not . . . it's entirely up to you."

On the tray were individual servings of mashed potatoes, mixed vegetables, and a hamburger patty smothered in red sauce. Clumps in the sauce looked like blood clots.

The nurse brought her head close to the tray and inhaled deeply through her nose. Tiny black hairs stuck out of her nostrils.

"Mmmmm . . . it certainly smells good, don't you think so?" she said, pushing the tray to me.

I pushed it away.

She pushed it back.

"Just a few mouthfuls, all right?" She cut off a piece of the hamburger patty with a plastic spoon and brought it to my mouth. I pursed my lips together and knocked the spoon away from my face.

"All right, enough is enough . . . either you eat it yourself or I'll have to call Doctor Soza." Her eyes were bulging and her face was turning red.

I looked at her, then at the food on the tray. I tilted my head forward and inhaled. The food didn't have any smell. I spooned some of the mashed potato into my mouth and began to chew. It tasted like chalk. I spat it out in her face. Bits of potato hung onto her nose and chin. I lifted the tray and threw it at her. She stepped backwards. I began throwing whatever was in reach. She bolted from the room, shouting.

She returned with two large men who held me down on the bed while she emptied a syringe into one of my arms. This was followed by a sudden sensation of asphyxiation.

"You'd be surprised what people are capable of," the doctor said. "There's always a first time for everything. Have you thought of taking your own life very often?"

Then nothing.

It wasn't until the doctor arrived the following morning that I learned I'd been suffering a side effect from one of the medications they'd been pumping into me since my arrival.

The following night, I had just managed to fall asleep when I was awakened by a hand shaking my shoulder. It was the night nurse. She was pulling me out of bed.

"I'm sorry," she muttered. "We need your bed. You are being transferred to the open ward. We have a bed for you there."

* * *

JARED AND KRISTINA were considered veterans on the open ward. Both of them had been admitted to Metro-Mercy so many times that they were on a first-name basis with the staff. For some reason, when visiting hours came around, we were the only three patients on the ward without any visitors. Perhaps it was the stigma of mental illness. Perhaps people thought we were contagious. Perhaps nobody knew we were there. I don't know.

Jared was my roommate in the open ward. Unlike the security wing, where there was just one patient to each room, the rooms on the open ward contained two men, or two women. Day or night, Jared was constantly talking. He was a paranoid schizophrenic who kept hearing voices. The voices all said the same thing over and over: Kill yourself. His parents would find him hanging in the closet of his bedroom, dangling from the bathroom shower rod, or lying in a pool of his own blood in the kitchenette of their small apartment. It was difficult to find an apartment when your only child brought the entire emergency services department to your home every other month. Again and again, Jared would be rushed to Metro-Mercy's emergency, then to ICU, then to psychiatry. It happened like clockwork. Each time he was admitted, he'd have bandages on his throat, or on his wrists and forearms.

Jared's cogwheels were always turning. He'd talk nonstop, all day long, his voice becoming increasingly louder as he spoke, as if he were trying to talk above the voice of someone else. Then, suddenly, he would stop talking, and tilt his head to one side as if something had caught his attention. Then his ceaseless monologue would continue as if nothing had happened.

Kristina was a married mother of three in her early forties. She suffered from post-partum psychosis. She had lost count how many times she had been admitted to Metro Mercy in the past two years or so. Probably more than ten times but less than twenty. She'd already attempted suicide twice. Her previous psychiatrist had wrongly diagnosed her as a paranoid schizophrenic and pumped her so full of an anti-psychotic medication that she thought her husband was the Devil and her children, three demons. Instead of slitting their throats, she took all her sleeping pills. After a week in ICU, three days on the security wing, she was transferred to the open ward with the rest of the walking wounded.

While other patients visited with friends or family, we hung outside by the medical waste incinerator smoking cigarettes, or down in Metro-Mercy's basement cafeteria. It was early Saturday afternoon and we were seated in the busy cafeteria. I was drinking hot chocolate, which was better than the watered-down crap they gave us up on the ward. I took a sip from the Styrofoam cup. The hot sweet liquid made my teeth ache momentarily.

Jared was counting off his scars again, as usual. It was like a complete medical history he showed to anyone whether or not they were really interested. He had scars up and down his arms from the time he took a box cutter to them. Scars on his neck from all of his attempted hangings. He had scars all over his body. Some were self-inflicted. Some were the result of attempts to save his life. The scar on his chest was by far Jared's favorite. "That's where they cut my chest open to massage my heart." He said. "It stopped, you know."

> *After shock therapy, Kristina took to masturbation like an Olympic sport, with whatever was conveniently at hand. She tried to hide her favorite bottles from the orderlies, but you can't hide anything on a psychiatric ward for long, especially a makeshift dildo.*

"We know," Kristina and I said, almost in unison. We'd heard this before, many times. Jared just continued talking. Kristina treated Jared like the little younger brother she had never had.

"This one," he said, pointing to the back of his neck, "this one's from when I tried hanging myself from my parent's shower rod last year. That's where my head hit the bathtub when I fell. . . ."

Meanwhile, under the cafeteria table, Kristina had one of her legs outstretched with the sole of her foot between my legs, rubbing my crotch. I had an erection. She rubbed the outline of my cock with the toes of her foot. Her eyes stared into mine like some sexual predator focusing on her chosen prey. I could feel the heat of her body in the sole of her foot. I didn't want her to stop but I didn't want to come in these one-size-fits-all light-blue hospital pajamas we psyche patients wore, either. Might as well just piss my pants.

"Let's go for a smoke, okay?" I say, stumbling to my feet.

Mondays, Wednesdays and Fridays were agonizing days for Kristina. Those were the days she had her Electro-Convulsive Therapy (ECT). A few other women on the ward also underwent the procedure. It was reserved for those patients who were no longer responding to traditional psycho-pharmaceuticals. They'd each be given a muscle relaxant just before an anesthetic made them unconscious. Then their brains would be given an electrical shock. The hope was that the electric shock would change the patient's thought pattern. Whether or not this worked for Kristina or any of the other patients, I don't know. The treatment did cause her to lose all memory of her marriage, and to enter into a state of extreme horniness.

Soon, Kristina became the ward's resident nymphomaniac. At least that's how the male orderlies referred to her, after one of them was caught having sex with her in the bathroom, by her visiting husband, during a previous admission. Now the male staff just avoided her to protect their jobs. That left the other patients, most of whom were so chemically castrated by their cocktails of psycho-pharmaceuticals they could barely shuffle around the ward, let alone get it up. So, after ECT days, out of desperation, Kristina took to masturbation like an Olympic sport with whatever was conveniently at hand. Shampoo bottles, deodorant sticks, soda pop bottles, whatever—until the staff caught on and confiscated all the bottles on the ward and started dispensing shampoo and deodorant from the nursing station as required. She tried to hide her favorite bottles, but you can't hide anything on a psychiatric ward for long, especially a makeshift dildo the staff is on the lookout for. The female staff made a point of interrupting Kristina's self-abuse as often as possible. "Doctor's orders," they told her. "You're disturbing the other patients."

One time, we were walking along the first-floor corridor, with Jared about fifty feet ahead of us, when Kristina pulled me into one of the custodial rooms and closed the door behind us. Her mouth was immediately on mine, her tongue poking and probing my mouth as she tugged at the elastic of my hospital blues. The room was full of mops and brooms and various cleaning supplies. Any sound from the corridor outside was quickly muffled by the slurping sounds of me fucking her moist mouth. I held onto the sides of her head while she bobbed back and forth.

As soon as I was hard enough, she stood up, turned around and slid down her light blue hospital blues, grasped my cock and slid me inside her. Fuck was she wet. She held onto the door handle as I rammed into her again and again. She was a screamer. With each plunge, she moaned loudly. In the corridor, I could hear Jared calling our names. With one of her hands still holding onto the door handle for balance and leverage, she took my left hand and guided it up under her hospital blues to her engorged breast. I cupped her breast in my hand and felt her nipple hardening against my palm. Almost at once she began expressing into my cupped hand. I rubbed the liquid over her breast and stomach. By now, she was bucking against my prick. Her moaning had evidently brought us to somebody's attention, because someone on the other side of the door was trying to get in. They pushed on the door. We pushed back with the combined weight of our bodies. This went on for several minutes, perhaps longer. When Kristina finally came, she was like a wild woman, bobbing her ass back and forth and from side to side. I slipped out of her and ejaculated across her buttocks. Maybe it was the meds I was on, but when I came, it felt like tiny razor blades running up the length of my urethra.

* * *

Later that afternoon, I watched as Kristina wrapped her arms around each of her three children in their strollers—first one, then another—then, lastly, tentatively, her husband. I could plainly see the dark blue stain on the ass of her blue hospital pajamas bottoms. I suppose I should have felt like a shit or something, but I didn't. Thanks to the meds, all I felt was "blah." No ups, no downs. Just "blah." It's hard to believe people live their entire lives this way.

Back in the smoking room, on the television, a large purple monster was singing to several small, smiling children. The children didn't appear to be frightened by the monster, even though its tail kept hitting them when it turned from side to side or swept around in circles.

Nothing in this place seemed to make any sense. When people asked to bum a smoke, I let them take cigarette after cigarette until the package was empty. Fuck it. Fuck everything. I didn't care anymore.

* * *

After twenty-one days on the psychiatric ward, it wasn't the doctor or even the nurses who informed me I was being released, but the Metro-Mercy resident social worker. Apparently, someone was more in need of my bed than I was. The social worker gave me a large brown envelope with ten bus tickets inside, and vouchers for rent, food and utilities. At the nursing station, I was given a brown paper bag containing two weeks worth of psycho-pharmaceuticals and a card spelling out the date of my nearest appointment.

Before catching the bus back to my apartment, I threw the brown paper bag into the first trash bin I came across.

When I got home, what furniture had remained after the divorce was now gone. The landlady had taken the liberty of selling what she could to cover the overdue rent. All that was left was a dingy single mattress, a kitchen chair, and a television. I sat down on the chair and lit a cigarette. The apartment smelled of dirty bath water and aging mold. I bent forward and switched the television on.

Contributors

Mike Hudson, founder and lead singer of seminal seventies punk rock band the Pagans, has spent the past 35 years working for different magazines and newspapers, writing mostly journalism, criticism and essays but a small stream of fiction as well. He recently published *Never Trust the World*, his fifth book. In 2011, he had a nationwide booktour along with Bob Pfeiffer of Human Switchboard, David Thomas of Pere Ubu and Cheetah Chrome of the Dead Boys, all ex–punk rockers from Cleveland who have since become authors.

Karen Lillis is the author of four books of fiction, most recently *Watch the Doors as They Close* (Spuyten Duyvil, February 2012). She is currently working on a memoir called *Bagging the Beats at Midnight*, about her years behind the counter at St Mark's Bookshop. She blogs at *Karen the Small Press Librarian*: karenslibraryblog.blogspot.com.

Jim Feast is the author (with Ron Kolm) of the novel *Neo Phobe*, and with Gary Null of the health book *Germs, Biological Warfare and Vaccinations: What You Need to Know*. He is a member of the Unbearables writers group.

Chavisa Woods is a Brooklyn-based author whose work focuses on issues of class, culture, gender, and sexuality. She is the recipient of the 2009 Jerome Foundation Award for emerging writers. Her debut collection of short stories, *Love Does Not Make Me Gentle or Kind* (Fly By Night Press, 2009) was a Lambda Literary Award finalist for Debut Fiction. Woods recently completed her second work of fiction, *The Albino Album*, a novel, which is set to be released by Seven Stories Press in the Spring of 2013. Woods' poetry, short stories and essays have been published nationally and internationally in a number of magazines and journals, including the *New York Quarterly*, *The Evergreen Review*, and *Union Station*.

James Greer is the author of the novels *Artificial Light* (LHotB/Akashic 2006) and *The Failure* (Akashic 2010), and the non-fiction book *Guided By Voices: A Brief History*, a biography of a band for which he played bass guitar. He's written or co-written movies for Lindsay Lohan, Jackie Chan, and Steven Soderbergh, among others. He is a Contributing Editor for the *Los Angeles Review of Books*.

Todd Colby has published four books of poetry: *Ripsnort*, *Cush*, *Riot in the Charm Factory: New and Selected Writings*, and *Tremble & Shine*, all published by Soft Skull Press. Colby, also a visual artist and performer, has been broadcast nationally on PBS, MTV and NPR for Garrison Keillor's *Writer's Almanac*. He was the lead singer for the critically acclaimed band Drunken Boat. Todd is a frequent collaborator with artist Marianne Vitale and art collective Kunstverein. His books and paintings with the artist David Lantow can be seen in the Brooklyn Museum of Art and The Museum of Modern Art special collections libraries. Colby serves on the Board of Directors for The Poetry Project, where he teaches poetry workshops. He also serves on the Editorial Board of *LungFull! Magazine* and is a contributing editor for *Cousin Corrine's Reminder*. He posts new work on gleefarm.blogspot.com.

Su Byron is a poet and freelance writer living in Sarasota, Florida. Her poetry and short stories have been published in numerous anthologies and magazines. She is currently working on two new collections of poems, *Fire Burns Less Than This* and *Lying in a Filthy Bed with a Dying Cat.* She works as a freelance writer and editor to earn her daily dose of wine and bread. For more, visit www.subyron.com.

Les Bridges says: "It was, it was a heady mix of fabulous cash and crazy ideas. I lived on planes . . . LA, Chicago . . . then in a great house in the East Village. My life was a fireball. Cannot this do forever, right? The stroke was a massive thunderbolt."

William Lessard's work has appeared in *Maintenant 6*, an international journal of Dada and other literary hijinks. He's also a fan of the New York Mets.

Mark McCawley is the author of a collection of poetry, *Voices from Earth*, and eight chapbooks, including *Stories for People with Brief Attention Spans* and *Just Another Asshole: Short Stories*. His fiction has appeared in anthologies such as *Burning Ambitions: The Anthology of Short-Shorts*, *Grunt & Groan: The New Fiction Anthology of Work and Sex* and *Front & Centre #9*.

Rob Hardin is the author of *Distorture*, a callously florid collection of short stories that seduced the Firecracker Award into being won and then told the award it should really start seeing other people. His fiction and essays have manipulated their way into the anthologies *Avant-Pop: Fiction for a Daydream Nation*, *Postmodern Culture*, *In the Slipstream*, *Forbidden Acts*, *Storming the Reality Studio: A Casebook of Cyberpunk & Postmodern Science Fiction*, *Mississippi Review* and *An Exaltation of Forms*. As a studio musician, he has intimidated others into using him on more than forty albums.

Ray Jicha was born in Cleveland, OH and grew up in South Carolina. A frequent traveler and occasional scholar, he found youthful purpose in fronting microcosmic rock bands. Since relocating to Portlandia in 1999 he has learned to miss the South, but not much. His novella, *Requiem for a Cornerman*, is now available.

Tom McGlynn is an artist, writer, and independent curator based in the NYC area. His work is represented in many national and international collections, including the permanent collections of the Whitney Museum, The Museum of Modern Art, and The Cooper-Hewitt National Design Museum of the Smithsonian. His art has been reproduced on the cover of *Artforum* magazine and featured in articles in *The New York Times*. Mr. McGlynn has taught as an Assistant Professor at Castleton State College, Vermont, and has previously been a Visiting Artist Lecturer at the Mason Gross School of Fine Arts at Rutgers University, NJ.

Ruby Ray got her start as staff photographer and muse at seminal punk culture rag, *Search & Destroy Magazine*, and co-founded *Re/Search Publications*; her iconic Burroughs photo graced the cover of issue 4/5. Ray's historic documentation of California's 1970s and 1980s underground music and art scene provides a rare insider's look at this pivotal time in musical history. A new hardback book, *From the Edge of the World, California Punk 77-81,* will be published in the Fall of 2012 and her Ebook is going to go live any day now on Amusedom: www.amusedom.com.

The New Monsters are Dan Plonsey (tenor sax), Steve Horowitz (bass), Jim Bove (drums), Steve Adams (flute, soprano sax and alto sax) and Scott Looney (piano). They perform compositions by Dan Plonsey.

Thaddeus Rutkowski is the author of the innovative novels *Haywire, Tetched* and *Roughhouse*. He teaches literature at City University of New York and fiction writing at the Writer's Voice of the West Side YMCA in Manhattan. His web site is www.thaddeusrutkowski.com.

After a decade and a half spent in Chicago, where she wrote freelance and served as a founding contributing editor of a magazine about digital photography, **Jennifer Adams** moved to New York to be closer to The Strand. Her first book, based on her blog TheBooksTheyGaveMe.com, will be published by Free Press in early 2013. She is at work on a variety of fiction projects, including a zombie novel for kids, and she blogs sporadically at jen-adams.com. She lives in Astoria, New York and is the mother of two boys.

James Romberger is an American fine artist and cartoonist known for his depictions of New York City's Lower East Side. Romberger's pastel drawings of the ravaged landscape of the Lower East Side and its citizens are in many public and private collections, including the Metropolitan Museum of Art and Brooklyn Museums. His solo and collaborative exhibitions have appeared at Ground Zero Gallery NY, the Grace Borgenicht Gallery, Gracie Mansion, The Proposition and the New Museum of Contemporary Art. Romberger has long contributed work in the comics medium to alternative publications such as *World War 3 Illustrated*. *Ground Zero*, his science-fiction strip collaboration with his wife, filmmaker Marguerite Van Cook, was serialized through the 1980s and 1990s in various downtown literary magazines. *Seven Miles A Second*, Romberger and Van Cook's graphic novel done in collaboration with artist, writer, and AIDS activist David Wojnarowicz.Romberger is also a critic and writer for *Publisher's Weekly* and the comics blog the Hooded Utilitarian.

Justine Frischmann is an artist and musician who has performed and exhibited in Europe, North America, Japan and Australia. She wrote and performed with Elastica and, more recently, has written and produced for a number of artists including M.I.A. She has a degree in architecture from University College London, has studied Contemplative Art at Naropa University, and Fine Art at the San Francisco Art Institute. Her work has been reviewed in many publications including the *London Sunday Times* (Art and Culture), the *LA Times*, and the *London Telegraph*. She was a presenter and writer on *The South Bank Show,* the UK's oldest and most respected arts program, and has presented programs on art, music and architecture for BBC TV, BBC World TV (Arts), and BBC Radio 6. She has written about art and culture for magazines such as *ID* and *The Face (UK),* and was a judge for the Sterling Prize. She now lives and works in the Bay Area.

Sensitive Skin Books—on sale now!

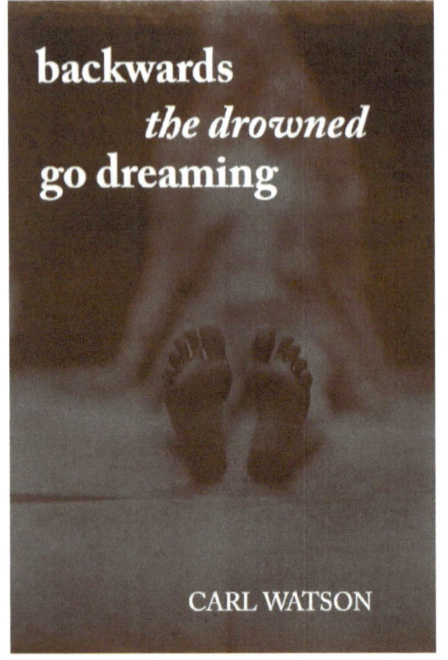

"[Watson] writes like someone who pushed himself to the wall, then pushed through it to the void and came back with stories to tell. Here he reclaims the Seventies, one of the more desolate of recent epochs, with the clarity of Proust, the balefulness of Bodenheim, and the raw honesty of an Iggy song."

—John Strausbaugh, author of *Black Like You* and *Sissy Nation*

"With prose unfurling like cigarette smoke bleeding into that cloud of half-forgotten memories forever shadowing missed opportunities that hangs over a noonday dive somewhere during the twilight of the last blown century, heartbreak rock-n-roll on the radio crackling in exquisite precision between am stations and windswept interstates, Carl Watson daydreams before silent black-and-white televisions in SRO lobbies or as he drinks himself sober in crumbling Chicago tenements. *Backwards the Drowned Go Dreaming* explodes the bleary-eyed myth of the American road."

—Donald Breckenridge, author of *This Young Girl Passing*

"Carl Watson's work is desolate poetry. He writes with sharp nostalgia for a past that really wasn't all that great. It feels like a stay in a down-and-out motel, but right on the other side of the paper-thin wall is transcendence. Watson never lets you forget that even in the most desperate situations, there is humor (even if it's mostly black) and greatness of the spirit."

—Emily XYZ, contributor, *United States of Poetry*

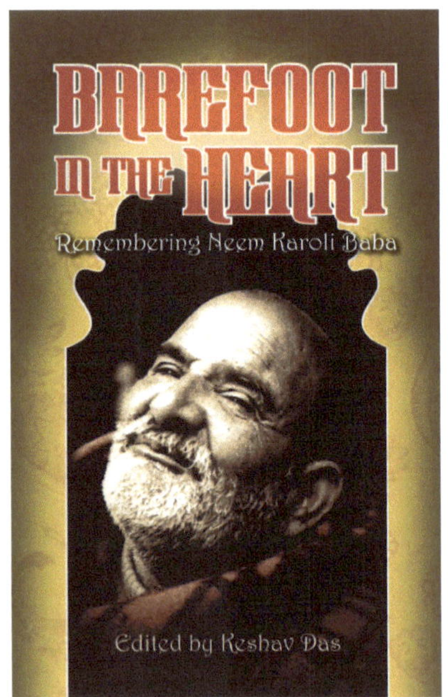

Barefoot in the Heart is a collection of transcribed oral stories of the Indian saint Neem Karoli Baba (Maharaji). It includes many anecdotes and first-person retellings of stories collected in India and the in the USA over a period of 9 years, by Keshav Das, including a small selection of unpublished stories originally intended for inclusion in *Miracle Of Love* by Ram Dass.

"*Barefoot In The Heart* is a divine raft to take us across the ocean of darkness to the glorious land of light. Every page is filled with Maharajji's nectar. Profound gratitude to Keshav Das and his collaborators."

—Jai Uttal

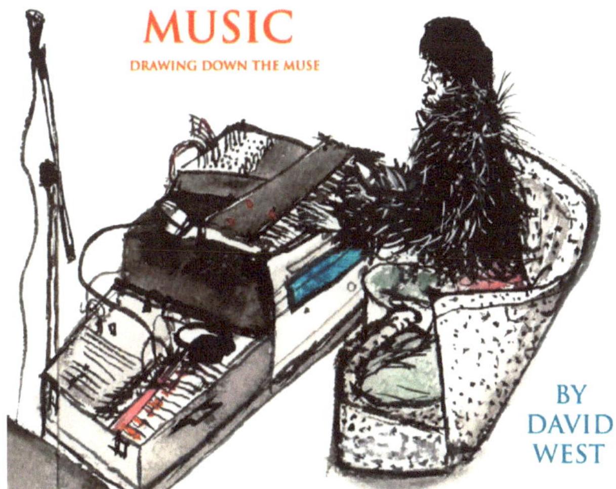

"Inside this book you get *portraiture vérité* of bands in action. Banging away in rehearsal. The appreciative eye watching the battle of the bands as they try to navigate their way through the sometimes complicated maze of illusions, delusions and solutions of grandeur before asphyxiation and evaporation of all the notes into the air. I'm the wrong person to comment on rehearsal as I work in a more backward way. I don't care if a performance is anally-retentive-perfect because a computer can do that now. I'll work hard on something to a point then I stop, as what I want surprises myself, especially in a live situation. It's a viewpoint probably not shared by most of the bands in this book but that's what makes things interesting. It's up to others to state theirs and that takes us to the artist.

David West hits the target dead center BOOM with his beautifully liquid renderings of NYC bands in rehearsal. Mr. West captures a scene in the late 1990s largely ignored. These aren't vacuous American Idols but musicians who are The Real Deal. Like a fly on the wall, David gives you an inside view from his own multifaceted eye. There is a dripping aquatic fluidity to his drawings. Mr. West is not afraid to let the ink, gouache, and watercolor run and flow never betraying the nature of his medium. That's why he's The Real Deal. If you the viewer can't understand, appreciate and see that in his work then go out and get corrective eye surgery!"

—Monte Cazazza, Psychic TV

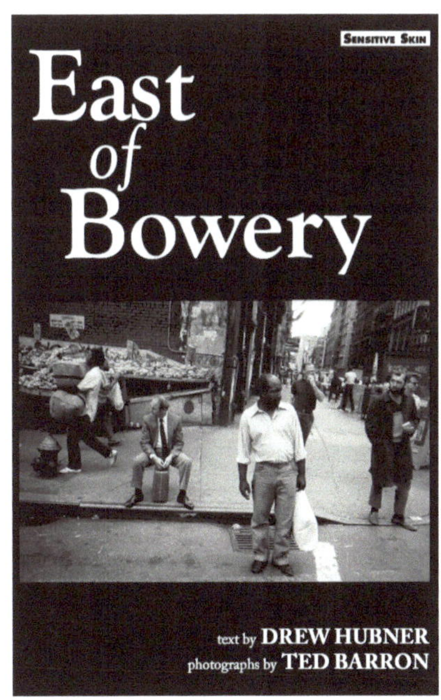

East of Bowery began as a collaborative web project between writer Drew Hubner (*American by Blood, We Pierce*) and photographer Ted Barron in 2008. It was subsequently performed as a multimedia performance with live musical accompaniment at The Gershwin Hotel and The Bowery Poetry Club. This is the first print publication of the project.

"Drew Hubner's prose and Ted Barron's photos are kin, at once raw and lyrical, grit and grace, which is what the city was like back then. The combination is magic, the essence of the time and place."

—Luc Sante, author of *Low Life* and *Kill All Your Darlings*

"*East of Bowery* is a sharply focused, street-level view of Downtown before the real estate agents started renaming everything."

—Steve Earle, author of *Doghouse Roses* and *I'll Never Get Out of This World Alive*

"Drew Hubner writes like people used to."

—William Georgiades, *New York Magazine*

"The voice is loose, jazzy, and fast, the memories liquid and hot, avoiding the romance of macho drug memoirs with black humor, verisimilitude and a knack for the absurd."

—Kate Christensen, author of *In the Drink* and *The Astral*

more great stuff from some friends...

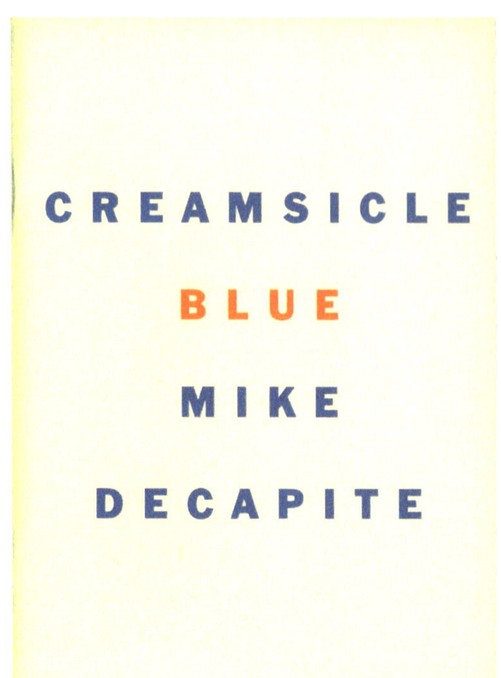

"*Creamsicle Blue* is a spectacular piece of writing."

—Karen Lillis, author of *Watch the Doors as They Close*

"I'm excited about this form. *Creamsicle Blue* is as close as I've gotten to the kind of thing I've always wanted to do."

—Mike DeCapite

$10 postage-paid at www.sparklestreet.com

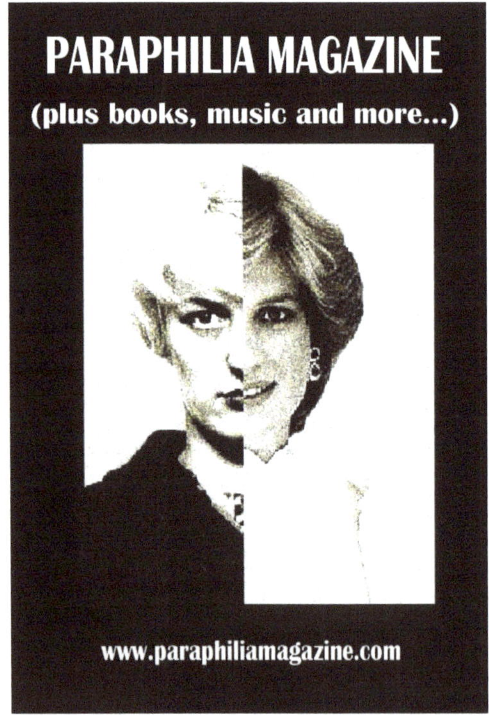

Paraphilia, an unlicensed, underground enterprise that renounces established and arbitrary rules, regulations, guidelines, genres, categories, and all other manmade shackles. *Paraphilia* recognizes that expression is a fundamental function of the human organism, and within these walls, it will only be presented in the purest, rawest, most unfettered form. The sole requirement for admission is an open mind, so do come in, we embrace your presence.

www.ingramcontent.com/pod-product-compliance
Lightning Source LLC
LaVergne TN
LVHW070128110826
845147LV00002B/210

* 9 7 8 0 9 8 3 9 2 7 1 5 0 *